A Grimm Haunting

Book 4 of the Mari Fable Mysteries

Emily Fluke

Copyright © 2022 by Emily Fluke

All rights reserved.

No part of this book may be reproduced in any form or by any electronic or mechanical means, including information storage and retrieval systems, without written permission from the author, except for the use of brief quotations in a book review.

Also by Emily Fluke

-THE MARI FABLE MYSTERIES

Death of a Fairy Tale

Kidnapping the Classics

The Pinocchio Project

A Grimm Haunting

Book 5 (releasing spring 2023)

-THE SUPERNATURAL MAMAS OF BEWITCHER'S BEACH SERIES

Momsters and Minivans (releasing October 2023)

Book 2 (releasing November 2023)

Book 3 (releasing December 2023)

-FOLKLORE FALLS ROMANCE RETELLINGS

Until Theft Do Us Part

Fake Dating's a Beast

...and more (releasing spring 2023)

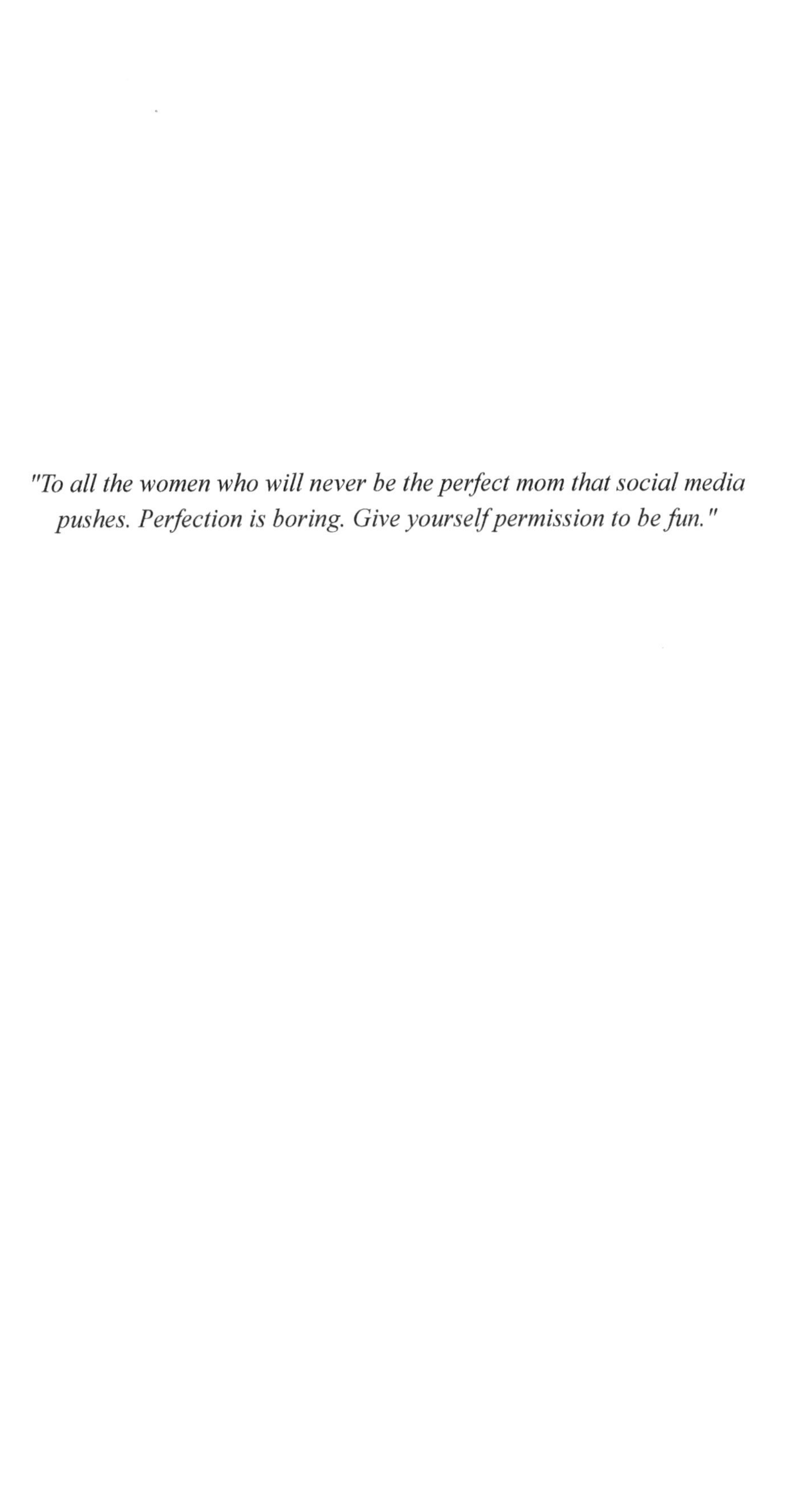

"To all the women who will never be the perfect mom that social media pushes. Perfection is boring. Give yourself permission to be fun."

Prologue

Dear Journal,

Whew. How long has it been? When life is peachy, I forget to record it. Maybe I need to get a gratitude jar because not a single dangerous fairy tale has reared its ugly face in almost three years, and that is certainly something to be grateful for.

How did I get so lucky, but also so screwed at the same time? Look, I know hunting gods of another world wouldn't be easy, but I thought by <u>now</u> I'd have a clue or two. If they're the all-powerful gods of stories that Johnson claimed, I suspect the Brothers Grimm are the key to saving Wendy from her fairy tale.

Alas, the combined research between Scarlet, Kai, and me, yielded nothing. Now Scarlet is gone trying to become an official investigative journalist and Kai is swamped with teaching.

In the meantime, I guided two gentle stories along to seal their endings. The first one started out real kidnappy, but ended with a happy marriage. The guy begged a lady for her friendship, which reminded me of a borderline stalker, but then plot twist! — it was the lady demanded who he move in with her. After he did, BOOM, no more frog face, and his body temperature issues resolved.

Oh, and I can't forget the old lady that wandered into a frat house.

Apparently, the Omega Iota lodge looked just like her assisted living home. When she fell asleep and ate all their food, the frat guys got pissed. Good thing I was already monitoring her thanks to the golden story aura she emanated.

Anywho, Wendy wants a snack. I need to wrap this up and run to the grocery store, considering she's munching on pieces of the Gingerbread house kit before we even had time to build it.

P.S. I'm writing this as a reminder that the quieted story cycle, literally leaves me <u>no excuse</u> not to be a better mom. To-do list: exercise, eat healthily, be like the social media moms who always have perfect hair, and dinners, and their houses probably smell like laundry-scented candles.

Ebenezer Scrooge. I'm going to fail at this, aren't I?

Chapter 1

Building Bridges With Villains

R ed Riding's hood solved a lot of supernatural issues, but my favorite way to use it was to hide my greasy hair and the pajamas I wore at the after-school pickup. Being an ex-fairy tale character didn't have a lot of perks, but a magical hood was one of them.

Except this trip to Wendy's classroom was a special one rather than the everyday pickup after school. So much for the 'walk of shame' after a one-night stand. That was peanuts compared to the looks other parents gave when the principal at May Alcott Elementary School had approached me during pickup and asked that my husband and I return for a meeting with our daughter's substitute teacher, Mrs. Skipper.

So, now we marched down a hall that smelled like chicken nuggets two hours after Wendy's bell had released her from class. Most of the teachers locked up their classrooms, but a few stayed late for after-school programs, one of which supervised Wendy while we waited outside her First-Grade classroom.

A yoga-pants-wearing-homemade-cupcake-wielding mom I recognized from Wendy's friend's birthday party, emerged from the double doors at the end of the hall. Her perfectly shiny, smooth ponytail swung back and forth as she bounced toward us with a spring in her step.

Before she looked up from her phone, I willed the hood to materialize. The nearly non-existent fabric filled in, bringing with it the soft but heavy feel on my arms and shoulders. Not only had I learned to shift and control its visibility, but I'd honed the skill of changing its appearance to whatever I felt like wearing. Today, I chose a comfy, red hoodie. Classic, but cozy. I flipped the hood over my messy bun and sunk in the shadow it cast across my face, hoping to conceal the bags under my eyes.

Don't see me. Don't see me. I'd begged the opposite, praying to the Brothers Grimm gods for the past two years, but after months of trailing the only fairy tales I could find, I'd come up dry and ready to quit. If I didn't know better, I'd say the hood was an invisibility cloak for fictional deities.

Yoga Mom bounded by like a bunny rabbit with a reusable tote full of homemade, organic lunches for the kids in after-school clubs. At least, that was what I'd overhead her brag about at the birthday party last week.

Kai leaned forward, making the plastic chair squeal as it slid slightly on the linoleum. "Let me guess, she's Peter Rabbit?" He discreetly nodded after Yoga Mom. She disappeared into a classroom with a paper sign marking the door as the *Mathlete Meeting* room.

The bunny comment confirmed my husband, and I were on the same wavelength. Not unusual, but his guess landed miles from the truth this time. I'd grown lax with the hood, using it for clothing alongside its guidance to the story aura—something that Yoga Mom did not have.

"No proof of Beatrix Potter here," I confirmed with a shake of my head. "I just didn't want her to see me. Then we'd have to explain that we haven't met the substitute teacher taking over during Mrs. Terri's maternity leave." I frowned and folded my arms. "I bet Yoga Mom knows all the teachers here personally. She probably brings them coffee every morning while I forget to put on pants—"

"Mari," Kai interrupted my pity party with *the look*. What? I tilted my head and bugged my eyes. The recent fairy tales were nothing more than a sweet old lady snoozing at a frat house and a dental hygienist married to a dude who vaguely looked like a frog. I had zero excuses for failing on the organic lunch front considering no bloodthirsty wolves hunted me and I'd already freed my imprisoned shape-shifting mother.

Kai waved his hand in front of my face. "Did you hear me?"

"What?"

"You need to chill. Not even Yoda Mom is perfect. I mean, her nickname follows a master Jedi, and that's pretty killer." Kai's eyes glazed over as he disappeared into his imagination of Tattoo-Town or whatever the planets in Star Wars were called. I was a Trekkie girl, myself.

"I said 'yo-gah' mom." I enunciated clearly but Kai didn't hear. The classroom door swung open with a creak. A shockingly familiar face appeared, restricting all the blood in mine. Kai glanced at me, presumably because he recognized her too, then double-backed. I could only imagine I looked like I'd seen a ghost if I hadn't turned pale enough to be mistaken for one myself.

The perky blonde forced a grin that quickly twisted into a grimace. "Didn't you know it was me?" Miss Jenna asked. The same teacher from Wendy's preschool classroom almost three years ago stood before me now and the surrounding glow was impossible to ignore. Apparently, she'd graduated from teaching the alphabet to a full-blown fairy tale villain. Oh, and substituting for elementary classes.

"I-I," I struggled to find the words. "I thought your name was Mrs. Skipper?" The moment the words came out of my mouth, I realized the stupidity of my mistake. I palmed my forehead, shielding my eyes with my hand. "Oh my gosh, Skipper is another word for a captain isn't it?"

Kai glanced between us, catching on but slowly. Poor guy couldn't see the bright green aura that glowed around the teacher's body and screamed *Hey, look at me! I'm bound by a fairy tale's plot because the fabric between reality and fiction is thin.*

"Oh, yeah," Miss Jenna—or Mrs. Skipper—whatever her name was, said. "I got married and go by my last name now." She raised her hand to swipe hair out of her face. A lump gathered in my throat as the picture came together. Wendy's former preschool teacher and the current substitute in her first-grade class was, without a shadow of a doubt, Captain Hook.

"And yes." Her head bobbed. "They're synonymous. I'm a Hook at heart if you know what I mean." Was it the dying bulb in the track lights above us or did her eyes just sparkle? Hook held my gaze and tilted her head in the faintest nod, before looking both ways down the hall as if about to cross a street. "And Peter, your daughter, has found me." With her wink, my suspicions were confirmed. Somehow, someway, this random school teacher knew.

Hopefully, May Alcott Elementary employed a skilled janitor because they'd be cleaning my jaw off the linoleum tonight. How in the fairy-tale nightmare did Wendy's teacher know about the stories coming to life?

"How?" I squeaked but couldn't finish.

Hook frowned. "I'm a spiritual woman. The gods have answered my prayers."

If the plot held true, my daughter would dismember her first-grade substitute teacher then feed the hand to a crocodile. Of course, modern society tweaked the stories a little, so, it might look more like Wendy tricking a dog to bit her nemesis' hand. Hook mistook me for staring at her when really my brain had frozen, unable to process the next chapter in the children's tale.

"P-Peter cuts off…" I couldn't finish the sentence but with my eyes glued on her arm, Hook filled in the blanks.

She cupped her wrist with her other hand and stroked the skin. "I'm worried too, but nothing like that has come close to happening, yet."

I eased from a whole-body exhale. My senses returned to me, the smell of chicken nuggets, whiteboard markers, and Hook's strawberry perfume. The weight of the hood on my shoulders and my exhaustion teamed up to drag my posture into a half-melted position.

"Wait…" Kai held up both hands and glanced between us. "What am I missing? Is she…?"

Maybe my head nodded, I couldn't be sure. I wasn't even certain if we stood in an elementary school or an alternate universe. As far as I knew, only Reese, Johnson, Scarlet, Kai, and I knew about the story cycle. And my mother...and father...and his mother. *Ebenezer Scrooge.* What I didn't know definitely could hurt me. Our little world of supernatural story stuff had spread to a lot more people than I'd realized.

Hook sighed and checked the hall for eavesdroppers. "Follow me." Blonde hair flew behind her as she spun around and beckoned for us to follow her into the privacy of the classroom. I floated behind her in a state of shock that the villain of my child's story stood right in front of me. Should I dig out the switchblade from my boot or the pepper spray in my purse? Would it be appropriate to throat-punch my daughter's teacher under the claim that she'll inevitably become a murderous villain? Or had she already?

"Will somebody, for the love of all that is story, fill me in here?" Kai asked.

Questions inundated my mind as we sunk into the child-sized chairs across from the teacher's desk. Posters with baby animals decorated the classroom with inspirational phrases. The 'hang in there' picture of a kitten holding onto a tree branch didn't fit with the villainous vibes the teacher sent. Her perky, stylish look clashed with the daggers in her eyes and twisted grimace.

Hook settled into the spinning chair and pulled herself closer to the desk. When she clasped her hands and rested them on top of a colorful table calendar, I expected her to explain. Or launch across the desk and strangle me. Or do something, anything. Instead, she muttered something unintelligible and picked up a pen and paper.

I cupped a hand to my mouth and answered Kai's question under my breath. "Remember how we suspected Wendy had the story aura? It's true, she's Peter, and this is her antagonist."

My husband raised his brows. "Mari, we've been solving fairy tales for almost seven years now. I know how it works. But how does—" he paused and wiggled his pointer finger under the table, repeatedly curling and straightening to direct my attention to Hook, "she know?"

I widened my eyes and lifted my shoulders into a discreet shrug. Kai shook his head and mouthed something about being lost. *Join the club, Buddy.*

A bang caused us both to jump and interrupted our private conversation. In a flash, I pulled out the blade in my boot and stood, leaning across the table. Instead of flesh, the weapon poked at a piece of paper that I first mistook as Hook's attempt at a shield.

The unamused look on her face told me she didn't call us here to fight. "Sit down, Mrs. Fable."

"Rowan," I corrected with my married name. My maiden name reminded me too much of stories and all the danger they brought into the world. When I eased back into my seat and tucked the blade away, my cheeks burned. I'd jumped the gun because Hook's self-awareness caught me off guard. Did she know she was being steered into a life of villainy by the story aura? What crimes had she already committed that attracted the aura of an evil character?

Hook licked her finger and straightened the crease my switchblade had poked into the paper. A crudely drawn diamond shape had been scribbled in the middle of the paper. "This is Neverland. It's where your daughter and I both belong."

"Hell n—"

"Trust me," Hook interrupted, slamming the paper face down against the desk. "I don't want her there either. That is why I called you both here today." Again with the clasped hands. It was her version of the cliche villain when they'd tap the tips of their fingers together and laugh maniacally.

I scooted to the edge of my chair and held Hook's icy, blue-eyed gaze. The shine of the fluorescent lights against her lip gloss nearly blinded me. I squinted. "Start from the beginning and tell me how you know you're a fairy tale character before you go claiming you know who my child is."

The corner of her mouth curved up, and her eyes drifted into an unseeing glaze. "I like to think of myself as a prophet."

I arched my eyebrow and exchanged a 'what in the wonderland' look with Kai. The flop of his thick hair partially blocked the evidence of his wariness as creases on his forehead.

"I've always been a believer in things beyond our understanding and when Wendy enrolled in my preschool classroom, I started praying, no—begging—to a higher power to get that terror away from me."

Kai's knees bumped the table as he shot to his feet. "Hey!" A half-empty water bottle toppled off the edge of the desk. Hook raised her hand in calm surrender.

"Look, I get it, she's your precious baby. But Wendy tortures me. She is everything I'm not, wild, loud, and skeptical. She's not a proper girl with manners and honor."

"Proper girl?" I spat. *Sexist much? Are you from the eighteen hundreds?* "She's six!"

"And she'll forever be a child if she goes to Neverland." Hook dropped her voice to a low, growling tone that clashed with her colorful clothes and the shimmering highlighter brushed across her cheekbones. "Do not let her go to Neverland, it's my home."

No matter how rapidly I blinked, Wendy's villain still sat in front of me. "She's not going anywhere."

Hook threw her head back and laughed. "If she feels the pull to Neverland as strongly as I do she'll be there."

Kai pointed to the picture. "Where? How...?" The words wouldn't come and I couldn't blame him. The sheer absurdity of the situation froze my brain too.

"I told you, I'm spiritual. So when I prayed, the gods came to me in a dream and they showed me Neverland."

So was that how the Brothers Grimm showed themselves? In dreams? Or was Hook hallucinating? I shot Kai another look and his slight nod told me he agreed. *This lady has a case of the Nutter Butters.*

Hook's crystal-clear voice cut through my thoughts. "Apparently that hood of yours is quite the concealing cloak. They're looking for you, Red."

The name chilled my blood and my heart slowed to Department of Motor Vehicles-level speed. Nobody had referred to me as Red Riding Hood. Ever. Not even Scarlet since she'd tried to trick me into believing Wendy was Red. But right there, in that single word, Hook proved her entire story.

A knock rapped at the door, and I startled, my heart jumpstarting to a rapid beat again. Kai laid his hand on my knee, a common gesture to tell me he recognized my fear or shock or whatever it was, and that he was there if I needed him.

Yoga Mom's head popped through the door, and she lifted a plate of Christmas cutout cookies. "For my favorite substitute!" She sang.

"I'll be right with you Mrs. Harrington," Hook said.

Yoga Mom waved her hand. "No rush, I'll pop over to peek at Remy's choir practice. I just can't wait to chat with you about his advanced academics."

I had to hand it to Hook—no pun intended—her narrowed eyes and slightly curled smile conveyed a stern, but not unpleasant message that told off Yoga Mom's pushy behavior.

Hook rubbed her temples after Yoga Mom disappeared. "I've got to go. This is my last day substituting in this class so I had to find a way to meet with you on neutral ground. I'm not the villain the stories say I am, I've been tempted to steal, but I never did. It's not the honorable thing to do. I just wanted decent pay so I could afford nice makeup, maybe a Botox injection or two. But when the gods showed me Neverland in my dream, I realized I didn't want to just look young, I want to live forever. The gold treasure is just a bonus."

She paused to sigh with another glazed-over look but I couldn't get a word in before she spoke again. Hook snapped back to reality and stared me down, slapping her palm against the scribble of Neverland on the desk. "This is all I can remember from my dream. A Christmas Tree with no lights, rubber ground, child's laughter, and a full moon." A crack in her voice caused her to choke up. She brought her hand to her lips and coughed. "I-I wasn't faithful enough. I tried to figure out where they were and what else they wanted to tell me, but I can't recall everything after I woke up." Her voice dropped to a whisper, and I got the feeling she wasn't speaking to us anymore. "Forgive me."

Kai had discreetly typed something on his phone with his free hand under the desk then tilted the screen for me to see. *Do we call the cops?*

I lifted my shoulders in a faint shrug. It was a valid question. A villain sat across from us, a pirate one at that—though I figured it was more of the illegally downloading music kind than the swashbuckler. That alone could warrant a visit from law enforcement but we had no proof Hook had done anything wrong. In fact, in all my study of *Peter Pan*, Hook merely wanted revenge against the child who'd injured her. The distance Hook wanted between her and Wendy wasn't unreasonable.

Another knock banged on the door.

Hook leaped to her feet, leaned across the desk, and spoke under her breath. "They stopped answering my prayers, so please, use what I told you to find the gods and tell them to keep Wendy away from me, and from Neverland." When she straightened, she smoothed her blouse and cheerfully invited the person at the door to come inside.

My mind was reeling with the barrage of information but it circled one reality I never expected—the villain in my child's story and I shared the same goal.

Find the gods and get Wendy the hell away from Neverland. Oh, and free Wendy from the cycle that bound her to the plot of a fictional story, effectively stripping her of her life and freedom.

Screw the Brothers Grimm and their stupid stories.

Chapter 2

Eat, Drink, and Be Worried

Thick liquid dripped off the tip of my knife and landed with a plop in my lap. Thankfully, I'd thrown on pajamas before butchering the hard-as-rock bagel with jam that hadn't entirely defrosted. The stain of the strawberry condiment only ruined the clothes I wore at home...and in the drop-off line at school. And sometimes for a coffee run, but I manifested the hood to cover me in those situations.

Maybe I wore it too much. Maybe the Brothers Grimm gods would have found me months, or even years ago if I'd let it hang off my shoulders in its invisible state.

Maybe I shouldn't go down a rabbit hole right before dinner.

I scraped the last bit of not-frozen jam over the stale bagel and set it on my plate next to applesauce and a bowl of pumpkin-spiced oatmeal left over from fall. The night I'd planned to go grocery shopping had fallen on the same day as our parent-teacher meeting. Needless to say, a family huddle won out against the scavenger hunt for the freshest batch of cranberries. Not that I ever got around to making the sauce. I bet Yoga Mom home-cooked the perfect cranberry dish every day in December while I was scrounging food out of the freezer for the last two days and pretending it was the meal plan all along.

I frowned and balanced mine and Wendy's plates, carefully leaning in the opposite direction as her tower of Eggo Waffles so they wouldn't topple and decorate the kitchen floor. Once it balanced, I shuffled around the tall counter that separated the kitchen and living room.

We often ate on the couch over the short table in the center of the room. The Coffee Table of Evidence was covered in sticky notes with the four items Hook had mentioned written in dozens of questions.

Rubber ground = tires on the street?

A Christmas tree with no presents = the Grinch's house?

Child's laughter = a classroom? Cartoons? Wendy every time Kai told her a dad joke?

A full moon = werewolves. No. Vampires? Cheese, definitely cheese.

Wendy peeled two orange Post-It notes from the tabletop to make room for her plate while Kai used the lists of clues as a placemat.

I flopped onto the couch, sinking into the cushion that'd worn to the shape of my hips and butt after bearing a genius, and apparently spirited, child. The same child that the story aura targeted and bound to the plot of *Peter Pan*.

Kai gave me a discreet nod from the chair sitting kitty-corner to the couch. While she was too busy stabbing the tower of waffles, Wendy didn't notice we'd planned our third 'mintervention,' AKA a kid-sized intervention we'd coined with the word mini. For the past two nights, we carefully questioned her about her behavior issues at school. Unfortunately, Hook hadn't been the only one at the receiving end of Wendy's teacher tricks. She was smart, too smart, and knew that if she distracted the adults in the room, whether it be school or dinner time, she'd get out of doing assignments and eating vegetables.

Was that the Peter Pan spirit inside her? If so, it'd only get worse as time went on.

I needed to stop twiddling my thumbs over sticky notes, find the Brothers Grimm with Hook's clues, and threaten to mess up their stories even more than simply saving the victims of their more gruesome tales. Twisting the original plots was the only leverage I had to bargain for Wendy's freedom from the story aura.

But life demanded multitasking and, first, I needed to make sure Wendy wasn't going to run off to find Neverland soon. Before diving into the conversation, I tapped the password into my phone and double-checked the text I'd sent Scarlet. It remained on 'delivered' which meant she'd yet to read it from days ago. I tried not to worry, considering Carlo insisted she was fine—just focused after our boss at Bay Side Media had sent her on her first real assignment in Hollywood to track news for our celebrity column. It wasn't the murder investigations Scarlet had wanted to center her journalism career around, but it was an official shoe in the door as a lowly intern.

I'd give Carlo another call after dinner.

"So," I started, trying to remain casual. If Wendy sensed trouble, she'd do one of two things, curl up and sob or snap back with total denial that she'd fallen under the allure of the prankster life. "What'd you learn in class today?"

Wendy gulped down a too-big bite of Eggos and then tilted her head. "I don't know."

"Any phonics practice?" Kai asked.

"Yeah." She shrugged then shoved hair out of her face. Like me, she preferred to keep it chin-length, neither of us had the patience for brushing. "We do that every day. Can I watch Jake and the Neverland Pirates before bed?"

"No!" Kai and I both shouted at the same time. We scolded each other with silent looks over Wendy's head. The capital *They* of child development specialization said not to overreact when having serious conversations with your kid. Wendy would surely pick up on our paranoia and start to worry too. Though she was only six, I feared the worst —teenage behavior. The more we denied her knowledge of and access to anything about Neverland, the more she'd want it and possibly sneak around to find it.

"Please," Wendy dragged out the word.

"Let's wait for Christmas break," Kai said in his teacherly wisdom. It diffused the situation, for now. Come the first day of vacation, Wendy would beg for screen time. I took a bite of the stale bagel and frowned.

"Want to play the question game?" I suggested. Games were a good way to get Wendy's attention. She nodded with sparkling eyes. The kid inherited my competitive streak, now I needed to redirect that ambition from pranks and mischief to school or solving murders like her mama. "If you could go anywhere right now, where would you go?"

Wendy gulped her apple juice as if she'd never had a drink in her life then picked locks of hair from the sticky syrup on her cheeks. "Nowhere."

Kai and I took a collective sigh.

"Grown-ups go places and I don't want to grow up."

If I didn't know better, I'd think an imaginary vacuum sucked the air from my lungs. Hair flopped into Kai's face as he sat up and scooted to the edge of the cushion. We cringed.

Wendy hopped to her feet and carried her empty plate to the sink. Only the top of her head peeked out from the other side of the counter as she milled about the kitchen, refilling her apple juice and examining the slim pickings of leftover Halloween candy in the cabinet.

Kai leaned over the coffee table and whispered. "Do you think she meant—"

I shot my arm out like a crosswalk volunteer, holding my palm out to Kai. "Don't say it." I hissed.

"Can I have this?" A tiny arm poked above the counter with a bag of M&M's in hand.

Chocolate and Eggos, the dinner of champions. Wasn't I just the star pupil in Mom Class? Not to mention I'd yet to find the gods of the story who doomed my daughter to the plot of a book.

I sighed. "Sure, Wednesday."

Wendy skipped into the living room while struggling to tear the bag open. She did an entire six-year-old-style dance routine as she waited for Kai to rip it.

"Mommy," she said with all the seriousness in the world at the same time as doing a half-hearted cartwheel. After landing on her side, she rolled to her stomach and reached for the bag of M&M's. "Did you know there's a planet where you can play all day? I bet they eat candy always, too."

I dropped the rock-hard bagel to the plate and gave up. My appetite was gone. Maybe I should take over the diet column at Bay Side Media because I had the secret to never wanting to eat again: I knew my child's future. Sure, that sounded cool on paper, like I could prevent her from a fall where she scraped her knee or knew she'd get into a good college someday. But paper was where stories were immortalized. Crap always sounded good when it was merely a means of entertainment.

"I want to live there." Wendy bounded around the living room, doing something akin to parkour about as well as Michael Scott. "I could climb up the slides the wrong way and eat a lollipop and swing at the same time. And no grown-ups could tell me not to and…" she continued babbling about Neverland—the world where all her dreams came true, apparently. A place where no parents were around to warn kids they might fall from the monkey bars and choke if they have candy in their mouths while they play.

I muttered about Neverland's imaginary playground. "It better have rubber or grass underneath because—" I jolted straight up, the plate sliding from my lap and clattering to the floor. "Rubber ground!" I shouted. Wendy rolled out of a half-hearted cartwheel and Kai snapped his attention to me with an arched eyebrow. I ignored his judgmental look as the pieces of the puzzle came together. "The clues," I said, pointing to the sticky notes, "rubber ground and child's laughter equals a playground!"

Kai's Adam's Apple bobbed as he swallowed the last of his random-item dinner. "What about this one?" he scooted to the edge of his seat and leaned over the coffee table. "A Christmas tree with no presents and a full moon?"

I waved my hand. "I don't know. One step at a time. A playground is at least part of it." Though I didn't know why I'd find the Brothers Grimm at a child's play area. It was disturbing at best. I headed for the door where I slid my foot into a pair of slip-on shoes. "Maybe it makes sense because we consider fairy tales children's stories?"

"Can I come?" Wendy hopped over to me on one foot, sticky fingers grabbing my shirt to help her balance.

"No, it's early bedtime every night this week for teasing your teacher. You know that." I twisted the doorknob, backing out of the house quickly before Kai could negotiate that I take over bedtime while he grades papers. Technically, it was my night to read stories and help Wendy brush her teeth, but this lead couldn't wait.

"What's your plan?" Kai had twisted in his chair to face the door. He ran a hand through his overgrown hair. The guy didn't have a free moment for a haircut, not with the holidays and finals at his school coming up. As a dedicated history teacher, he took the time to read each paper carefully rather than skim.

"I don't know, but I need to find them. Maybe they'll meet me at a playground. I'll run down to the little play area in the complex and be back in a second." I didn't bother with a sweater or anything extra. Our condominium had installed a tiny playground for residents a few months ago. Really, it was just a reason to raise the Homeowner's Association fee. Nobody used the pathetic play structure that was already too small for kids Wendy's age and too big for toddlers.

A rush of crisp air blasted down the condo's outdoor hall. I greeted our neighbor Tala as she returned from a walk with her dog.

"Something wrong?" she asked, likely because of my resting-witch face.

"Opposite actually," I said, as I passed her and paused at the top of the concrete staircase. "I have a lead on an investigation."

She wished me luck with a warm smile and then disappeared into her boyfriend's condo one door down from her house. One of these days Mr. Geppetto would make an honest woman out of Tala but I knew it wouldn't happen until Carlo, AKA Pinocchio, had fully recovered from his PTSD after becoming trapped in virtual reality.

I pulled out my phone and tapped Carlo's contact information. The line rang once before he answered.

"She's still alive," he said without even a greeting.

I paused at the top of the stairs. "I—what if I wanted to call and talk to my buddy Carlo? You know, the old DoorDash driver dude turned technological genius?"

Carlo laughed, breathing too loud into the phone. "Sure, Mari. I know you're worried about Scar but she shared her location with me so I can keep an eye on her. Plus, she called me last night."

"Last night, huh?" My voice dipped, and I wiggled my eyebrows even though he couldn't see me. "So, are you guys…"

"What?"

They'd been flirting for months but neither wanted to admit their attraction. *"Best friends" my butt.* I snorted and started down the steps.

"Never mind," I said. "Just call me if you hear anything. I could use her help on a case."

He agreed to the promise and asked me to tell Kai to get online to beta-test a new game Carlo had created.

I considered Carlo, Kai's, and Mr. Geppetto's friendship as I hurried down to the first floor of the sky-high building. They'd bonded over a video game before it blossomed into Mr. Geppetto counseling Carlo through his post-traumatic stress. Kai stuck to the gaming side of the group while Mr. Geppetto took counseling seriously, even putting his proposal to Tala on hold until Carlo showed signs of improvement. In reality, it seemed they were both healing one another as Mr. Geppetto worked through the grief of losing his daughter to a serial killer-turned-werewolf.

A lump gathered in my throat at the memory of the innocent young woman torn apart at the hands of Jameson. It was another murder intended for me. I shoved the thought away and focused on finding the spirits of the men who'd immortalized Red Riding Hood into a story. I couldn't let them subject my daughter to the story's control. She was Wendy Rowan, not a fictional character, and not a mischievous, forever child who tormented Captain Hook.

Another wave of wind blew through the parking lot, sending brown and red leaves littering the concrete. They crunched under the soles of my shoes. A blinking streetlamp struggled to illuminate the play structure, and instead, only shined off the plastic slide.

The gate creaked as I opened it and stepped inside. I hugged myself and willed the hood to materialize. The thick, soft fabric covered my bare arms and protected me against another blasting breeze that rolled up from the coast of California and slithered through the skyscrapers in San Francisco.

"Okay, show yourselves you selfish old Scrooges," I whispered. The irony of the Christmas-inspired name-calling wasn't lost on me. I wasn't ready for the hustle and bustle of the holidays. The last two years of fairy tale reform had been quiet, and easy, and allowed me to enjoy time with my family. Nostalgia for last year's simple Christmas Eve dinner hit me with a wave of emotion. Carlo and Scarlet still hadn't admitted their feelings for one another but they'd sat beside each other and flirted all night. Mr. Geppetto and Tala acted as Wendy's grandparents while I kept my mother's memory alive through pictures and stories for my daughter's sake. This year, I'd played with the idea of going to visit Kai's family across the country but we'd never committed to airplane tickets and it was just as well. With the clues from Hook, I wouldn't waste any time on my hunt for the brothers.

"Hello! I'm at the playground. Come out you old creeps." I dared to raise my voice.

Footsteps had me spinning around. A teenage couple eyed me warily, and I forced a smile.

"Bluetooth," I lied, pointing to non-existent earbuds in my ears. Thankfully, the hood covered the truth, though I hadn't put the effort into willing the fabric into the illusion of a normal outfit. So, I stood alone on a child's playground at twilight with a full-length Renaissance-looking cape. No wonder the couple hurried past me without a word.

I plopped onto the bench and pulled the bottom of the hood around my legs. With the sun completely gone now, the chill set in.

Full moon and a Christmas tree?

The rest of the puzzle didn't fit, but I committed to waiting. I folded my legs into my chest and hugged them.

"Wendy belongs with us, not in Neverland," I said as if the Brothers Grimm had arrived. But nothing changed, only the light of the streetlamp blinked overhead and the wind responded every so often with another gust.

"Mommy?"

A small voice broke through my thoughts. I dropped my feet and whirled around. Wendy stood with her hands on the play area's gate, with Kai running up behind her.

"I told her no, but she ran out the door," he huffed.

My heart skipped a beat. She was getting bolder and listening less and less. The story aura glowed brightly around her, taking its hold.

Pressure built behind my eyes but I wouldn't cry, not in front of her. I could figure this out. Christmas tree, full moon, playground. Playground, Christmas tree…full moon.

I looked up at and squinted past the streetlamp. Clouds obscured the yellow moon. It wasn't full. Not until tomorrow night.

"You'd better show yourselves," I muttered, twisting my fear into determination.

Chapter 3

For Here or To-Go

Crayons, classrooms, and Captain Hook. Not a good combination for my nerves, or nose. I wrinkled my face at the scent of wax from the melted crayons in Wendy's backpack. It hung off my wrist as I paced the length of the principal's office. Kai and I waited outside her door for an emergency meeting. With this second call in one week and my nerves were shot, mangled, annihilated.

The receptionist tapped away at her computer behind the tall desk. She offered me a closed-lipped smile when I turned and shuffled back in her direction.

Kai ran his fingers through his hair and turned to our daughter in the chair beside him. "Tell us what happened."

"She started it." Wendy sat in the same folded position that I had at the park the night before. With her legs plastered to her chest and arms squeezing her knees, she'd curled into herself.

"Started what?" Kai kept his voice even. His dad skills far surpassed my ability to stay calm right now.

"Miss Jenna is mean," she pouted. "She told me Santa put me on the naughty list and I didn't like it."

I paused to crouch in front of her chair, balancing on the balls of my feet. I brushed unruly hair from her face and took a steadying breath.

"I hear you, Wendy. We need you to tell us everything."

She opened her mouth but before she could get a word out, the office door swung open. Out stepped Principal Clearly and a wild-looking Hook. Her blonde hair stuck out in all directions as if she were an electrocuted cartoon character. Tears filled her eyes as she nervously tugged at the strands and inspected a pinkish substance that stained her hair.

Hook opened her mouth, and a sob escaped. "I'll have to shave my head!"

I seethed and glanced at Kai.

"Come inside," Principal Clearly herded us into her office and told the receptionist to let Wendy pick a coloring book off of a shelf by the receptionist.

Once inside, Hook refused to sit down, instead leaning against a bookcase and picking incessantly at her hair. Long stringy strands of gum peeled away from her matted hair. Thankfully, the principal praised Wendy's behavior with other teachers, calling her focused, kind, and delightful…until Mrs. Skipper came to substitute. Then the pranks started, from putting glue in the teacher's seat to shaking Mrs. Skipper's soda bottles when she wasn't looking, our daughter had mastered the art of a practical joke gone too far.

"Wendy is usually an exceptional student but we draw the line at harmful pranks," Principal Clearly said as she wrinkled her brow. "We don't suspend children younger than fourth grade but now might be a great opportunity to start her holiday break early. She's ahead in math and language arts so it won't be a loss to her academics. We expected her teacher's maternity leave to end last week but the teacher has extended it. She'll be back after Christmas vacation."

"That sounds reasonable," Kai said as we exchanged glances. I gazed past him at Hook who still picked at her hair. She looked up, glaring at me through her brow.

I narrowed my eyes, and she nodded slightly. I didn't know what that meant until she discreetly gestured prayer hands.

"Thank you both for coming down here on short notice." Principal Clearly stood, and we followed suit as she opened the door. "I hope Wendy remembers that pranks and putting gum in anyone's hair are not allowed when she comes back. Have a wonderful holiday."

Hook shuffled beside me and spoke just above a whisper. "Did you find them?"

"Your clues are too cryptic," I said between my teeth. "And do they look like their portraits? How will I know it's them?"

The crooked way she smirked matched her villain persona. "It's the best I have. And about their appearance, just trust me, you'll know if it's them."

We stopped in the hallway outside the office while Kai helped Wendy pull her backpack on.

I grabbed Hook's arm before she could walk away. "What does the Christmas tree mean?"

She shrugged. "You're the investigator. Now, if you'll excuse me, I have to go wig shopping because your daughter snuck up behind me and squished gum against my head." The way she forced the last few words out felt like a slap to the face. She pointed at the spot where the gum stuck to her scalp.

"I'm sorry about your hair—"

Hook stepped too close to me, breaking my personal bubble. "Do whatever you must to get her away from Neverland."

"I don't even know how you know about Neverland or if it's real." As soon as the words came out of my mouth, heat snaked up my neck. The statement was about as embarrassing as the time I went to work in slippers and got crime scene blood on my fuzzy bunnies. This admitted that Hook, this random storybook character, and a villain no less, might know more about the fairy tales than me.

I was supposed to be the lead on the Story Aura Case, but it didn't feel that way when my daughter's substitute teacher knew more about fairy tale magic than I did. I pinched the edge of the hood, which materialized now as one of those sweaters knitted by grandmas, and I rubbed it between my forefinger and thumb. Johnson had threatened my role as The Keeper of Stories, now Hook tread dangerously close to that line.

Hook snorted. "I saw it. That's how I know. The gods called it a rip, but I thought it looked more like a crack. I'm going to find it and I'm going to step through. But if your daughter follows me, I can't promise I won't make it my mission to send her back by whatever means necessary."

And for that I was thankful. Not the 'whatever means necessary' part, of course. I wouldn't let Wendy get hurt, but she didn't belong in a fictional place, worlds away from us. As far as I knew, only the gods could stop it. But they were MIA and apparently couldn't locate me, either.

I blinked to the present to see Hook's back. She marched for the double doors, shoving them open and letting sunlight flood the hall. The blinding brightness obscured her until her silhouette stepped out of view.

Kai pressed his hand to the center of my back. "Ready?"

My gaze dropped to Wendy who giggled with a friend in the hall. They discussed what they planned to ask for in their letter to Santa Claus.

"I have to take off the hood," I mumbled, as I stared at the girls. Wendy's pigtails flung from side to side as she shook her head. Her friend's eyes bugged when she insisted Wendy was on Santa's naughty list.

"Then I'll go to the North Pole and find him," Wendy said, hands on her hips. "I know how to go to other worlds. You just walk through it like a door."

Breath hitched in my throat and I sputtered a cough. It wouldn't matter which list she ended up on, Santa wouldn't find Wendy in Neverland anyway.

"You can't," Kai said, interrupting my focus on our daughter.

"Of course, she can't. She…she, it's a portal." I scrubbed my fingers through my hair as I stuttered out the words.

"No, you." My husband held my shoulders, grounding me. "Remember what happened last time you took the hood off?"

I finally tore my attention from Wendy and met Kai's gaze. Dark rings cupped his eyes and worry wrinkled his brow. Finals and grading papers swamped him at this time of year and he'd have to add holiday shopping to the list because I didn't have a second to spare. Despite all of his stress, Kai never failed to be there for me, standing by my side and shaking reality into me.

I swallowed. "The stories that join the cycle won't manifest until the next century. In seventy-whatever years I'll be a pro. It's fine—" I waved my hand but Kai caught it and laced his fingers through mine.

"Johnson tried to take it," he said what I'd been avoiding. "And if he gets it, the stories won't be twisted." With a quick glance at our daughter, he sighed.

I read between the lines. If I wasn't the Keeper of Stories, and Johnson somehow stole this role away from me, Wendy's story would play out as the plot of Peter Pan. And Peter Pan wasn't like the other stories. This wasn't Pride and Prejudice where Elizabeth and Mr. Darcy fall in love and the story ends, effectively ridding them of the aura. Thankfully, it also didn't include a violent death like Red Riding Hood where I should have been eaten by the wolf, then completing the plot. Peter Pan never ended, he lived on, unable to grow up, eternally hunted by his nemesis. I hadn't a clue if Wendy's story *could* be completed.

So, it had to be removed.

The aura must go. I pictured the thoughts as a banner outside of a furniture store.

A dull pain throbbed in my head, pulsing with every beat of my heart. My thoughts blurred, and the colors I'd imagined organizing my plans, melted into one another. I winced and Kai gently squeezed my hand.

"Headache again?" he asked.

I cringed and nodded.

"It's getting worse," he said. "Maybe you should go to the doctor—"

"No." I pulled away from him. "I'm fine. Everything is fine." I shrugged. Thank goodness Wendy was elbows-deep in a debate about

Rudolph because I couldn't hold my tongue. "Wendy's basically suspended. The only lead I have on finding the Brothers Grimm is something about a Christmas tree with no presents. And speaking of Christmas, it's two weeks away and I haven't even started shopping!"

Kai pursed his lips and tucked a strand of my thinning hair behind my ear. It had fallen out in clumps lately, filling my brush with dark tangles of dead strands. Stress did a number on hair and nails.

His worried look lifted and, either the fluorescent lights caught his iris just right, or a spark ignited in his eyes. "Wait, didn't Hook say it was a Christmas tree with no lights?"

"Mommy?" Wendy inserted herself between us, looking up with enormous eyes. Her missing front tooth only reminded me of another recent mistake I'd made. Apparently, the Tooth Fairy wasn't real, or else she'd have backed me up with a shiny coin under Wendy's pillow when I'd forgotten.

"No, I swear it was 'with no presents'." I shook my head, but it only made me dizzy. "That's what I wrote in my notes." The color red came to mind, like Rudolph's nose. I'd assigned the holiday-adjacent color to organize that thought in the filing system of my brain. The dull throb intensified until it forced me to squeeze my eyes shut.

"Mommy, I'm hungry."

"Are you okay?" Kai asked.

I opened my eyes. "A Christmas tree with no lights could be any pine tree. It had to be *no presents*." Could I trust my brain right now? Another dizzy wave struck me.

"Right." He nodded. Overgrown hair flopped into his face. Stubble decorated his chin and joined in the lack-of-grooming look. Though I liked the shadow, it gave him a distinguished, college-professor look, and reminded me how busy and stressed we both were.

"So if you're right, I'm looking for a pine tree, at a playground, during the full moon. Which is tonight." I struggled to shift the clues around in my brain, assigning colors to each one the same way I organized evidence on a case.

"And Colonel Mustard did it in the library with a candlestick," he joked.

I cracked a smile, and Kai squeezed my hand.

"Can we get a Happy Meal?" Wendy persisted.

"Good luck," Kai said. He leaned forward and kissed me. It ended too quickly but we couldn't exactly have a passionate make-out sesh in the middle of our daughter's elementary school. Speaking of Wendy, her unofficial suspension would turn into an expulsion if I didn't get food into the hangry monster soon. Who knows what hungry Wendy-slash-Peter would do to the nemesis named Hook?

Kai continued. "The Teacher's Aide is covering my classroom right now but he can't give the last lecture before finals. I've got to head back. Do you need me to take Wendy? She can sit and color at my desk—"

"No," Wendy complained as we turned and finally headed for the door. "It's so boring."

"Gee thanks," Kai joked. Though the sun shone brightly today, rare for a winter afternoon in San Francisco, a chill still bit through my clothes. "In fact, my students find my government lectures, mingled with humor, quite amusing."

Wendy's shoulders slumped. Though she misbehaved and didn't deserve the luxury of choice, I couldn't leave her with Kai. He was too busy and too stressed. It'd be much easier to set her up with crayons and coloring pages in the corner of my cubicle at Bay Side Media while I finished writing an article update about routine muggings at the pier.

"I've got this," I said. A sharp bolt of pain joined the dull ache. My hand shot to my forehead, but I blinked the dizziness away before Kai got concerned all over again. I quickly changed the subject and lowered my voice. "If you have time, make a run to Target and grab stocking stuffers before they're sold out. Oh, and some freezer meals, maybe?"

"Done." Kai nodded then planted a quick kiss on Wendy's head. He turned and walked in the opposite direction while I took our daughter's hand and pulled her toward Bay Side Media's building.

Cars honked and left exhaust behind for us to breathe. Wendy tugged me toward the McDonald's on the corner.

By the time we'd retrieved fast food, eaten it, and made it to the office, I'd popped another aspirin. Writing the article proved easy, but time flew by. When I submitted it to my boss, it was time for a second trip to McDonald's. I helped Wendy stuff her load of printed coloring pages into her backpack and followed her into the elevator.

My coworkers rambled during the ride down to the first floor of Bay Side Media's building. I asked, again, when Scarlet would be back from her assignment following a lead on a story in Hollywood but Pam didn't have answers. The sliding doors rolled open, and I bid goodbye to my boss Pam, Elsie, and the others. Evening had fallen and brought with it an icy breeze. San Francisco in the dark didn't bother me until I had a child at my side to protect.

I was used to crime scenes and the constant threat of danger for a woman walking alone—it was the purpose of Red Riding Hood's story, after all. But Red Riding Hood never lived long enough to become a mother. If she had, she'd definitely have developed severe anxiety as she tried to protect her child from untrustworthy people, wolves, and… Neverland. I knew how to keep her safe from all of those, except the last one.

How long did I have to find the Brothers Grimm and change their minds before Wendy found the rip, crack, or whatever invited her into the fictional world?

I tightened my grip on her hand as we hurried into the bright and colorful building with the giant glowing 'M' for the second round of french fries.

We stood in line until it was our turn to order two cheeseburgers, sans Happy Meal since Wendy was grounded from getting new toys for putting gum in her teacher's hair. No *happy* for her until she'd served her time. We shuffled forward, drawing closer to the registers. While we waited, my mind wandered. After a quiet afternoon in the office, my migraine had subsided to near-invisible levels, clearing room for thoughts of the Grimm Case.

The tree equaled green for the color-coding system in my head. Basic. The playground was orange, and I pictured the full moon in all its yellow glory.

A park with pine trees during the full moon. And a full moon means what, werewolves? How did I not think of it before? I blamed the headaches.

As I placed our order, my stomach grumbled. I wanted to blame nausea on fast food but the truth twisted my insides. Everything suddenly made sense.

Rubber floor. Child's laughter. And trees. All signs pointed to the park, at night, apparently with the added lead of a full moon.

The site of my near-death experience, well, one of them, was where I'd find the gods.

The answer should have been obvious when Hook had given me the clues. Memories flooded my mind of the first time I saw Jameson transform into the wolf from Red Riding Hood. Scarlet was there, to stop him from killing me out of turn.

Pioneer Park was a playground full of trees, tall pines. We hadn't paid it a visit since Wendy was younger. At almost seven, she was busy with school, karate classes, playdates, and piano recitals. The fact that I hadn't put the clues together before now was embarrassing at best. Stupid migraine.

"For here or to-go?" The McDonald's cashier repeated, cutting into my thoughts. The smell of over-salted, fried foods stung my nose, but memories were strong and my brain tricked me into believing the scent of Christmas surrounded us. Between the oil they dropped potatoes in and the tang of ketchup, I smelled the pines of Pioneer Park.

"To-go," I said, eager to get there. But as soon as they handed us the bags full of burgers, black dots spotted my vision and the pounding returned to my head.

"Mommy?" Wendy looked up at me as I paused with one foot on the sidewalk's concrete and one still firmly standing on the tile inside the McDonald's lobby.

I swayed and grabbed the door frame but a quick blink and a breath of cool air recovered me.

I swallowed the pain and managed a smile. "Want to have a picnic at the park?"

Chapter 4

Wild Ghost Chase

A large crack snaked through the rubber ground beneath the play structure. Was this the rip between worlds? Were we close to Neverland?

Wendy ran for the slide after shoving the last bites of cheeseburger into her cheeks like a chipmunk. I opened my mouth to warn her about the dangers of choking. *Don't run while chewing.* The words never reached my voice, dying in my throat instead.

The clock on my Apple Watch struck seven and buzzed with a reminder that I only had five hours left to meet my daily step goal. The early evening meant other city-dwellers should be out, walking their dogs, or jogging for their own daily exercise. But I heard no footsteps.

I kept my eyes glued to Wendy as she threw herself into the air to reach the monkey bars.

"Careful!" I intended to shout it but it came out as a whisper. Would my warnings drive her closer to Neverland? Screw it, mother knows best, not the Brothers Grimm. "Wendy, slow down!"

She listened, considering she only reached for the next bar rather than swung like the animal the bars were named for. I breathed and allowed myself to take in the surroundings. The play structure stood near the park's entrance with benches surrounding it. A drinking fountain and a sign with complimentary doggie doo bags were on the other side where the fences lined the pathways. The pathways were made for jogging, cycling, and long romantic walks through the forest of trees, thick enough to make you forget you were in the center of San Francisco city. The concrete sidewalk broke off into several directions at the back of the park where the trees obscured the paths. The moon, though full, didn't shine bright enough to break through the tree cover leaving us at the mercy of the dim streetlamps scattered throughout the park.

Thankfully, I carried plenty of weapons at all times. Monster-hunting didn't come without its perks—one of those being fearlessness when it came to werewolves and evil stepmothers. But Neverland was a different sort of beast. Not a monster like Frankenstein or a fractured fairy tale like Pinocchio trapped inside a virtual reality.

I couldn't solve it or stop it. I could only hope the Brothers Grimm would listen. Maybe if I spoke in my best, stern mom-voice, they'd hear me out.

Still scanning the park, my gaze landed on a lump in the shadows.

"Are you here?" I whispered to the gods. I edged around a bench and closed the distance between me and the object. *You'll know if it's them.* Hook's words came back to me. How would I know? It still boggled my mind that *she* knew about any of this.

"Mommy?"

I glanced back to see Wendy standing on the bench only a few steps behind me.

"Stay there," I said.

A bolt of pain lanced through my temples but I ignored it. I shuffled toward the shadow, blinking away the ache in my head and squinting. Before my eyes could adjust to the darkness and make out the shape, something splashed beneath my feet.

I whipped out my phone and flicked the flashlight on—an action I should have taken before walking toward the unknown object. But, of course, my stupid brain wasn't working right. Stress led to pain and pain led to a muddled mind, all of which I wouldn't let Wendy see. She needed a strong mother.

Dark blood stained the soles of my boots. I swallowed the gasp that rose in my throat as my tired mind slowly registered what lay before me. Murder wasn't new to me but the mangled woman's body far surpassed the gore I'd seen in previous cases. She was half-eaten as if attacked by a horde of zombies with enough blood loss to feed a family of vampires. A third of her head was completely gone. The bite marks obscured her facial features but the partial view of her thin nose and full lips looked freakishly familiar.

My gaze trailed the frame of her face until my heart slowed. The victim's short, dark hair was cut in a style identical to mine.

I glanced back at Wendy to see she'd hopped off the bench and returned to the playground/ There, she grabbed the end of a stainless-steel talk tube and spoke into it, though nobody was at the other tube to hear her.

Female victim, possibly mid-thirties, hack job. Was it a murder or a wild animal attack? I'd come here to find the Brothers Grimm, but stumbled upon a case to investigate instead. At least this made the trip up the hill to Pioneer Park on nothing but salt and potatoes, worth it.

I knelt and inspected her clothes. Her red sweater meant she likely intended to go outside. This showed she wasn't dragged from her home but attacked here, instead. Light reflected against the smooth, cold surface of a pistol's barrel. The weapon was peeking out from beneath where her right arm was twisted and partially covered by her body. *Gun. 9 millimeter. A Sig... just like mine.*

Pain seared through my skull as I tried to list more details.

"Ebenezer Scrooge," I cursed.

An icy chill swept over me, leaving a flood of goosebumps down my neck and over my arms. I willed the hood to materialize and pulled the heavy fabric tighter around me, but it didn't help.

I swiped the screen open on my phone again. After a quick scroll, I landed on Detective Wilhelm's contact information. The pain built, leaving my head spinning and my hands shaking.

I tried to tap the picture of the frowning-faced emoji I'd inserted into his contact information, but my depth perception was off. What the hell was happening to me? After this investigation, and once I found the gods of story, of course, I'd sleep long and hard after a self-care bubble bath. That'd fix everything.

I blinked and refocused.

Wendy's sweet singing sounded haunting in the empty park. I glanced back to see she still sang into the talk tube, apparently serenading an imaginary friend.

"I want to play all day, all day, all day. Take me away to the land of play!"

Though she belted out the last of her improvised lyrics, I could have sworn it came with a whisper.

"*Mommy.*"

The chill grew heavier, like a frost on my shoulders, but the breeze hadn't picked up. In fact, the tree cover should have kept us relatively warm in the center of Pioneer Park. Speaking of warm, my breath clashed with the frigid air, sending swirls that curled in the shape of my own, personal miniature cloud.

The whisper repeated itself and I blinked at the dead woman.

"*Mommy.*"

My gut knotted. I'd interviewed psychopathic serial killers before. Rarely did I feel fear beyond the threat of failure or worry for my daughter. But something here was different. I half-expected the victim to rise and speak to me. Did any fairy tales from long ago include zombies? I'd already faced down Frankenstein's monster. What else did the story cycle have in store for me?

I tapped my phone again, and the screen lit up. Quickly, I jammed my finger where the contact information spelled out the detective's phone number.

The whisper repeated, louder and with more clarity now. The word wasn't mommy but my brain couldn't wrap around what it'd said.

"*Mari…*"

It echoed now. The trill of my phone fell into the background, distant from my senses. I moved the bright screen from my view and leaned closer to the bloody body.

"Are you…alive?" I asked the mangled woman.

A thousand thoughts pounded me all at once. What the hell was I doing? I took my daughter to the park, hoping to find the gods that doomed her to Neverland but found murder instead. This wasn't the time to inspect a case. I needed to return her to the safety of our home and come back with the detective in a professional and official capacity. What kind of sick, messed-up mother was I to lean over a mutilated body while my daughter played only a few feet away? Not just played, but sang about the place that would basically kidnap her one day…soon.

"Rowan." Detective Wilhelm's voice joined the other haunting sounds. My eyes never left the dead woman's mouth.

"*Mari.*"

Did her lips move? Was that the flutter of her eyelashes or the wind? This victim had no chance of survival, that was clear. And yet I could hear her voice. I barely breathed but the chill still picked up my breath and carried it into the wisp of a cloud between me and the dead.

"Hey, Rowan!" Detective Wilhelm shouted from the phone. "You in some kind of trouble again?" He mumbled something about *women and their scattered brains* but I didn't catch all of it.

"*Mari Fable. Mari Fable.*"

The whisper surrounded me, enveloping me in the icy chill of a winter storm. As it became clearer, the voice seemed to drop two octaves, and another one joined it.

My heart pounded, keeping time with the throbbing in my skull.

I tore my gaze away from the victim and straightened from the crouched position. The phone fell from my shaking hands and I stumbled back.

"Did you butt-dial me, Rowan?" Detective Wilhelm's voice stuttered and broke into what sounded like a robot. Static blocked his rant at me, growing louder. I could make out his last words before the line went dead. "What a waste of—"

I forced my feet to move, stepping backward, ready to pivot and run for my daughter.

"*Can you hear us?*"

The cold intensified, and my shivering shifted into violent shaking.

If I didn't get out of here, I'd succumb to frostbite or my heart would slow from freezing.

I knew I needed to grab Wendy and bolt, but my brain cleared long enough to make sense of the situation. All at once, the clues came together—a full moon, the pine trees, the playground, and even Wendy's giggles in the background completed the picture Hook had given me. This was where she'd seen the Brothers Grimm in her dream. Now I had real confirmation, rather than a theory.

"I hear you," I answered.

Like the hood, something materialized in thin air. Silver clouds formed into the shape of spectral, wispy, and barely visible creatures. With a faint glow, the shapes filled in.

"Spirits," I whispered.

Two men stood over the dead woman wearing old-timey clothes. Kai would know the exact era from which they came. As a history teacher, he could name the style and the men's social status. But I didn't have a clue. To me, they looked like the male love interest in a Jane Austen novel or carolers in an old-fashioned Christmas play.

"Don't you know she can't hear you, you blunderbuss?" said the slightly older man in the black coat and perfectly pressed pants. Existence as a spirit clearly had its perks, like never ironing and yet always wearing clothes with no wrinkles, though his counterpart's appearance didn't match. His thick German accent was unmistakable.

The other man donned a collared, white shirt with his gray coat hanging open, and hair slightly disheveled. He grimaced and narrowed his eyes. "Dare you call me the blunderbuss when you're fussing about with your glorious artwork?" His tongue rolled over the last word, exaggerating it as if he didn't believe what he said. "It's hideous, really. We could do without the exposed brain matter."

"Who am I to be cursed with a brother whose weak stomach cannot handle a little death?" He added a word in a language I didn't recognize, likely German but I wasn't a linguist.

"If she cannot hear us, then I believe your little girl's voice is to blame. I insist you allow me to do the talking when we show her the future." Gray Coat raised his arm and extended his long, crooked finger. It pointed at nothing in the dark down one of the forked pathways. "As well as the present. Perhaps, the past as well." The slight waves in his hair didn't budge as he looked at the body beneath their feet.

Their argument continued and I stood there like a dolt, just watching. Add the static from the interrupted phone call earlier, their unrealistic appearance, and my invested interest in their fight, and it felt like I was a couch potato enjoying a sitcom. Alas, I was shivering in a park over a dead body—in the real world.

"Won't you leave my masterpiece alone?"

Gray Coat threw his head back and laughed. "I suppose you consider that awful story about the boy and girl eaten by a witch a masterpiece as well?"

Each time they spoke, the chill grew colder. I'd frozen in place, both literally and figuratively. The sight before me scrambled my brain, but I still tried to turn, to open my mouth, and call out for my daughter. Worry lingered but took a backseat as my mind filled in the clues from their conversation and cleared enough for me to realize neither Wendy nor I were in immediate danger from these…what had he said? Blunderbusses?

Fancy Pants scoffed. "Are you accusing me of inventing famines and cannibalism? Hansel and Gretel was history to be preserved, was it not? Is that not the job of a dedicated librarian?"

A small hand slipped into mine, and I squeezed.

"I'm cold," Wendy said. "Are they ghosts?"

I glanced at my daughter to see her undaunted by the spectral figures before us. Pride swelled at her bravery until the ache in my skull zapped my focus. I blinked and returned my attention to the gods of story.

"They're brothers," I said.

Chapter 5

Loose Cannon

The ghosts behaved more like annoyed brothers than timeless gods who controlled the story cycle. They flung old-fashioned insults at one another, arguing relentlessly about magic beans and giants in the sky. Nothing of which related to Neverland.

I cleared my throat loud enough to startle them.

"Do you see us?" Fancy Pants, who I'd identified as Jacob between the name-calling, asked. He, apparently, only spoke in questions, which I'd find annoying real fast.

"Of course not," Wilhelm, the one for which the detective must have been named, said. "She's looking right through—"

"Yep," Wendy interrupted. Thankfully, she'd been so intrigued by the ghosts that she hadn't noticed the body beneath their feet. The shadow that was cast over her likely helped obscure her from my daughter's notice.

I swallowed and tugged her away before I crouched in front of her. "Wendy, Honey, it's past your bedtime."

"Kids don't have bedtime on the Play Planet," she said, confidence exuding from her every word. Play Planet equaled Neverland which meant I needed to minus the story aura from the equation ASAP.

I sighed. Gods or not, I needed to get my daughter away from the dead body.

"Mommy needs to have a chat with these guys. Will you try the monkey bars again and then we'll go?"

Wendy chewed on her bottom lip, licked the salt from around her mouth, then twisted. I gently yanked her back to look at me before she could see the victim.

Finally, she shrugged and skipped past me toward the playground.

"Aren't you the elusive Keeper, Mari Fable?" Jacob said with a jab of his elbow through his brother's ribcage. "Isn't that right, Willy?"

'Willy' shot his brother a piercing glare and bared his glowing teeth. "It's Will. And you're taking this rather lightly considering the crack has grown—"

Jacob coughed loud enough to pop my eardrums. "Have you forgotten the plan?" He mumbled between his teeth.

"I miss Agnes," Will said with a sigh. He stared wistfully at the trees hanging over the center of Pioneer Park. The crooked branches stretched out like long fingers, casting jagged shadows across the concrete.

I didn't know who Agnes was, but I didn't care. I straightened and inhaled. "I wasn't intentionally hiding. How was I supposed to know the hood made me invisible to you? And why can't you appear in my dreams like you did in Hook's? Where the hell have you creeps been for the past several centuries?" Apparently, Jacob's question-talking had influenced my word vomit. Embarrassing.

The blunt end of my words shocked both brothers to silence. Will's jaw hung open, but he quickly shut it and swallowed.

"Dare you blame us?" Jacob's eyes bugged, and he glanced at Will before looking at me again. "Did you hear that, brother?"

Will frowned. "I'm quite capable of hearing, Jake."

"Jacob," he corrected—his first sentence without a question mark. Color me shocked.

"It's the twenty-first century, *Jake*," his brother insisted.

I stepped forward, all too aware of the dead body when my boot splashed in blood again. "I don't have time for this. I've got a daughter to put to bed and a murder to investigate. I'm here to demand that you remove the story aura from Wendy. ASAP." My arms flung around wildly as I spoke. The temporary adrenaline dulled the pain from searing through my skull. "I mean, as. Soon. As. Possible." I spoke slowly and explained the acronym, unsure what these seventeenth-century dudes would understand. Or was it the eighteenth century? Kai had explained it to me several times, but I always forgot—my brain was too busy storing other, more important, information.

Jacob tried to elbow Will again but his arm went right through his brother's torso. "Did you hear that?" he laughed.

Will groaned and turned to him. "Stop asking me that." He gritted his teeth. "If you weren't already dead, I would off you."

I snapped my fingers. "Hey, Jake, Willy, focus." They turned to me in time to see me point two fingers at my eyes and then back at them. Like Wendy, these gods, ghosts, librarians, or whatever they were, didn't intimidate me. Now that I knew where the voice came from and confirmed the victim wasn't ready to rise from the dead, I could return to Mama Bear mode and focus on breaking Wendy free from her story's plot. "See that faint glow around my daughter? You're going to abracadabra that godly magic and vanish it, capiche?" I tossed my thumb over my shoulder.

Jacob squinted until his bushy brows completely obscured his eyes. "What daughter?"

My heart slammed into my stomach and all at once the migraine bolted through my temple with pain intense enough to fell a horse. I spun around to find the monkey bars vacant and the park devoid of a child's laughter.

"No." I breathed, my voice shaking from the heavy pounding in my chest. "Wendy!" The heel of my boots slammed into the concrete. I ran for the path that led to the street, the closest walkway to the playground —a poor design, really, then double-backed to the playground.

"Hurry back, won't you?" Jacob shouted.

I glanced back. Bloody, red footprints followed me from where I'd stepped too close to the victim. On top of everything else, I still needed to call the police and inform them of the crime scene. Plus, I'd have to admit that I'd accidentally trampled it, spreading blood with my feet.

The playground's rubber floor squeaked beneath the soles of my shoes. I collapsed to my knees to check inside the plastic tunnel then jumped to my tiptoes to see if Wendy had hid at the top of the staircase. With the top of the play structure cleared, I dropped to my knees and ture cleared, I dropped to my knees and scaled the tunnel slide's walls, shouting for Wendy along the way.

My heartbeat seemed to echo through the slide and bounce off the enclosed walls. I scrambled out and ran for the park's entrance. Before now, I hadn't let myself think the worse. If she left the park, finding her would be much harder. And what if someone took her? My throat squeezed while the trees along the sidewalk seemed to close in on me, reaching with the long branches.

Somewhere, behind me, the Brothers Grimm were yelling. Despite the distance between us, their words struck me, crystal clear.

"Solve this murder and we'll help you," Will's voice echoed as I rounded the corner.

"We want to go home!" Jacob added, shouting in a high-pitched voice that didn't match his ghostly existence.

As soon as I emerged from the park, I nearly collided with a wisp of a woman. The elderly lady's terrier yapped at me and then bore his sharp, tiny teeth for coming too close to his beloved owner. The dog trembled but growled as viciously as if he were the wolf who'd tried to eat me. Nothing could frighten me more than I already was. The woman slapped her hand to her chest, reflecting how I felt on the inside.

"Sorry, I'm sorry." Words tumbled over one another. "Did you see a little girl? About yea high?" I indicated at the height of my belly button. My stomach churned like the sea during a storm while my mind rolled through all the worst-case scenarios.

The stunned woman only shook her head. She stooped to pick up her pooch and hurried down the street. I scraped my fingers over my scalp, tangling them in my hair. My heart banged hard enough that I must have looked like a cartoon character with the shape of it extending from my chest.

"Wendy," I squeaked out her name as I scanned the street. A couple sauntered along the sidewalk on the other side, their hands in each other's back pockets. A wiry man jogged with his earbuds in, flying past me before I could ask if he'd seen a six-year-old nearby.

I scrambled across the street before the headlights of an oncoming car drew too close. It whizzed past, flinging my hair into my face. I begged the couple to tell me if they'd witnessed anything but they shook their heads.

After stumbling past them, I stopped a man speaking into his cell phone, my hand on his chest. He didn't like the personal invasion and I didn't blame him. Thankfully, he still paused long enough to hear me out. But, the answer was no.

"Wendy!" I screamed, desperation taking control. *The crack.* Was Neverland beneath the play structure? Did it open up and swallow her whole? I stepped into the street and a car screeched its brakes until it swerved a tire onto the curb to avoid hitting me.

The man honked and wailed at me but I disappeared into the park.

"Wendy…" I coughed, running out of breath.

A tiny body slammed into my legs and wrapped her arms tightly around me.

Tears flooded my eyes before my brain even registered she'd returned. My body knew my daughter's hug before my mind could process the action. I fell to my knees and pulled her into me, likely squeezing the life out of her.

I buried my face in her small, bony shoulder and silently sobbed.

"I'm sorry," she repeated. "I'm sorry."

It's my fault. How did I let her out of my sight? She was only a few feet behind me and I could hear her humming the song she'd created while she played.

Despite the panic raging within me, I forced myself to calm down before letting her see my face. Wendy needed a strong mother. I sucked in a slow breath through my nose and then blew it out. *Always strong.* The headache reminded me of its presence and a wave of dizziness threatened to topple me. I sniffed and discreetly reached up to wipe the tears from my face before holding her at arm's length.

"Are you okay? What happened?" I asked.

Wendy nodded, her eyes huge and round, catching the glow of the streetlamp that barely illuminated the playground. "I heard other kids playing a game, and I wanted to play too." She shrugged, calmer now. I glanced around the park but saw no children, not a single soul. "I asked if they'd let me play but they said I had to have pixie dust and I didn't have pixie dust so I came to find you to see if we could buy some pixie dust but you left and I thought I was lost. Then the ghost called me a lost boy, so I stuck my tongue out at him and said I wasn't lost and then I heard you calling my name." Her strung-along sentences left her breathless.

The explanation didn't make sense, and yet I understood. The visions of Neverland were growing stronger, just as they had for me when the plot of Red Riding Hood seeped into my life all those years ago. I'd seen fangs on my OBGYN and had heard a wolf's howl. None of it was real and yet all of it existed somewhere between the story world and San Francisco, guiding me to the plot of the fairy tale that had taken hold of me.

"Oh, Wednesday," I called her by her nickname and brushed the hair from her face. "I didn't leave you. I'd never leave you anywhere alone."

A dark shadow beneath us caught my eye. My gaze flicked to the ground where the rubber flooring had cracked. Had it widened or was that my paranoia? The potatoes threatened to come back up my throat as I inspected the crack. It ran right between us, like a warning that we'd soon be separated again—daughter in Neverland and mother distraught.

Tears welled in Wendy's eyes again. She threw herself against me and looped her arms around my neck. "I just wanted to play!"

I feel Neverland's pull. I read between the lines, correcting what she didn't understand. Thank not-the-gods for Hook. Never did I expect to be in cahoots with a villain but Hook was different, and because of her willingness to share her dreamlike knowledge, or faithful beliefs, or whatever they were, I knew what to expect for Wendy's situation.

I swept the crook of my arm under her rear-end and stood, lifting her with me.

"Let's go home and get into our cozy jammies. We'll have a snuggle—"

"And a bedtime story?" Wendy asked between sniffles.

My throat squeezed. *Don't ask for a fairy tale.*

"Of course." A promise was all I could manage. I couldn't deny my baby the comfort she needed despite how unsettling it was to read those books to her.

I turned to where the brothers were but only the shape of the dead body was in the shadow. It served as a reminder that I needed to call the cops again since my communication with Detective Wilhelm had been interrupted.

Jacob and Will Grimm were gone just when I needed them the most. Will's words finally registered in my panicked mind.

Solve the murder and we'll help you.

I frowned and turned toward the street. I'd be back, and I'd solve that murder so hard the brothers wouldn't know what hit them.

Okay, that didn't make sense. But what did in this crazy, messed-up existence I called immortal life, did?

Chapter 6

More Fun Than a Barrel of Murder

Armed with my notebook in hand, a block of blank sticky notes in my fist, and, of course, my small pistol tucked into the front of my jeans, I returned to the scene of the crime. I'd called the police and alerted them of the situation which meant I'd be walking into a crowded crime scene. But that wouldn't stop me from picking up clues and recording leads.

Despite all the crap in my arms, the questions were the heaviest thing I carried. I pulled the hood closed across my chest, tightening the strings and willing it to appear as a trench coat. Trench coats were intimidating, right?

The questions cycled in my mind. When would Scarlet call me back? Why did the Brothers Grimm want me to solve this murder? As gods of story, didn't they already know which fairy tale she came from? Or were they not all-knowing spirits and they needed my help?

A small smile curved at the edge of my mouth. The Brothers had let their hand show. If they needed me to deal with the story cycle, I had an extra bargaining tool for Wendy's freedom. The epiphany was the only thing keeping me from losing my mind at all the pieces that didn't make sense.

Jake and *Willy* thought they had the winning cards, but I carried a royal flush. I pulled the hood over my head and stalked into the park.

A female cop nearly collided shoulders with me as she marched past the playground. I spun around to ask where they were on the investigation but she was busy trying to get her walkie-talkie to work. It blew a steady stream of static as she repeated her partner's name.

"Excuse me," I said, but my voice came out quieter than I'd expected. I cleared my throat and opened my mouth to try again but she was engrossed in the conversation now.

The further she walked from the center of Pioneer Park, the clearer the person's voice on the other line spoke.

"So it's clear?" The static-covered voice asked.

The cop sighed and clicked the talk button. "Yep, it was just a stupid prank. Probably by some kids who knew about the murders here from a few years ago. They're just trying to stir up drama."

What? I whipped around on my heels and saw a body. But this one was thick and sweaty despite the chilly December wind. The shirtless torso showcased abs made of steel, and he wore laced Nikes that looked special edition and probably cost more than my mortgage payment.

My jaw dropped but not at the runner's sculpted physique. The overpriced jogging shoes ran straight through the victim's body. For a moment, I thought my brain glitched like a botched computer program, but nope, Gym Dude's foot slammed the concrete right between the victim's hip bones.

Ebenezer Scrooge. Was the murdered woman a figment of my imagination? Was she just a mirage in my desperate hope to find a lead that I could trade with the Brothers for Wendy's freedom?

Gym Dude flashed me a grin with a nauseating wink.

I rolled my eyes. "I'm not checking you out," I muttered. The pool of blood didn't splash from his footsteps or stain the sole of his shoes. My stomach churned and Gym Dude's ego didn't help.

He stopped right in front of me and took that moment to stretch his arms over his head, expanding his chest and sending wafts of body odor from his pits. I grimaced.

"Do you see that?" I pointed, hoping beyond all hope that he answered the way I had on my wedding day. *I do.*

Gym Dude only furrowed his waxed brows and shifted his stretching into an extra twist. His gaze followed to where I pointed a few steps behind him.

"Do you see her?" I repeated.

He turned back and cracked a forced smile. "Her?"

"The woman!" My heart pounded now as the cop's words haunted me. *Just a stupid prank.* As much as I didn't want this victim to have suffered, I *needed* this murder to be real. I needed to know I hadn't lost my marbles. I needed confirmation that it wasn't a hallucination. Did I find the gods of story and received the promise that would save my daughter, or not?

We'll help you.

How much longer did Wendy have until her visions became reality and she found Neverland? The metaphorical clock ticked and another minute was taken away from my chance to save her from eternity as a lost child, with no family, and a target for Captain Hook.

"Her," I said, again. "Right there!"

Gym Dude shook his head and widened his eyes in a look that told me my marbles had spilled all over the park, tumbling, rolling into the bushes, and filling the crack in the playground's rubber floor.

"Drugs are bad," he said, as he popped earbuds in and resumed his jog.

"What?" I struggled to catch up with his accusation. He disappeared around the corner and into the street.

I squeezed my eyes shut. *She's not real.* Did that make the Brothers fake too? How could I continue my hunt to find them if these dang headaches gave me hallucinations?

When I opened my eyes, I expected the body to be gone. But the woman didn't move, didn't glitch, nor did she waver as the spectral figures had. The attacked woman was as solid in my sight as my own two feet.

I closed the distance between us, pulled out my phone, and crouched. I flicked open the camera app and positioned the victim in the center of the screen. It sickened me to save a photo of this brutal murder in my storage alongside pictures of Wendy's smile with her first missing tooth, and selfies of Kai and me at the Renaissance festival. But I needed to know if she existed. A photo would confirm the chaos.

The flash brightened the shadow for a second before darkness surrounded me again and a lump caught in my throat. The photo showed nothing more than the squished gum on the concrete. No woman. No body. Nothing. It was the ultimate confirmation that I'd made it all up.

I caught the slight shape of something white and oval in the photograph at the corner of the screen. I zoomed in and squinted. It looked like the toe of a shoe as if Gym Dude had returned for a photo shoot of his feet.

"Ghosts," I said. "Wendy called them ghosts. She saw them too." I stood and scanned the park. "Jake and Willy," I called in a singsong voice. "Come out, come out wherever you are."

I used the camera to pan the park and spot the vague grayish-white of their spirits but it was no use. Nothing showed in the rapid-fire photos I took and nobody responded.

Still, the chill had settled, and I hadn't noticed until the cloud from my breath swirled in front of me.

"You're here. Why can't I see?" I raised my voice. "Hello?" I opened my arms, ready to attack nothing. "Are you cowards? Come on!"

The streetlamp above flickered, and the temperature dropped again, forcing me to shudder.

"Fine. Fine!" I threw up my hands in surrender and turned to the victim. "I'll play your little game. As soon as I solve this pretend murder, I better not see that glow around my daughter anymore. Do you hear me?" I crouched again, pulled a pen from my pocket, and ripped off a sticky note from the block.

I scribbled detail after detail on the brightly colored pieces of paper and slapped them inside my notebook, the same way I arranged clues in a regular murder investigation. After a list of basic information from her approximate age to her clothes and injuries, I added theories.

Claw and teeth marks + weapon = a huntsman?

I crossed out the equation, knowing the original Little Red Riding Hood story didn't include a huntsman, besides, I'd already fulfilled that fairy tale for this century's cycle.

I sighed and swiped my palm over my forehead. Pain needled my temples and the freezing air didn't help. In the past, I'd solved cases like these with the help of identifying the fairy tale.

"What story is she from?" I asked the air, or rather, the ghosts I couldn't see. "Or don't you know? You dummies need me, don't you?"

The breeze bit into my nose as it blasted against my face.

"Oh, real nice. Put on your big boy pants and use your words." I glared around, eyes narrowed. I must have looked like a gremlin, crouched in the center of the park, threatening nobody. "If I freeze to death, you won't have me to solve your precious murder." Of course, I couldn't die. I felt the pain, I came close to death, but I persisted as the Keeper of Stories.

I settled into crisscross applesauce and shot Kai a text.

I'll be here awhile. Don't wait up, I love you.

The bar above the message froze, and the message hung in purgatory.

"Stupid phone," I grumbled and tore off a fresh sticky note. It was time for the minute details.

Carefully, I poked and prodded the body to check inside what was left of her mouth, and in her pockets. Her jeans produced a crumpled, green sticky note, a Starbucks receipt for a caramel macchiato with extra caramel and decaf—the same order I'd requested after Wendy was born and my taste buds had shifted to crave sugar but my breast-feeding schedule demanded caffeine-free.

"Weird," I breathed. The swirl of breath curled and formed into the shape of something familiar, like a dog's head. I blinked and waved it away. No more lost marbles.

I smoothed the sticky note. The scribbles looked familiar, like my handwriting. I squinted to make out the words. Some of the notes had faded because of its crumpled state.

"Selkie?" I pieced together the first word but the next few were too far gone. I passed my thumb over the paper, smoothing it more. "Coming out of San Fran boy? No, bay? Coming out of San Fran bay…" My voice tapered as breath left my lungs. The note was all-too-familiar. I'd written it six years ago when trying to solve Jameson's murders. My coworker-turned-serial-killer-wolf had left me a trail of dead women as he tried to track me, his personal Little Red Riding Hood.

The thumping in my ribcage picked up its pace. I coughed and gasped for breath as the icy air dried my throat.

"No…" The note slipped from between my fingers and floated to the ground, not flying away despite the rush of wind. I scrambled to perch on my knees and check the victim.

I pulled up her shirt to find stretch marks identical to my own.

My throat tightened.

I yanked her pant leg away from her ankle to find the tiny, minimalist tattoo of a slice of cheesecake Kai and I had gotten on our honeymoon to commemorate our wedding cake.

My inhale sounded like a dying breath as I gasped for air.

Finally, I settled my gaze on the victim's half-eaten face. Did I willfully ignore it before? How did I miss the small diamond studs in her ear? The same earrings Kai had given me the morning of our wedding.

My lung constricted and I could have sworn an invisible elephant slammed into my chest. Black spots dotted my vision as I clawed at my throat. I managed a cough and sucked in a straw-size of air.

"It's me." Did tears fill my eyes? My vision blurred, but I blinked it away when a low growl jarred me from the horrifying epiphany.

I snapped my gaze up, but the shadows obscured most of the park now. The nearest streetlamp's bulb has burned out, but I didn't notice before now.

Wasn't this meant to be my moment of victory? I'd solved it. I'd kept my end of the bargain. But why? Why me? Why a fake murder?

A movement in the shadows triggered me back to the present. Or the alternate reality. Wherever I was, there was a hulking figure too. The shape of furry, muscular haunches came into view.

The wolf stepped from the shadows, baring glistening, wet fangs. His growl rumbled deep within me, sending a shudder through my whole body.

Frozen in time and place, I met his gaze and recognized the deep brown eyes as the man who'd tried to murder me. The wolf who'd eaten me. The beast I'd cut myself from six years ago.

Jameson was back.

Chapter 7

Sour Ghosts

I shot to my feet and yanked my pistol from where it was concealed between my hip bone and belly button.

The wolf's growl split into a wide, haunting grin that showed rows of teeth stained with blood—my blood.

I cocked the gun and flexed my arms, ready for the kickback from firing the bullet. Jameson threw back his head and shook his gray and white ears, taunting me. His long tongue slithered from between his fangs and licked his snout, matting the fur that hung over his teeth.

How was he here? I'd sliced through his stomach, destroying him from the inside out half a decade ago.

The wolf stalked forward, front paws crossing over one another and claws scraping against the concrete.

I slowly applied pressure to the trigger.

A whistle rang out behind me, and my head stopped. It wasn't the gun; I hadn't followed through and fired yet.

Red caught the corner of my eye as a woman stepped into my view. The long, familiar hood dusted the sidewalk at the Keeper's feet.

Thankfully, it wasn't a third version of myself and the momentary relief almost had me bursting into fits of insane laughter. Maybe I had one marble left still rattling around in my brain.

Scarlet's huge, gorgeous eyes fixed on Jameson. Her red curls tumbled over her shoulders, each strand in place. Her laced boots clicked against the concrete as she stepped forward and beckoned for the wolf to close the rest of the distance between them. With one hand she curled her fingers and taunted Jameson to answer her, while she held an ax behind her back with the other.

The wolf, the egotistical serial killer that he was, lunged for her, ready to make Scarlet his second meal.

"Scar, watch out!" My brain rushed, worried for my friend. Though she didn't look like the Scarlet I knew now, I didn't have time to mull it over.

She didn't need my warning. Scarlet whipped out the ax, gripped it with both hands, and swung at the wolf's throat as he leaped into the air above her. Blood spilled over her in a shower of red as the ax's blade sliced through the beast's neck like butter. The blood beaded and washed over the hood with ease.

Scarlet stepped back and let the heavy weapon fall as the wolf came down. Before he hit the ground, his body cracked and shifted, with joints and bones protruding from every angle. Once he landed, he was Jameson again, human and naked.

The former Keeper of Stories turned, unaware of me, then knelt over the concrete and traced the shape of a door. Before I could gather my voice, she fell through the portal to another location with the story aura.

I raised my shaking hand to my forehead to apply pressure to the intense headache. Frost fell from my brows, catching in my lashes. Had my sweat frozen on my face? The excitement kept me warm momentarily, but the chill set in, deeper now.

"What is this?" I asked. "I solved the murder and I don't understand why you won't answer me. This isn't real, so why am I seeing it?"

I shivered and tugged the hood tighter against my ears before they turned to ice and snapped off my head.

"Wait."

Will's voice filled the surrounding air. Time seemed to speed up as footsteps pounded the concrete. The nearly empty park quickly filled with bodies, paramedics, cops, and detectives.

Detective Wilhelm barked orders at a female cop as he rounded the corner.

"Time of death?" he asked the coroner then ignored the answer. I watched, as the detective stepped closer to the dead version of me.

"I know this woman." He nudged the body with the toe of his boot and peered at the gun. "Yep, that's her piece. This is Mari Rowan. Reckless journalist. I've worked with her before."

"Hey!" I snapped, but he couldn't hear me. No matter how it felt, it wasn't real. It was a vision, an alternate reality, or something I couldn't wrap my exhausted mind around. Of course, the stupid detective recognized me by my weapon because he barely gave me the time of day, rarely even looking at me when I spoke. But he'd always admired the limited edition Sig I'd acquired. According to him, it wasn't fit for a woman.

I folded my arms, both in frustration and to keep myself warm.

A familiar cry rang out, prickling my senses. I almost expected my boobs to leak at the sound of the baby's dry wailing. Once a mom, always a mom.

My heart stopped as I spun around to see Kai, a thicker, younger version of him holding a bundle in his arms. Wendy wailed while tears streamed down his face. He walked right past me, eyes fixed on the body.

Detective Wilhelm blocked him, placing his hand on my husband's chest.

"That's my wife!" he screamed.

I slapped my hand over my mouth and the squeeze in my throat told me tears were coming. My eyes stung as I watched the fire in Kai's eyes. I knew that look. If he wasn't holding our baby, he'd have punched the detective right in the nose. But Wendy wailed louder now, and all he could do was sob and tighten his hold on her.

"She's gone, Mr. Rowan," the detective said in a matter-of-fact voice, no tact, no sensitivity.

"How?" Kai asked.

"We don't know yet."

"Detective," the coroner interrupted. She was an odd person, I'd worked with her on a few investigations and she didn't have the tact or professionalism needed in these situations, either. "It's fascinating, really. He appears to have scratched her with his fingernails. Then she shot him as he ate her."

"That doesn't look like a bullet wound." Detective Wilhelm nodded toward Jameson. The slice in his neck didn't match an injury from a gun.

"The bullet grazed him at just the right angle, severing the carotid artery. He bled out," the coroner explained.

Kai raked fingers from his free hand through his hair and sobbed. He collapsed on a nearby bench, rocking his whole body back and forth, but it didn't soothe Wendy. Hair fell into his face, soaking with his tears and sticking to his wet cheeks. She screamed and screamed and screamed for her mama.

But I was dead.

"I can't watch this," I whispered. "I won't." I shook my head and marched for the park's entrance.

"Don't you want help?" Jake's voice this time, and always as a question.

I froze by the playground and stared at the crack in the ground. It wasn't a portal, but that didn't mean Neverland wasn't real. I swallowed the lump in my throat as the world brightened around me.

It was daytime. Kids laughed and played at the park. Kai, thinner now, maybe too thin, sat at the bench that faced the monkey bars. Wendy in her six-year-old self swung from one bar to the next as her dad cheered and clapped for her success.

After Wendy hopped down and started for the sandpit, Kai turned his attention to his phone where he pulled up a text message thread.

Pain seared through my head as my eyes scanned the small screen. I stooped to read over Kai's shoulder.

Kai: *I did it. I returned to the park where Mari was killed.*

Mom: *Does it feel like it's healing you or making your grief worse?*

Kai didn't respond. Instead, he swiped the messaging app closed and pulled up a news article dated six years before. His knuckles turned white as he gripped the phone tighter. *Investigative Journalist Sacrifices Life to Stop Serial Killer.*

"Don't you see, Keeper?" Jacob said.

Wind swept into my face, turning my lips to prunes and biting my nose with frost though there was no snow in sight.

Jacob's body materialized, and his brother soon followed. The spectral figures stood in front of Kai and my protective urge was triggered. I wanted to leap over the bench and strangle the ghosts with my bare hands.

"Your death saved those other women," Will spoke now, as he tugged his coat closed over his chest. Even he seemed chilled by his ghostly presence.

"Is it clear what we're saying?" Jacob's nostrils flared as he spoke and I had half a mind to sock him in the nose.

"You are Red Riding Hood. The story should have ended with you eaten and the wolf asleep." Will snorted, then added. "Permanent sleep."

"Just like the original?" Jacob prodded with raised brows, though I couldn't fathom how he lifted those monstrosities without some kind of eyebrow exercise.

I folded my arms and frowned. "I get it. I should have died. But I didn't and Jameson is gone. What was the point of all of this?"

Jacob and Will exchanged glances. They spoke a silent language of shared expressions I didn't understand, but I recognized the interaction because Kai and I often did the same. My heart joined the ache in my head. Now, I hurt all over, my muscles exhausted, migraine pounding, and the pain of seeing Kai's grief left me weak in the knees and my arms feeling like noodles. Would a noodle hurt if I used it to slap? Of course, my hand would go right through the ghost's faces. I had no hold over them except my role as the Keeper. They wanted something from me but I couldn't figure out what it was.

"You can't change the past," Will said, with a nod. "That is correct. But you have the present to do with what you will, and some people need to die in order to save others."

"Does that make sense?" Jacob again.

I gritted my teeth and glared at them with my chin tilted down. I was like the wolf, on my haunches and ready to pounce, to rip them to shreds if they kept taunting me, holding Wendy's freedom or their elusive promise of 'help,' over my head. Hot anger kept me from freezing over as my blood boiled. I imagined steam rising from my skin against the cold air around me. I was a cartoon character again with fire replacing my irises and puffs of air expelling from my nose like a penned bull.

"I'm not in the business of letting people die if that's what you're getting at," I said, between my teeth.

"She isn't ready, is she?" Jacob's stiff neck barely twisted, so he turned his whole body to face his brother, who nodded in agreement. I realized my gun was still in my hand as my fingers tightened into a fist, squeezing the grip.

"There's no time like the present for another lesson," Will answered his brother, but didn't take his eyes off me.

"What the hell does—"

My phone chimed, louder than our voices. The piercing ring startled me and intensified my headache. The hallucination of Kai and Wendy and the other unnamed people in the park dissipated and darkness fell again. I shifted my gun into my other hand and dug my phone out of my pocket.

Detective Wilhelm's contact information covered the screen and the green answer button rippled, waiting for me to respond.

I glanced at the Brothers, then back to my phone. He was likely returning my call from earlier, or a new investigation had surfaced and he needed my help. But I didn't have time to traipse around San Francisco and gather clues right now.

"Go ahead." Will waved his hand. "This is important. Use the contraption to contact your partner."

"He's not—ugh." I swiped at the last second.

"Rowan?" Detective Wilhelm's voice grated on my raw nerves.

"What is it?"

"There's been a murder at a house on Elm. Thought you'd want to know." With that, he hung up. The detective would never admit he needed my expertise on a case, but I knew how to read between the lines. *Thought you'd want to know*, really meant, *please help, I'm stumped*, in the detective's language.

I sighed and stared at the screen. The phone call blinked away and returned to a picture of Wendy on Kai's shoulders watching a parade. The memory was perfect, sweet, a moment in time when fairy tales had lulled and murder wasn't at the forefront of my mind. Wendy's story aura often wavered and shifted, sometimes so weak I could ignore it. I'd still hunted for the Brothers Grimm but allowed myself to enjoy the present.

No time like the present for another lesson.

My lip twitched as I frowned.

"Solve it," Will's voice carved into my private memories.

"Excuse me?"

"The deal was to solve the murder then we'll help you, was it not?" Jacob's questions made my arm itch. I nearly raised the gun to aim between his eyes. "We are *dying* to go home. The faster you solve this, the quicker we can do that."

"It's already done, I solved it." I nodded toward the center of Pioneer Park. "I held up my side of the bargain."

Will pursed his lips then unfolded his arms. "We said to solve the murder, but we didn't say which one."

That was it. I lifted my pistol, pointed it at Willy, and pulled the trigger.

Was shooting a ghost the stupidest thing I'd ever done? Maybe. Yes. But it felt so good to fire a bullet into the man's chest who controlled the story aura that trapped my daughter into a never-ending childhood.

The bullet wedged itself into the trunk of a tall tree on the other side of the playground, while Will dropped his head to look at the temporary hole, wispy and swirling, through his chest cavity.

Jake lifted his hands to inspect his fingernails. "Told you she wasn't ready, didn't I?"

"I just want to save my daughter," I said.

"Sure, sure." Will nodded. It was as much of a promise as I could weasel out of them at the moment. Better than nothing. I had no other leads for how to help Wendy avoid her fate as one of the lost children of Neverland island.

The rhythmic thump of a blaring song filled the air. A car rolled by on the street outside the park, blasting Deck the Halls as loud as its speakers would allow.

Jake's interest was piqued, and he dropped his hand, looking for the source of the music. "Delightful song, isn't it?" He asked, trying to nudge his brother with his elbow.

I shifted my arm to aim at the second Grimm, or was Jacob the first since he was the oldest? Either way, he'd have a hole between his eyes in a second. I pulled the trigger.

Okay, shooting a ghost a second time was the stupidest thing I'd ever done.

Chapter 8

The Girl Who Cried Wolf

A flickering fireplace and Christmas-tree-scented candle greeted me. If I took off my shoes, I'd never make it back out of the house. All the ghostly activity had killed my phone battery, so I stopped home on my way to the house on Elm for my portable charger.

The door didn't even fall shut before the ambiance drew me in and made me ready to kick off my boots. Kai's tongue cupped the edge of his top lip as he arched his feet and stretched to hang our tenth-year anniversary ornament near the top of the fake pine tree. Once it was secure on the branch, he turned to me with a smile.

Relief flooded me and the headache, blurry vision, aching knees, and chill, subsided for a moment. Seeing him happy again, after witnessing the painful alternate reality, gave me a second wind. I couldn't help but grin back like a goofy college girl with a crush on her nerdy, *Global History of Architecture* classmate again. I'd taken it hoping for an easy A and an excuse to travel to Europe. While Kai, well, he just loved history.

"Check it out, I doubled the number of light strands this year." He hopped over a cardboard box labeled *keep away from The Hulk*, which was our personal way of saying *fragile, breakable items inside*. Kai crouched behind the tree and popped the plug into the wall.

The tree lit up with hundreds of twinkling lights. He stood and placed his hands on his hips, surveying his decorative work. The tree sparkled with dozens of different colors, contrasted against the forest shade of green.

Immediately, I marched from the entry and threw myself into my husband's arms. He held me without asking any questions. Investigating murder is hard, and reporting on it was often harder. My need for his comfort wasn't unusual, and I predicted he'd offer to order cheesecake any moment.

"Rough night?" he asked, releasing me and pressing his palm to my lower back. He guided me to the couch, but I refused to sit. I'd never get back up. If I let the cushions and the warmth of his arms take me, a murder victim might not get justice. Not to mention the agreement I had with the Brothers Grimm. No, an all-nighter was necessary. I'd solve a murder, for the second time today and they'd have to grant Wendy freedom from the plot of her story.

I shook my head, then nodded, then shrugged. Everything was confusing, and stressful, and too much, but I had no choice other than to caffeinate, put my big girl pants on, and work through the night.

"You look like you need sugar," he said, as he grabbed a blanket covered in reindeer from a plastic tub on the floor and flung it over my shoulders. The soft fleece enveloped my neck and beckoned for me to collapse on the couch and curl up. "I'm going to order some dessert."

"No." I sighed. "I'm not done. I–I found the Brothers Grimm."

"The gods?" Kai looked up from his phone, eyes bugged.

I nodded and let my eyes fall shut for a moment. I caught the faint scent of apple spice in the air and I knew he'd plugged the slow cooker in with our favorite warm drink recipe, full of cinnamon sticks and floating apples. Our home was small and full of intense, crazy moments from portals that appeared in the walls, to werewolves killing innocent women on our doorstep.

But it was home.

It was also full of love, and family memories. Like when Kai had tried to bribe Wendy to take her first steps with a cookie. This was the rug she'd learned to crawl on, and the coffee table where Kai and I spent many nights putting pieces of case puzzles together. It was the place that called me back when Johnson and I were trapped inside the portal between virtual reality.

Wendy's voice and Kai's hand had guided me back here.

Home.

Neverland could never compare to the love we shared in our little family.

"So, what does that mean?" Kai took a seat in the armchair that sat kitty-corner to the couch. He offered me a sip of warm apple cider from his *History's Greatest Dude* mug, where *Dude* was crossed out and replaced with *Dad*.

Instead of taking the drink, I perched on the couch's hard armrest. I refused to get too comfortable knowing a victim waited for justice and my daughter's visions grew stronger.

I palmed my forehead, letting the bone at the bottom of my hand apply pressure to my skull.

"They showed me the past as they think it should have happened."

"Whoa, whoa, whoa. The past?" Kai raised his hands in a gesture telling me to pump the brakes. "Who do these chumps think they are? History teachers? Should I be jealous?" He narrowed his eyes in mock jealousy. "You already have one of those. I might not compare to a god but I'd battle them for your honor."

I rolled my eyes but smirked, allowing myself a moment of light-hearted conversation with my husband before I returned to reality.

"Chumps." I snorted. "Yeah. No fighting is necessary unless you want to fall right through them. They're ghosts."

"Ah." He snapped his fingers and pointed to the closed door across the house that was Wendy's room. "That's what she was talking about. I thought maybe she'd just seen a dead body."

I leaned forward and took the mug off the coffee table. A Post-It note stuck to the bottom, as I lifted it to my mouth and savored the cinnamon apple flavor on my tongue. I peeled the note off and read it.

A full moon = werewolves. No. Vampires? Cheese, definitely cheese.

If only cheese could solve everything like it did back in college.

Back then I'd cram for an exam so boring, it'd make me fall asleep on my textbooks. Kai had wooed me with a pumpkin-flavored cheesecake that'd given me enough energy to finish studying and pass the history of architecture class with a solid C plus.

"Was this past revelation like a movie? Projected on the trees at Pioneer Park? No wait, don't tell me, the ghosts acted it out like a two-man play. Which of the brothers played me? Did I look—" he paused and smoothed his hair back in a slick, flattened style. "Old fashioned?"

I didn't want to think about how Kai had looked, thin and stricken with grief. I shook my head. "We're definitely not doing seventeenth-century roleplay unless we're going to be Vikings."

Kai's eyes bugged. "Wow, it's amazing you passed any history classes."

"Whatever." I waved my hand. "You know what I mean. Besides, I'm Miss Librarian now, I know all the classics," I said. I wiggled my eyebrows and Kai's eyes glazed over, as he grinned with a faraway look. Unfortunately, I'd have to burst his fantasy bubble where he probably imagined me in glasses, ripping out a tight bun to let my hair fall around my face.

"Anyway, I have to pull an all-nighter," I said.

"Yeah, you do." He winked, but it wasn't with the annoying pretentious air of Gym Dude. Kai was all teddy bear love in the streets and sexy, pirate roleplay in the sheets.

"No, I'm being real." I stood and handed him the mug.

"I'm glad you're real, my fake wife is really boring," he joked. He nodded toward the virtual assistant technology speaker that was a knockoff of Amazon's Alexa. It sat on the tall counter that divided the large room into a living area and kitchen. Next to it was the portable charger with a small white cord coiled on top.

"Detective Wilhelm called and the Brothers Grimm told me to solve the murder. I have no idea why but they want me to follow through with this investigation. If I do, they might help us save Wendy from Neverland."

I palmed my forehead and stooped, using my free hand to balance against the back of the armchair.

"Are you okay?" Kai set the mug down and stood. He leveled me, holding my shoulders in his big hands. " You look pale and glazed like when you have a fever. You need to rest."

I hummed in agreement, but quickly added my plan of action before I let the lull of exhaustion convince me it was okay to take a break. "I need to save our daughter."

"Tonight? She's in bed where it's safe. I know, because she had me check for monsters."

My heart skipped a beat. "Monsters?"

"Mermaids actually," he said. "But the way she described them sounded demonic with all black and red eyes and sharp teeth. Plus, crocodiles. She said she sees them when she closes her eyes."

I pushed passed Kai and squatted in front of the little bookshelf that we used as a TV stand. I pulled Peter Pan from the stack and flipped it open. "Like these?" I flipped the book around and held it up, pointing to the smiling women with shining, scaly tails in place of their legs. The sanitized children's book version of the tale was much cuter with its bright colors and cherub-like illustrations.

"Yeah," he said, "if they looked more like the creatures Sam and Dean Winchester hunt."

I nodded. "It's Neverland. All the more reason I need to go, now." But even as I said it, I dropped my hand to the short, cubby shelf and used it for balance. My head spun, then my stomach joined the chaos of misery with nauseating twists and groans.

I shoved one foot in front of the other and made my way into the kitchen to grab a handful of aspirin and the charger.

"Mari, you can't pour from an empty cup," Kai said. "Tell Detective W you'll catch up with the investigation tomorrow."

After popping two capsules of medicine into my mouth, I stepped out of the kitchen, and scooped up the charger on my way.

"Mari, stop." Kai marched passed me.

I shook my head and stumbled for the door.

As soon as I grabbed the doorknob and yanked, he pressed his palm against the door and pushed it shut again.

"Kai." I glared at him.

"Mari."

The back and forth could fall into an eternal loop if I didn't stop it now. But I didn't have the energy to muster anything except his name. "Kai…"

"Your eyes are crossed right now. They'll never be unstuck if you don't close them immediately and go to sleep," he said. He waved his finger in my face, pointing at both my eyes.

"Uh-huh, sure." I grabbed his hand and laced my fingers through his. "I have to do this. Sleep can wait."

"Then promise me you'll get a coffee on the way. No dozing off at the wheel."

"I don't even have to drive," I said. "The victim is at a house on Elm."

"Still. Coffee," he demanded.

"I promise."

Kai squeezed my hand. He slipped his free hand beneath my hair at the base of my neck, then pulled me into a kiss. I melted against him, tasting the lingering hints of apple cider on his tongue. For a moment, I forgot the headache, the investigation, and Neverland, long enough to focus on nothing but my husband's mouth.

Reality returned when our lips parted and I sucked in a last breath of his scent, mingled with the smell of Christmas. I left without another word and didn't look back.

Tonight required focus and I couldn't fall prey to the distraction of daydreaming. I longed to be home with them where I could drift to sleep, knowing my family was safe. But it was a false sense of security and the guilt of wasting time would eat me alive.

I pulled out my phone and tapped Scarlet's picture in my contact list. The other line trilled and trilled, as I made my way down the staircase and onto the city streets. Scattered people still stalked San Francisco's sidewalks late into the night, but it came with a calmer atmosphere, quieter without the excessive vehicle traffic.

I followed the city's grid to Elm as I continued trying Scarlet's line. After seeing the Brothers Grimm, I needed to speak with her, share my experience and see if it triggered anything in her memory about the story cycle.

Cars honked at each other from somewhere in the city. Patrons at a pub laughed too loudly and the thwack of pool balls smacked into one another as I passed by.

As I turned onto Elm, the businesses steadily got more expensive. Decorative lights brightened the window of a clothing boutique that displayed a glamorous, glittering dress for New Year's parties next to a red coat. I logged the style of the coat away in my memory for a time I'd will the hood to behave as my Christmas stylist. Not that I'd have a moment to spare for a holiday party this season. Christmas loomed only a matter of days away. If I didn't settle the matter of Wendy's story aura before then, I'd have shopping, baking, decorating, and work at Bay Side Media that wouldn't get done.

I sighed and tapped my phone for a dose of warm fuzzies from the picture of last year's light parade. The colorful Christmas lights reflected in Wendy's enormous eyes and Kai beamed, as only a proud father could do.

The heels of my boots rapped the concrete, as I picked up the pace downhill into the residential area. These houses were built closer to the water, the most luxurious of them right on the San Francisco bay. View of the rhythmic waves should bring peace but this late into the night and away from the dense center of the city, the bright lights had faded. The ocean was a black abyss, yawning into the horizon. It taunted me with its endlessness.

Though I stopped well before the bottom of the street, the salty air stung my nose. I identified the victim's house by the collection of cop cars announcing their presence with red and blue flashes.

I ducked under the yellow tape and marched up to the pink house with white trim. It looked like Barbie's mansion if Barbie had lived in the Victorian era. Inside, the furniture matched the nineteenth-century exterior, with dark finishes on the embellished wood that framed the overstuffed couches and chairs. The collection of antiques came with a unique, musty scent that made me wrinkle my nose like a kid with broccoli on their plate.

"Rowan," Detective Wilhelm barked. He yanked his arm, waving for me to follow him from the top of the steep staircase. "Up here."

A team of crime scene investigators worked throughout the house. An analyst flashed photographs while others gathered evidence.

I waited at the bottom of the steps while several paramedics carried a stretcher down the narrow staircase. The patient weakly kicked at the blanket and squirmed in her bed.

A faint black glow hovered over her. Her thin, scraggly hair was plastered to her skin, which was pale enough to be a sheet of paper. Or a ghost.

I snorted. This poor lady was wispy, but nothing like the spectral figures of the Brothers' manifestations. Though the rim of black around her confirmed she belonged to the plot of a story. I didn't know whether to be relieved it would be easier to solve due, to it being a fairy tale investigation or that I needed to worry about twisting a story for a happily-ever-after, on top of solving a murder.

She rolled her head back and forth against the flat mattress, further matting her hair, while her arms lay limp at her sides.

"The big, furry beast came right through," she babbled in a faint voice. "Right through my window. It was a wolf!"

Somebody better watch their step or they'd trip over my jaw on the floor.

"You've got to be kidding me..." I muttered. A wolf? *A mother-fluffing WOLF?* If the voice in my head could scream, it'd earn a role in horror movie sound effects.

A paramedic glanced in my direction and I forced a closed-lip smile, though I doubted it concealed my rage. Was rage the right word? Frustration? Disbelief. Confusion. Absolute rage.

If this was another trick from Jake and Willy, I would waste a full round of bullets firing at them. *Note to self, research how Sam and Dean Winchester kill ghosts.* Really, I needed to look into historical stories. The Grimm brothers were actual humans in history, but ghosts came from the imagination, just like plots and characters.

I shook my head and made my way up the stairs. The sharp stench of blood filled my nose, but I didn't let Detective Wilhelm find an excuse to pick on me, and I refused to let my discomfort show. The feeling wasn't new, but that combined with the emotional rollercoaster of the last twenty-four hours nearly sent me to the ambulance.

"This isn't another Red Riding Hood," I whispered to myself. "It can't be." I knew Scarlet had mentioned that the modern era disrupted fairy tales, like when The Ugly Duckling had committed suicide because of online bullying before she grew into the beautiful swan. But I'd been The Keeper of Stories for six years now and never heard of a plot repeating itself. Of course, I *had* just seen the Big Bad Wolf with my own eyes only hours earlier.

Detective Wilhelm shouted for me to hurry down the hall.

Glass littered the floor in the bedroom. A plump woman lay sprawled on the floor, one hand on her chest and the other disappearing under the bed skirt. She'd died with her eyes open, frozen in fear. A large window took up most of the wall across the room. It was shattered with a gaping hole that brought in fresh air. I gulped in the sea breeze.

The room was a disaster, but that wasn't what shocked me. Despite the iron scent hanging in the air, there wasn't a drop of blood in sight.

I scanned the victim but found no weapon, no injury, and no bite marks.

"How'd she die?" I asked, peering over the coroner's shoulder.

The coroner sighed and paused her examination. "Looks to be as simple as cardiac arrest. But heart disease doesn't explain the obvious forced entry."

"Quite the mystery, huh?" Detective Wilhelm said too close to my face, and I wondered if rebelling against dental hygiene was his midlife crisis.

I straightened and tapped the screen on my watch. It was almost one in the morning and I swore I could hear my bed begging for me. It sounded eerily similar to Jacob Grimm calling my name, but they weren't here, no spectral figures, no chill, nothing of the sort.

Last marble, gone.

"You called me several hours ago, how is the investigation still this fresh?" I asked, nodding at the untouched evidence around the room, which included shards of glass jutting from the carpet like tiny knives.

"The, uh, psycho—"

The coroner cleared her throat exaggeratedly loudly and Detective Wilhelm rolled his eyes. He placed his hands on his hips. "The patient," he corrected, "was…" he paused, searching for the right word? "She was difficult, to say the least. Her caretaker was in the middle of routine treatment."

He lifted his chin, then pointed to the side table next to the head of the bed. On it sat a glass of water, a candelabra that looked like it belonged in the Phantom of the Opera's lair complete with candles dripping wax, and a bag of blood.

I peeled off a sticky note and pulled the notebook from underneath my arm. After slapping a fresh note onto a blank page, I used my teeth to uncap the pen.

"Name?" I asked.

The detective went down the list of basics. "Shannon Dew. Fifties. Retired antique dealer turned full-time caretaker of her daughter Lindsay."

The coroner excused herself, after announcing she'd continue her job once the body arrived at the lab.

"What's up with Lindsay?" I eyed the bag of blood.

He blew out a breath through his nose and folded his meaty arms. "Transfusions. Her nurse said its official diagnosis was anemia but only because doctors couldn't find another explanation. Apparently, Mommy Dearest here, insisted the in-home nurse teach her how to do the transfusions. That way they wouldn't have to pay the nurse as much."

I scribbled theories as quickly as I could across a column of sticky notes.

Which fairy tale starred a sick character? Was Shannon part of the story or an accidental death?

"So, somebody broke in here, caused Shannon to have a heart attack, stole nothing, and then bounced?" I asked. I wrinkled my brow for emphasis on my confusion.

Detective Wilhelm only shrugged. "You're an investigator too. Investigate."

I scoffed. *Just admit it, you're begging for my help.* But I didn't care to tease the detective. Though it'd be easy when the chill settled.

Icy air gently, but suddenly sucked the warmth from me. Detective Wilhelm shuddered and tightened his folded arms against his chest. His teeth chattered like a skeleton in a Halloween decoration and I only smirked, as he stiffened and tried to conceal his discomfort.

"Cold?" I asked, allowing myself to shiver freely. The brothers were nowhere in sight but their presence was undeniable.

He shook his head.

"Annoying isn't it? It arrives unexpectedly and demands endless work from you, but gives nothing in return." I said. I scanned the room for any glimpse of the spectral figures' shoes or mussy hair or cheesy Christmas caroler-looking overcoat.

"What?" he asked.

I blinked at the detective then shook my head. "It's, uh, a poem… about…" My gaze wandered to the open window. The shudder of a small object caught my eye. "The wind."

"Why the hell are you reciting poetry?"

I carefully stepped over the victim's body and made my way toward the window. The glass protruded, sharp and vicious-looking, in every direction. The small, gray piece of fabric was a clue I'd gladly risk getting near the glass for.

As I drew closer, I recognized the texture, and it didn't belong to an attacker's clothing.

"Of course," I mumbled. "Wolves don't wear clothes."

I plucked the tuft of gray fur from the glass and resisted screaming into the abyss of darkness beyond the open window.

Instead, I frowned at the spectral figures that manifested two stories above the ground.

"Is it Red Riding Hood?" I asked, with my voice plain and simple, all anger gone with my sapped energy.

Jake shook his head.

"We don't know which story it is. But we know it is happening right now, in the present. This is no manifestation and we are curious what you'll make of it," Will said.

So much for all-knowing gods. My shoulders slumped, defeated by the cryptic answer, though a surge of curiosity swelled in me, too. I lived for answers, for investigations with a challenge. The added benefit of knowing something the Brothers Grimm gods didn't know, only fueled my desire to find the murderer, or wolf, or whatever burst through this window and startled Mrs. Dew to death.

"Isn't there a holiday soon, Willy?" Jake tilted his chin back and eyed his brother.

Will nodded. "And it'd be such a shame for so many to suffer during this joyous time."

"Is that a threat?" I growled.

"An observation. We have something to show you when you're ready. We're not cruel like you might think, Keeper. In fact, we're not so different from you, but we have limited time and need to know you'll understand before we reveal more. We're giving you until the holiday to finish."

"I'm not a patient person—"

"Case closed," Will interrupted, and I nearly reached for my gun again.

"Christmas, isn't it?" Jake said, finally catching up with the earlier half of the conversation.

I knew I wasn't getting more out of the ghosts, so I curled my fist around the tuft of fur and spun around. The investigation would continue and it sounded like I had until Christmas morning to solve it.

"Bah, humbug," I muttered.

Chapter 9

You Snooze, You Lose

Shadows danced across the ceiling from cars that drove by on the street below. I gave up on tossing and turning and laid still, staring at the periodic lights that illuminated the top of the room. Kai snored softly beside me, a lump of weighted blanket and fresh laundry scent.

Tomorrow, I'd get to visit the hospital and interview Lindsay. Detective Wilhelm had insisted I go home and sleep, with the claim that I looked like I needed a transfusion myself. Whatever disease he thought I carried, he didn't want me near him. And since my legs nearly buckled beneath me, I agreed.

But sleep didn't come easily when your child could disappear into an alternate reality at any moment. Not to mention the ghosts that haunted my every step. After a solid four hours, which was more than I'd gotten on any given night for the first three months of Wendy's life and I'd survived then, I kicked off the covers.

I slipped my feet into corny, pointed, elf slippers and shuffled into the kitchen. The coffee maker whirred to life at the touch of my finger. I rested my elbows on the counter and took a long whiff of the bag of hazelnut roast.

"Mmm, magic," I whispered.

"And too much of it if she fails."

I jolted pin-straight and the bag of coffee slipped from my fingertips, sending a pile of brown grounds across my elf slippers. My head snapped up. In the darkness of the living room, the faint shape of Jacob and Will stood with their backs to me. They inspected the tree with childlike curiosity.

"We started this tradition, you know?" Jacob flicked the tree.

What in the wonderland were they doing inside my house? This was my sacred fortress, my lair where greedy story gods, and were-wolves, and people who are rude to their servers, weren't allowed. Home was off-limits.

Will shook his head. "I've never cut a tree down in my life."

"Not, *we*, we. We Germans."

His brother only laughed like the little twerp he was.

I rolled my eyes. Some men stay little boys forever, even the gods of story weren't immune to lame jokes. And these little boys were not welcome to turn this into their personal house of ghostly horrors.

I snatched the cylinder of salt from the cabinet and tiptoed around the counter. I wasn't about to shoot a gun at my Christmas tree, and I'd seen enough Supernatural and paranormal hunting shows to know my container of savory goodness would repel them better, anyway.

The floorboards creaked beneath my feet, and I froze at the end of the couch. Neither of them turned around.

"She's going to fail at being the Keeper, isn't she?" Jacob asked, eyeing his brother.

Will fiddled with the collar of his coat, trying to flatten it. "Most certainly."

I seethed, unable to keep quiet any longer. "You know I can hear you gossiping about me, right?" With my thumb, I popped open the little tab on the salt container. When they turned around, I'd get them right in the eye with thousands of stinging crystals.

Jacob turned first, likely eager to answer my question with another question. That'd earn him double the salty attack, whatever that meant.

When the shape of his body shifted to face me, I thrust the salt container out. Tiny grains soared right through his perfectly ironed coat and shirt. They scattered across the floor and both brothers looked at their feet, staring at the savory-seasoned Christmas tree skirt.

"Well, that was odd," Will said.

I dropped my arm and pursed my lips. Apparently, Sam and Dean Winchester were wrong about what repelled ghosts—or rather, the writers of the show made an incorrect guess. Or was it that Jacob and Will were actually the gods Johnson and Hook had claimed them to be? How could Wrinkly Willy and The Question-Talker be anything more than the confused spirits of old white men? I thought gods smote people with lightning bolts or at least looked like the muscular men in the Thor comics.

I folded my arms and sighed. "I thought you couldn't find me in the hood."

"Yes, but following you isn't difficult," Will said.

"Creepy…" I muttered.

Jacob tilted his head. "Do you understand your role as the Keeper?"

"Do I—" I narrowed my eyes and paused. What answer did they want? "I save people's lives against the monster you two wrote into fairy tales."

Jacob gingerly touched his fingertips to his chest, jaw-dropping. Dramatic response, really. I rolled my eyes and opened my mouth, but Will cut me off.

With a quick glance at his brother, he licked his lips and bore his gaze into me, as if he could see through me as easily I saw through his spectral skull. "The story world and this world do not belong together—"

"Agreed." I nodded, arms still folded. At least I had my Santa onesie to keep me warm from the ghostly chill.

"Unless it is bound by the magic of a library," Will finished. "None of us want them mixing." His voice lilted, dropping to a tone lower than I'd heard him speak before. "But modern technology treats stories differently, and it thinned the veil between both worlds. Then you came along and stabbed your knife right through it."

That sounded like me. I had to give him that. Wearing a holiday onesie came with a severe lack of storage for my switchblade or Sig, and I felt naked without them.

Jacob stuck his finger in the air. "Too much, Willy. Didn't we agree she isn't ready?"

An awkward silence fell as Will tugged on his open coat, pulling it across his chest. He sniffed and faced his brother with a look of pure pissed-off energy. The temperature dropped another few degrees, and I tightened my arms together.

I scoffed. "I'm ready to wreck you." I sounded like a ten-year-old harassing an opponent in his online game, but I didn't care. I needed coffee, a lasso that could wrangle ghostly gods, and a bucket load of answers that they would not give me.

Jacob blinked, clueless or careless about his little brother's anger. Finally, he groaned and arched his eyebrow at me. "I suppose Johnson already let the cat out of the bag." He rubbed his palm over his face, messing the long hairs of his bushy brows. "A Keeper keeps every plot thread, every character, and every theme where it belongs. This isn't the first time in history that technology has destroyed, confused, or hurt the stories. But it has grown far worse."

"You want me to solve this fairy tale murder so that I can help seal the story. And then what? You get to keep your little library in the sky happy?" *We get it. You're librarians who care about books, but this is life and death.*

"Monsters are coming." Will's voice cut through my thoughts, digging into my confidence and rattling my bones.

This wasn't new information. I knew I'd taken off the hood which triggered more stories to enter the cycle, next century. I knew technology ruined the stories. Like when The Ugly Duckling committed suicide because of online bullying before she had time to transform into the swan she was meant to become. I knew the crowded nature of modern cities caused the story aura to shift and waver since it had so many options of people that might fit into the character—just as when Jameson became the wolf in Little Red Riding Hood. Unfortunately, he wasn't the only man in San Francisco with serial killer tendencies.

Despite this knowledge, my hands shook, and a shiver trickled down my spine that had nothing to do with the spirit's icy presence. I swallowed a painful lump in my throat. My tongue had dried and seemed to expand enough to choke me. Still, I gathered my resolve, stiffening my back and curling my fingers into fists. I opened my mouth, but once again, Will stole my moment.

"Or should I say, your daughter is leaving?"

Before the words sunk in, distraction took hold of me and my brain didn't have the energy to split my focus. The pitter-patter of little footsteps echoed behind me. I twisted my neck to see Wendy in Christmas pajamas, marching up to us with her gaze fixed on the ghosts.

I instinctively offered my free hand, and she took it, wrapping both her hands around mine.

"Where am I going?" she asked.

Will's knees cracked, as he crouched to meet Wendy at eye-level. I tugged on her, but she didn't budge. Wendy was neither scared, nor particularly curious, about the spirits standing in front of her. The little smirk at the corner of her mouth told me she was…amused?

"Your clothes are funny," she said.

Will's brows furrowed, and he smoothed the fabric on his chest with both hands. "How would you like to go on an adventure?" He glanced at me, taunting me with the hold they both knew they had over me until I did my job. I seethed, but fighting the gods wouldn't help Wendy.

I'd solve the murder, so I could seal the story. This would allow me to help lock away another murderer, while also appeasing the story gods.

With the reminder of the goal at hand, my mind worked in overdrive, an overheated engine attempting not to smoke. I quickly organized the events of the day, from interviewing the living victim to tracking any clues Detective Wilhelm had gathered.

Wendy shrugged. "I've gone on adventures with my babysitters before. Scarlet took me to a bounce house, and we caught fish with our bare hands once. Once we played tic-tac-toe in the hospital because she tried to use a microwave and it exploded."

"Sounds dangerous." Jacob's eyes bugged but Will wasn't deterred.

"Don't worry, her eyebrows grew back," Wendy explained.

"Well, Neverland is far more fun than hospitals." Will's statement pulled me from the recesses of my brain, where I stored my schedules and filed evidence.

Oh, hell no. Coming after my daughter was off-limits.

"Get out."

Will stood and Jacob dusted off imaginary dirt, or wrinkles, or whatever he pretended to be interested in. "I told you she wasn't ready, did I not? Oh, well." He sighed. "Maybe we can make the best of being back in this messy, sticky world. Why is there always so much dust?" He waved at nothing in the air.

Wendy giggled. "You look like a cat when you do that."

"I said, get out," I repeated, eyes boring through Will's skull.

"The faster you solve it, the faster…" he tilted his forehead at Wendy, arching a discreet brow, then tapped the timepiece on his wrist. "We have a deal," he said before they both vanished and left us to thaw. His words lit a fire under me. As much as I didn't want to play by their rules, I had no choice. Even when I closed my eyes, the green aura around my daughter's body glowed through the thin layer of skin.

I picked up Wendy and headed for the kitchen. Now was the time to shift the gear into drive, not wallow in fear asking questions like; *what if* I couldn't uphold my end of the deal? First things first, I needed to speak with Lindsay about who, or what had attacked her.

"We have a long day. Do you want some oatmeal?" I asked. I stood on my tiptoes to lift Wendy onto the counter. She plopped down and swung her legs, banging her heels against the cabinets.

"Why oatmeal?" she wrinkled her nose, already forgetting about the *adventure*. Relief flooded me and I finally unclenched my jaw and pulled my shoulders out of my ears.

I smiled and tickled her sides. "Because it sticks to your ribs!"

If nothing else, I'd make the best of the day for Wendy's sake. Just because I needed to solve a murder and save her from Neverland, it didn't mean we couldn't have fun doing it.

I pulled milk from the refrigerator and started mixing chocolate syrup into it. As I watched the thick, dark liquid mix and swirl, I did everything I could to forget the ghosts, as well as Wendy's story aura glow, so that I could focus on the task at hand.

Find Mrs. Dew's murderer.

If I took one step at a time, I wouldn't trip and fall flat on my face, right?

Chapter 10

Don't Look a Murder Victim in the Mouth

Apparently, a six-year-old burned enough energy that a big bowl of oats couldn't sustain longer than two hours. By the time we reached the hospital, Wendy begged for a trip to the vending machine.

I scrounged in my purse for change and filled Wendy's hands with quarters. She happily skipped to the machine and pressed several buttons, while I turned to the woman at the administration desk to ask about Lindsay's room number.

Wendy returned with an armful of cheese puffs, apple chips, and a Gatorade that she balanced while following me into the elevator. At the top, the doors slid open to a long hallway on the second floor that brought back a flood of memories. The smell hit me first, with its sterilized sting. Then came the specific moments, from seeing Scarlet with the hood sweeping the linoleum for the first time, to watching Carlo slowly turn into the Pinocchio puppet.

I'd lost Wendy here right after giving birth. I'd found my second daughter here—or so Kai and I liked to believe that we were the loving parental figures that Scarlet had lost centuries ago. Emotion welled in my throat but quickly dissipated when we reached room 235.

Lindsay was as pale as the sheets she lay in, her skin melting into the pillow and her slight, frail arms lost in the wrinkles of the thin blanket. The squeeze of emotion in my throat switched to a gasp. I'd seen a man transform into a wooden doll, my coworker become a wolf, and my mother shift into a swan, but the skeletal, red-eyed woman in front of me still left me breathless.

Lindsay didn't just look sick, she looked inhuman in a way that I couldn't identify.

I stopped in the doorway and Wendy bumped into my butt, focusing on carefully screwing the cap back on her frost-flavored drink. I spun around and dropped to a crouch, pulling out my phone. "I have a good idea, why don't you try this cake-decorating game on my phone?"

Wendy wasn't scared of anything that I knew of, except, apparently, mermaids, but I still wanted to distract her from the dying woman in the bed. I tapped on the icon for the app store and quickly downloaded the game I'd deleted for wasting too much of my time. Then I added it to the pile in Wendy's arms.

I smiled at a nurse who squeezed past us, while I stepped inside.

"Be careful," the nurse said, glancing back over her shoulder. Was Lindsay so weak the nurse thought I'd break her with nothing but a quick visit? Or was it a warning?

Wires and tubes hung around Lindsay's bed, disappearing beneath the blanket and inside her flesh.

Her eyes shifted to me, and that's when I noticed the cold steel around her wrists. Handcuffs shackled her arms to the bed, keeping her lying flat. Clearly, they considered her dangerous, or unstable, possibly a risk to herself. I grimaced and pointed to a chair on the other side of the room.

"Want to sit and decorate a Christmas cake?" I asked. I sent Wendy to the corner where she'd be as far from Lindsay as possible. Except, whatever creature the victim might become likely wasn't contagious, and Wendy was unkillable—the only good thing about the story aura.

Wendy shuffled to the chair, hands full, and plopped down. With her tongue poised at the corner of her mouth and attention fixed on the screen, I knew it was safe to approach Lindsay without my shadow following.

I cleared my throat. "Miss Dew," I paused, waiting for a response, but her blood-red eyes stared at the ceiling. I stepped closer, and she snapped her neck to the side, eyes narrowed as she scanned me. "Is it okay if I ask you a few questions?"

Lindsay tried to lift her head to see Wendy behind me and then sniffed. Werewolf? My brain immediately started listing classic stories starring humans who turn into furry beasts.

Nordic folklore. Beowulf? No, it's Steppenwolf. I needed to ask Kai about wolves in history later. What about The Three Little Pigs? Maybe Lindsay wasn't a wolf at all, but a pig, and the murderer was Big Bad.

Her nostrils pinched inward as she took a long inhale, then licked her lips. *Okay, not a pig.* As far as I knew, pigs didn't look like they wanted to devour little girls. Lindsay blinked and her eyes focused on me again.

"Who are you?" she asked, her voice stronger and clearer than I expected.

"I'm an investigative journalist," I said. "I'm here to ask you a few questions about what happened if you're feeling up for it."

The predatory fix in her eyes faded and a worry line appeared between her shapely eyebrows. "My mom…"

"I'm sorry about your loss, Miss Dew." As always, I reached out to give a touch of comfort to the victim's family. Lindsay's gaze dropped to my hand, and she sniffed again. The reaction seemed more bloodhound than werewolf, but I didn't know any classic literature or fairy tales with a hunting dog as a named character.

I took a seat on a nearby chair and scooted it close, trying to get her eyes to focus again. With my notebook open and pen clicked, I was ready for the details. "Do you remember anything about the attack?"

Lindsay's tongue slithered out, licking her top lip. I glimpsed her teeth, noticing the extra-sharp, long canines, like fangs. The behavior reminded me of a snake that matched the sharp, thin pupil inside her red irises.

I scribbled the first stories with snakes that came to mind, at the top of the page. *Kaa from Jungle Book. Did Paradise Lost have one too?*

"It was a wolf," she finally said, eyes glazing over.

I nodded, as I added to the notes. *A wolf that can jump into a second-story building?* "And who broke the window?"

"The wolf."

This was going to be harder than I'd thought. Wolves didn't fly, not even in stories. But pigs… I shook my head, getting rid of my hangup on that particular fable.

"Did you see the wolf breaking through the window?"

Lindsay shook her head, rolling it back and forth against the pillow which further knotted her thin hair. "He wasn't a wolf."

I blinked, frustrated now. It wasn't Lindsay's fault, she'd been attacked, and traumatized. But I felt the pressure of solving the case with the Brothers' appearance inside my house, just hours before. Their unpredictable nature left me feeling flighty, and desperate, and…a sharp pain sliced through my temples. Despite the rest I'd gotten last night, my headache returned.

I crossed out *wolf* in my notes and looked up. "There was a wolf and someone else?"

Again, her hair tangled as she shook her head, with less energy now. "Just him."

"A man?"

Her lips curled into the faintest smile. "He can fly, too."

What? So far, it sounded like Peter Pan in Cruella Deville's fur coat —except that'd have spots.

"Miss Dew" I took her hand again to show her I cared, while asking the sensitive question. "Who killed your mother?"

The beep on her pulse monitor dropped to a crawl. The slow, rhythmic tick mirrored her lost energy, as her eyes rolled back into her head.

"Lindsay?" I squeezed her hand, and she gasped, eyes flying open again. She looked at me with tears in her eyes.

"My mama. She just fell over at the sight of him. The wolf scared her so badly, she just collapsed, and I screamed but she didn't get up. Then the man came for me again!" The words poured out of her now. I scribbled each detail as quickly as I could, not wanting to miss any clues.

She shook wispy hair from her face and tried to sit up, but the pull of the handcuffs made it difficult. The sudden energy surging through Lindsay didn't match the slower and slower crawl on her monitor.

"And now I'm hungry," she said, as she yanked her arms against the restraints. "I'm starving!"

"I'll call the nurse," I said, scrambling for the call button on the inside of the bed's frame. I couldn't see which button alerted the nurse from where I sat.

I stood and leaned over the bed, knowing she needed help now. My options were limited, scream and scare my daughter, or smash the button until help responded. I couldn't very well leave Wendy alone here to run into the hall.

"You smell…" Lindsay's voice faded, and she jolted, suddenly arching her back. The monitor dropped to a single, flat line with a long, endless beep. I smashed the button and tried to pull away, but Lindsay yanked her arms, snapping the handcuffs apart. With lightning speed, she grabbed my shoulders. Her fingernails dug into me and my stomach leaped into my throat—right where Lindsay's gaze landed.

My arms shot out to shove her back, but her intense, impossible strength overpowered me. I should have grabbed my switchblade. Except, if Lindsay was a zombie, it wouldn't have done much good, unless I could jab deep enough to reach her brains. Somewhere in the chaos, I heard Wendy squeal for me and glimpsed a man in scrubs running into the room.

Lindsay grabbed the hair at the back of my neck and dragged me down, her mouth wide open and the fangs clear now. Sharp, pain radiated from my neck as she sunk her teeth into my flesh.

Vampire.

For a moment, my brain summoned no other words or actions. Mind fog scrambled my thoughts. What did I just have an epiphany about? Why did my neck tickle? Where was Wendy?

Suddenly, clarity returned, and I strained against Lindsay's hold. I scrambled for my switchblade, ripping it from my back pocket and pressing the flat side of the cold iron against her face.

Lindsay dropped back onto the bed and seized, long enough for me to stumble back and let the army of nurses pin her down. The handcuffs burned her wrists and my blade had left a red mark across her cheek. I spun around to grab Wendy, but I spotted the nurse from earlier through the open door, holding a small hand.

Before I hurried out the door, I saw Lindsay cowering in the bed like a scared child. The sudden switch from predator to fearful piqued my interest. I dipped to pick up my notebook and caught sight of where Lindsay's gaze had landed. A shiny cross necklace dangled from one of the nurse's necks, grazing Lindsay's forehead as they pinned her against the bed. It sliced through Lindsay's flesh, leaving a thin cut just below her hairline.

I'd at least solved one piece of the puzzle. I cupped my neck with my palm and then pulled it away, confirming my theory with the sight of blood smeared across my hand.

This is a vampire story. But which one?

Chapter 11

To Be Bitten With Someone

The question stayed at the forefront of my mind, as I held tightly to Wendy's hand and we hurried down the hall.

Footsteps rushed up from behind us and I nearly whipped out my switchblade again, ready to stab Lindsay if she'd risen for another bite. I spun around to see the nurse who'd guided Wendy out of the room during the attack.

Her cheeks flushed and worry creased her brow. "I know it's not my place," she huffed, between breaths. "You're not a patient here, and this is unsolicited, but you're pale and she scratched you. Right? It'd be in your best interest to get checked." The nurse pointed to my neck.

Thankfully, it wasn't bleeding enough to scare me. "How about just a Band-Aid?" I asked.

"Are you sure? She scratched you pretty badly. I can't imagine where all that strength came from, she's been weak and faint all day."

I didn't need to imagine. It was obvious, and I didn't have time to waste chatting with the nurse about a little scratch—or, bite.

"I'm sure." I said.

She nodded and hurried to the nurse's station. With a glance at Wendy, I confirmed she, too, wasn't scared. But I asked, anyway. "Are you okay?"

She nodded. "It looked like that lady bit you."

"Don't worry about me," I said. "I just want to make sure you're not afraid."

"She's not a mermaid?" Wendy asked.

I shook my head. Wendy's fear of sea creatures was my second success of the day. Not that I could control her story aura. Still, it soothed my soul to know she wasn't fully Peter yet, since she still didn't like the mermaids she saw in her Neverland visions.

"Then, nope!" she went back to looking at my phone, tapping the screen until it brightened and brought up the cake decorating game again.

Before the nurse could inspect the 'scratch' and see that it was a bite, I slapped the Band-Aid over the injury and offered her a tight smile.

She opened her mouth. "You really have to stay, it's a legal—"

I waved my hand. "Oh, I'm fine. I won't sue. Really, I'm in a huge hurry." I held up the empty bandage wrapper and offered a bigger smile. "Thank you, for this."

With Wendy's hand in mine, I shuffled down the hall and rushed into the elevator before the doors slid shut. Once again, I was relieved to get the heck out of this hospital. Maybe I should have stayed to get a checkup or just a quick nap. But, as the Keeper, I couldn't die and what would they tell me, anyway? *A vampire bit you, so take one dose of garlic fries every day to repel another attack.*

The fact that I laughed at my own thoughts, meant I was feeling fine. Definitely.

"Totally fine," I mumbled, as we stepped out of the hospital and into the sprinkling rain.

I repeated it to myself when we drove home. Then again, after I finished a call with Detective Wilhelm who said he had no news on the case. I said it another time when I hobbled dinner together. And once more when I threw the stale bagels and burnt eggs into the trash and ordered Cheesecake Factory for mobile delivery.

Though the Oreo cheesecake with its crumbled cookies and whipped cream looked delicious, I only poked it with my plastic fork.

With my energy sapped, I barely stabbed through the sugary goodness and I still needed to hash over clues with Kai before the night ended. It felt like cheating to eat celebratory food in the middle of an investigation. Especially since the only lead I had was the story itself. Where would I find the vampire?

Kai emerged from Wendy's room after checking for creepy mermaids under her bed.

"Okay, so what's the story?" He marched through the small kitchen and took a seat beside me on the worn-out couch. I'd replaced the older Post-It notes with fresh ones, ready for lists of evidence and theories, but they remained as unused as my cheesecake did uneaten.

I sighed and peeled the Band-Aid off my neck. Kai's eyes bugged at the sight of the teeth marks. The two small holes had scabbed over, but they weren't entirely healed.

"It's fine," I said, repeating it for the sixth time. My husband's expression didn't match the sentiment as he waited for an explanation. "It's a vampire bite."

"I see that," he said, as he lightly brushed his thumb over the scabs. "If you can't go into the sun anymore, it's really going to put a damper on our anniversary cruise next summer."

I gave him a deadpan expression before giving in to the temptation to roll my eyes. "I'm literally unkillable. Turning into a vampire is the least of my worries. It can't happen."

He nodded, considering this. "So, you fought Dracula?"

"And there's my question." I scooted to the edge of the couch and closer to him. "Is Dracula really the only vampire in literature?"

Before I finished the question, Kai already had his phone out to pull up a list of stories about blood-suckers.

He paused, tapping on the screen. "Did you know Dracula is based on Vlad the Impaler, a ruler in the fourteen-hundreds?"

"Literature, Kai, I need books and characters, not history and real people."

I snuggled closer to him and leaned my head against his shoulder. Someday, I'd need a historian to help me solve a murder but today was not that day. Speaking of today, it flew by too fast. I needed to be out tracking down the vampire who'd turned Lindsay, not cuddling with my husband. But I had nowhere to start, and Detective Wilhelm had no leads.

"That's where you come in," I said as if he could read my thoughts.

"Huh?" Kai halted his scroll of the Google pages that listed vampires in literature.

"I need to scrape together what I have and pull out a lead." I sat up and grabbed a pencil from the coffee table. "Hopefully, the medical examiner will have a cause of death confirmation for Mrs. Dew tomorrow, then I can piece together what Lindsay told me."

Flying into the window.

Wolf attack.

Man = vampire, turned Lindsay.

Mrs. Dew died from… what?

"So, approach it like you do other cases," Kai said, running his hand in circles over my back. "Why was the victim targeted?"

The headache pulsed with my heartbeat, a rhythmic reminder screaming *get some rest!* "Because she had the story aura?" The response was lame but better than nothing. Modern society tweaked the stories. Likely, Lindsay still had an actual connection to her mother's murderer, or Mrs. Dew was in direct contact with the person who had attacked her.

"But why?" Kai asked. He leaned over the Coffee Table of Evidence and tapped the sticky note with Mrs. Dew's name scribbled on it. "What made this lady become a character?"

"What if she wasn't a character? Jameson killed a bunch of women who weren't characters before he found me because the condensed amount of people in one place confused the story. And the city gave him access to a lot of ladies going to their grandma's houses," I argued, playing devil's advocate. Kai and I regularly bounced off of one another, producing theories and trying to fit pieces of the puzzle together. We were partners against crime, always side-by-side. The thought made me sentimental, wanting to snuggle my head at the spot between his shoulder and collarbone and take a whiff of his scent.

He smelled so dang good.

"Then you still have to figure out what made Lindsay a character. Maybe her mom was just in the way," he said, as he peeled the sticky note off the table and moved it beside the one where he wrote Lindsay's name. "The murderer killed Mrs. Dew in the bedroom. Now, what's the weapon?"

"She had no visible injuries, but—"

An obnoxious ringing cut me off. Kai's phone lit up on the coffee table beside the tree of sticky notes. A picture of his sister covered the screen with her gap-toothed smile from the first and only time she'd flown out to California to meet Wendy. Gerda was a busy woman and rarely took the time to call her brother, which made the call about as shocking as a wolf diving through a second-story window.

We exchanged a surprised look as he picked up the phone to stare at his sister's face.

"Answer it," I said before the call went to voicemail. "I'll keep playing Clue."

Kai swiped right and stood, pressing the phone against his ear. He paced behind the couch while I scribbled a to-do list for the next day.

- *Grab one of Wendy's Christmas presents. Then tell her Santa's elf dropped off a sticker book for her to play with today.*
- *Stop by the office to check in with the boss and tell her I'm out on a case.*
- *Get the cause of death from Reese/medical examiner.*

I jumped at Kai's gasp and turned to give him a look, but he was engrossed in the conversation. Wrinkles lined his forehead, visible since he raked his fingers over his scalp, which pulled the hair back from his face.

"It's okay," he mouthed, before offering me a tight smile.

"Sure." The situation sounded about as okay as I felt, with a raging migraine, fang marks on my neck, and two old white men haunting my every move. Three, if you counted Detective Wilhelm. I gave Kai space, and returned to my notes, tucking my hair behind my ears.

- *Talk to Lindsay again and match her with a story.*
- *Use the story to track the murderer.*

The boundaries of a specific plot would always be a faster route to the answer than questioning potential witnesses, victim relations, and scraping the crime scene for clues. Only a handful of people became fairy tale characters. All I needed was a lead on a few suspects, and the story aura glow did the job for me from there. If only every murder case could be so cut and dry…though I preferred dealing with mere mortals over serial killers with superpowers.

The memory of Jameson's insane speed and massive jaws left me with a little shiver.

Kai hung up with a sigh. "It sounds like my dad is showing signs of dementia."

"I'm so sorry," I said.

He swallowed and nodded. "Yeah. Gerda wants my help to set up an in-home nurse for our dad. I might need to fly out there. Can you take Wendy again tomorrow?"

I seethed. "Do you really want your daughter tracking a vampire?"

Hair flopped into his face again as he leaned both hands against the back of the couch. "What I don't want, is a portal to appear and suck her into Neverland without you around. As always, she's safest by your side and it'll only be for a couple of days."

He was right, and I'd already added entertainment in the form of a Christmas sticker book for tomorrow's to-do list. If the story aura claimed her, Kai had no access to the Brothers Grimm and no protection like the immortality the hood gave me. Who knew what other fairy tale creatures roamed out there that I'd yet to encounter? The Big Bad Wolf could very well be on Kai's flight to go blow the pigs' house down in Montana.

I nodded and reached behind me, grabbing his shirt and pulling him down to kiss me.

I paused, with his mouth hovering over mine. "Take care of your dad, I've got Wendy. But don't you dare miss Christmas."

Our lips met, and he tasted so incredibly good, like… metal?

Chapter 12

Like Mother, Like Daughter

Everywhere we went, Wendy left a trail of stickers. Pam earned a Rudolph sticker that she accepted on her hand, despite my boss's aversion to children, she liked Wendy. Apparently, my daughter behaved more like a grown-up than most kids, and I didn't know whether to be proud or worried.

At the morgue, Reese scolded Wendy for sneaking a sticker of Santa's red toy bag on a cadaver's toe. My attempt to tell her it was a mannequin didn't work, Wendy knew the person had passed away, and that I investigated the reason. Still, the dead body didn't frighten her, at least not as much as mermaids.

"Sorry," I said, as I peeled Santa's bag off Mrs. Dew's yellowed toe.

Reese grumbled something from his stool where he stooped over a clipboard of the victim's report. The hump at the back of his neck had grown more pronounced, and it seemed he'd given in to his role as the hunchback of Notre Dame from Victor Hugo's story. He'd known, longer than I did, about the story cycle and accepted his fate, insisting that I only intervene to save Esmeralda when the time came. *Better to have loved and died, than not love at all.* It broke my heart, but I wouldn't meddle with his life without his consent.

Finally, he peered over his thick-rimmed glasses and confirmed what I'd suspected. "Cause of death is conclusively cardiac arrest and toxicology reports came back clean. She wasn't murdered unless her attacker knew she had a weak heart."

"She was literally scared to death?" I scanned Mrs. Dew's lifeless face. She looked calmer now, more peaceful in death, opposite of her daughter's undead rage.

Reese nodded and glared at Wendy again, as she peeled off another sticker. Undaunted by his grumpy stare, she held it up and offered to put it on his hand the way she had for Pam. Reese relented and thrust out his arm, which delighted my daughter. She skipped around the examination table, paying no attention to the dead body, and slapped a big ol' sparkly sticker of a Christmas tree on Reese's arthritic hands.

"Do you think a vampire would look scary enough to make you die?" I mused aloud.

"Me?" Reese pointed to himself and scoffed. "Definitely not. But the victim and I are two very different people. In any case, she didn't seem to be the attacker's target, or else she'd show signs of vampirism rather than lying dead on my table."

I nodded. "So, I still have to identify who the heck her daughter was, and then trace the people in her life to find the vampire."

"I guess," he said, shrugging.

"Thanks, Reese." I tried to smile but exhaustion tugged at my muscles, even the tiny ones in my face. I imagine I looked about as good as Mrs. Dew right now, even with half of a night's sleep. "You know where to find me if you ever change your mind about twisting The Hunchback—"

He held up his palm. "I'm happy with who I am."

I nodded and guided Wendy out the door. Before it swung shut to seal the freezing air-conditioner atmosphere inside, I glimpsed Reese's smile as he admired the sparkly Christmas tree on his hand.

With my hand on the top of Wendy's head, I continued guiding her up the street and toward the hospital. Whatever they'd diagnosed Lindsay with, I hoped it didn't require an induced coma or another form of unconsciousness since we needed to have another chat. What did her life look like before the attack? It'd narrow the character sketch as I tried to place her in Bram Stoker's novel.

I kept one hand on Wendy while digging for my buzzing phone at the bottom of my purse. The sticker book consumed her attention as she peeled off reindeer and placed them on reusable pages with open scenes like the night sky, a fireplace with stockings, and Santa's workshop.

I answered to the gruff, but familiar bark of my last name.

"Rowan," Detective Wilhelm said. "I just heard from the medical examiner. Mrs. Dew wasn't—"

"I know, heart attack. So, is it not considered murder in the records?"

He ignored my interruption, the only way I could get a word in edge-wise with a conversation plow like him. "Right before Reese's call, I heard from the hospital. Lindsay Dew passed early this morning."

I stopped dead in my tracks and Wendy spun around, bumping back into my leg as she stared at the stickers. How? Lindsay must not have fully turned, or I didn't understand vampires as the Brothers Grimm had said.

"This puts the case back to a murder." He took the words right out of my mouth. "I spoke with Lindsay's doctor. The guy who attacked her was a real creep. It sounds like he used medical equipment to drain her since she suffered significant blood loss. The doc identified needle marks on her neck. He might have been going for organ donation on the black market, but blood instead. Maybe to help people pass drug tests that use blood." Detective Wilhelm rambled and I let him believe the theory, while I scraped my brain for a new idea. "That doesn't explain why the dirtbag didn't just take the blood bag the nurse used for her transfusion treatments though."

"Did you locate any friends or family of the Dew women we could speak with?"

"A few." he breathed loudly into the phone. "Lindsay's nurse confirmed a best friend named Mindy, and another friend named Nolan."

"Can we interview them?" I asked.

"Already scheduled. If you're free tonight, I'll be chatting with Nolan at the station. Mindy is out of town, couldn't reach her."

"Thank you," I said, before clicking to end the call. With Lindsay's death, part of my to-do list went out the window and now I needed to pivot my plan of action until tonight's interview. If Nolan was a character, I'd see the glow, but I needed to know the novel then match it up to his life and personality to know which one.

Library. There I'd get acquainted with Bram Stoker's characters and keep Wendy busy along the way. The neighborhood's library offered my best bet with lots of picture books and plenty of quiet for me to focus on Dracula's plot.

I spun around, directing Wendy with me, and headed in the other direction.

The quiet, calming atmosphere greeted me. The smell of old books filled my nose, and the librarian's warm smile invited us inside. I posted up at a large, round table in the back corner near the horror section where we could spread out sticky notes and Christmas stickers. If Wendy was as like me in her fairy tale tendencies as she was in regular life, I wouldn't have to worry about her draw to Neverland— she'd fight it with everything she had.

With Wendy still in my view, I visited the aisle where the shelves stocked horror books and located a copy of Dracula. The dim corner of the old library suddenly brightened and flashbacks to Scarlet's portals came back. It was only a few aisles over where she'd appeared during my Red Riding Hood investigation to keep me from learning about stories come to life.

The vague glow of Jacob and Will Grimm appeared. They arrived, already arguing about the city library's basic organization of books. I groaned and let my forehead fall against the front of the shelf, then gently banged it twice.

"Dracula should be in the classics, not horror." Jacob said, with his arms crossed and nose literally in the air.

"But it *is* a horror, though, with the state of this Keeper's world, they should classify it as a true crime."

My jaw dropped as my brain caught up with the slight. "Hey!"

Jacob threw his head back and laughed. "On that, we agree, yes?"

"You two just can't get enough of me," I said, coming out with my guns blazing. "Maybe I'm not such a bad Keeper after all?"

Again with the laughing. Jacob guffawed, and I got a full view of the thick hair up his nose. Suddenly, his face dropped to a deadpan expression, and he stared straight at me.

"Do you have any more information?" he asked. All four eyes fixed on me, waiting tentatively as if I were a bomb about to explode. And I was. If they kept haunting me at every turn, I wouldn't get a chance to solve this crap before Christmas and save my daughter. That'd earn them another bullet *through* the chest. Speaking of Wendy, I took a step back and peered around the bookshelf to double-check she still sat at the table with a sticker stuck to each of her fingers.

"Information on what, exactly?" I asked, returning my focus to the ghosts.

Jacob opened his mouth but his brother cut him off. "Have you identified the fairy tale?"

I tapped my fingers against the book and turned it around for them to see the cover of the ominous castle. "You were literally just talking about it, and it's not a fairy tale."

Jacob waved his hand in my face. "Are you sure?"

That earned them my best strict-mom stance, with a hand on my hip and brows furrowed. "Is this the test? You knew the story all along but you want me to figure it out? Do you know who the murderer is too? What's the point of all this? It's a waste of my time."

"Certainly not," Will answered. "We…" he glanced at his brother. "We need the Keeper's insight. We're not part of this world anymore which means we cannot see who belongs to the stories. By rights, we shouldn't even be here. So *keep* the stories straight and correct the damage you've done."

"Me?" I slapped the book to my chest, palm pressing against it.

"Well, we certainly didn't rip a hole—" Will started, but his brother coughed and hacked so loudly it interrupted the rest of his sentence.

"Let us see if she makes the right choice, first," he said. Then he dropped his voice to library-level volume and turned to his brother's ear. "What if she wants to make it worse?"

"Make what worse?" I interjected, jabbing Bram Stoker's novel at them like an accusatory finger. A library patron turned the corner, saw me talking to myself, and skittered away with wide eyes. I cleared my throat and continued. "Twisting the stories? Because I'll twist your heads right off—" I clamped my mouth shut before my sharp tongue threatened the only beings who could help my daughter.

Will's eyebrows raised to his hairline.

Jacob's eyebrows followed suit but couldn't reach the receding line of his hair. "Have you gotten close to the answer?" he asked.

I sucked in a breath through my nose. "It's Dracula, duh."

"Dracula-da?" Jacob repeated, but I ignored it.

"Someone with the story aura died this morning—"

Jacob gasped. "Who? Who? Who?"

"You sound like an owl," Will said, shushing him. "Let her speak."

"Her real name is Lindsay but I don't know who she is in the story. That's why I'm here." I waved the book in their faces again.

"If this person was a character whose death takes place in the plot, this is positive news," Will said.

I curled my upper lip and gave them a disgusted look. Death was never good news. How out-of-touch with humanity were they? The Brothers Grimm were once humans, two regular librarians who somehow became gods. Or were the gods first and came to earth like aliens? I was inclined to believe the latter considering how cold-hearted they behaved.

"What?" Jacob said. "The stories are as the stories should be. It isn't our fault they've crossed over."

So, you're just chill with innocent people dying? Gross.

"Look," I said, "just stay out of my way and let me solve this so Dracula can seal and go back to Storyland or whatever."

They looked at each other and shrugged. Without so much as a 'good luck,' they turned and walked down the aisle. Pieces of their conversation floated back to me, as they fought over which books belonged in the classics section, and which stories should be arranged by their genre.

"Do you know what I find fascinating?" Jacob asked his brother. When Will didn't respond, Jacob kept talking. "To hurt a vampire, hunters can bless any weapon by carving a cross into it. Do you remember how Agnes did it when she hunted Dracula in the 1900s? Story aura vampires are not what these modern humans think."

Will grunted and their conversation faded. Whoever Agnes was, apparently she'd discovered a new way to attack those afflicted with vampirism. It sounded too good to be true but I filed the possibility away in my mental storage cabinet.

I sighed and returned to the table. By the time I sat down, Wendy had created full Christmas scenes with most of her stickers on the reusable pages. She complained of hunger. I produced an applesauce pouch and mini bag of pretzels from my purse to hold her over until I'd brushed up on all of Bram Stoker's characters. Lunch passed an hour ago, but my headache kept my appetite at bay. I offered Wendy the protein bar I'd packed for myself, too.

"Okay, so," I muttered to myself, "there's Dracula, of course, and Jonathan who goes to Dracula's castle. Mina is engaged to Jonathan and Lucy is Mina's friend. Lucy's engaged to…" I flipped the pages and double-checked the name I kept forgetting. "Morris, right? Morris and then there's Mrs. Westenra. Who the heck is that?"

I quickly scribbled a tree in my notebook to connect the characters. Wendy's interest was piqued, and she set down the applesauce pouch long enough to add ornament stickers to the 'tree's' branches between the character names. After shuffling through several pages, I identified Mrs. Westenra as Lucy's mother, and then continued, skimming for names and actions they take in the plot.

I whipped out my phone to pull up a summary of the novel and cross-reference the actual book with the internet's shortened version. A word caught my eye from the website with the list of characters. If only I could trust the quick notes version of fairy tales and novels online, my investigations would go a lot faster. But Scarlet had warned me too many times that technology messes with the stories, and I didn't want to make any mistakes like the one she had when The Ugly Duckling girl killed herself. But the word 'death' certainly piqued my curiosity.

"Wait! Mrs. Westenra dies?" I skimmed the website, then flipped through the book to confirm its accuracy. My eyes flew over the novel's words as I mumbled them.

"The window blind blew back with the wind that rushed in, and in the aperture of the broken panes there was the head of a great, gaunt grey wolf. Mother cried out in a fright, and struggled up into a sitting posture, and clutched wildly at anything that would help her. Yes! Yes, oh my gosh. Mrs. Westenra is Mrs. Dew which makes Lucy the same as Lindsay. Lucy, Lindsay, Lindsay, Lucy." I bounced in my seat as I recorded my triumph with the huge clue. "Now, how in the wonderland did they know Dracula?"

Wendy hopped out of her chair and climbed into my lap without an invitation. Such was the life of a mom. I made room for her by scooting back from the table, but I didn't stop my eager search through the novel.

"What're you doing?" she asked.

"Oh, just getting some reading in for my investigation. Remember? I solve puzzles to help keep people safe."

She twisted to look at me. "People that died because of bad people, right?"

A lump gathered in my throat. Did my six-year-old really need to lose her blissful innocence and learn about murderers? It seemed she already had. How much did she overhear of mine and Kai's theories at night, when she got up to use the potty, or get a fresh glass of water?

"That's right," I confirmed, not interested in lying to her. "I write news from the city about the puzzles and the bad guys. That way people can learn where danger is and stay safe from it."

"I'm bored," she said. "Can you read the book to me?" Her little hand reached out and patted the worn pages of the library's copy.

"Um, okay, sure." I continued, giving the character voices to keep her interested, though she quickly went back to playing with the stickers.

When I stopped reading, she didn't even notice. I picked up the pen and added a theory to my notes.

Nolan = Dracula? Considering his interview was scheduled with the detective after dark, it was the best guess I had so far. Otherwise, this Nolan dude could be any number of the characters in Dracula from Van Helsing, to Lucy's best friend Mina, not to mention the two men who ultimately kill the vampire: Jonathan and Morris. Despite popular belief, apparently, Van Helsing was not the original Buffy, it was a team effort between Mina's fiancée and Lucy's ex-fiancée.

While Wendy finished her last scene, a picture of elves making toys, I added more ideas to sticky notes that I could later peel out of the notebook if they ended up being wrong.

Where is Lindsay's in-home nurse? Nurse = Doctor Van Helsing since both have a medical job?

Not only did I need to find Dracula for Wendy's sake, according to my agreement with the Grimms, but if I located the murderer before Morris's death, I could intervene and spare an innocent person's life who'd lost their freedom to the story aura. Like Wendy, Morris needed help from the push and pull of the tale's plot.

Quincey Morris dies when Jonathan and Morris kill Dracula.

The second most important identification to Dracula was finding the person who'd been overtaken by Morris's story aura. If I could find Morris, I'd keep him out of the fight that hurt him.

I returned to my to-do list and added: *save Morris's life!*

Chapter 13

Like Taking Clues From a College Kid

Detective Wilhelm's office stank of beef and cheese. Taco Bell bags spilled out of the desk-high pile of trash in the bin behind his chair. I wrinkled my nose, if my migraine didn't steal my appetite, the smell of the sticky food wrappers certainly would.

The fast food stench didn't seem to bother Wendy, as she took a seat on the floor with my phone in her hand. A cartoon's opening theme song blared from the phone's speaker. She scooted against the back of my chair and got comfortable.

The detective plopped down across from me with a grunt. "Nolan's late. I hate it when people don't respect others' time." He continued griping, while I tuned him out and peered out the window behind him.

The glow of the setting sun was still visible outside. Though the streetlamps had come on, the night did not fully begin, yet. It was another strike against Nolan as the murderer in my book.

A slap against the desktop startled me back to the detective's one-sided conversation. He slid a piece of paper across the desk to me.

"These are all the relations I've contacted in Lindsay's life. She wasn't a very popular chick if you ask me."

I scanned the list, which included black-and-white printed pictures of some of the people's driver's licenses.

Nolan, friend.

Mindy, best friend. The story aura always landed on those for whom it made sense, which meant Mindy was likely Mina, Lucy's friend in the book. I snorted at the convenience of the name starting with the same letter. If nothing else, I could write Mindy off as the murderer.

Nurse Betty, was a nurse, duh. *Van Helsing?*

Brandon, Lindsay's fiancée. *That rules out Brandon as Dracula. He has to be Arthur Holmwood since Arthur is engaged to Lucy in the novel.* I quickly made note of that in the margin of my empty page, ready to record whatever we discovered during Nolan's interview.

That left Nolan still unidentified.

Speak of the devil, a knock sounded on the door. The detective shouted for him to enter, a power play move Wilhelm always used— make them to come you. A tall-dark, with a jawline that looked altered by plastic surgery, shoved through the door carrying all the confidence of a millionaire playboy. I scraped my brain, trying to remember which of Dracula's character had a lot of money. The black glow radiated around him and intensified my migraine.

"Sit," the detective instructed.

Nolan flashed me a shiny smile, full of ego. His eyes raked over me and I instantly regretted willing the hood to look like a tight, leather jacket. Thankfully, he put his creeper eyes away as soon as he heard the cartoon jingle and noticed Wendy posted up behind me.

The blank page filled quickly as I listed my observations. *Egotistical. Likely wealthy. Comes out at night.* Discreetly, I peered up from the notes to observe his tick of regularly wiping at the bottom of his nose. If I was careful, my visual inspection wouldn't make him believe I found him attractive.

"How well did you know Lindsay?" Detective Wilhelm asked.

Nolan leaned back in the chair, slouching with disinterest. "She's a friend of Mindy's—or was, or whatever."

As soon as he opened his mouth, the confidence dissipated though he kept his eyelids half-open, likely to keep up his superiority. Or he was tired.

How early in the evening did vampires wake? Had the interview interrupted his beauty rest?

"She wasn't your friend?" Detective Wilhelm asked. He glanced at me. He'd gotten lazier over the years, letting me take the lead on the questioning, despite his belief that women weren't as astute as men.

Today, though, the pulsing in my temples raged, and I didn't have the mental clarity to run the interview while also taking notes. Not to mention, the constant cross-referencing my life as the Keeper required. What pieces of this suspect matched with which character?

"We chilled." Nolan shrugged. "She's been on my yacht a few times."

Definitely rich. While Morris had money, Dracula lived in a castle. Nolan's wealth matched both.

"Look, No-lane." The detective purposely mispronounced his name, another lazy power-play. "Lindsay didn't have any relatives except her mother and she's dead now, too. I need you to work with us here."

A whiff of too much cologne nearly choked me, as Nolan shifted in his seat and looked at me. I offered a smile as fake as his teeth, capped in rows of veneers. Were they hiding sharp fangs?

"Did Lindsay have any enemies?" Detective Wilhelm asked, pulling Nolan's attention across the desk.

The playboy rubbed his finger under his nose again and sniffed. Either it was a nervous tick that made him look entirely guilty, or he smelled blood, which made him look guilty *and* vampiric. "She had a few exes before she settled for that Brandon guy. But she was sick a lot lately, and didn't hang out with us much anymore. Like I said, Mindy wanted me to help because she was feeling guilty."

The detective and I both straightened, exchanging curious looks.

"Guilty?" I inquired.

"Nah, Man." Nolan shook his head. "I mean Mindy wanted to visit Lindsay while she was sick but we just never really got around to it, you know? We both felt terrible about it." His lip twitched, the mask of confidence slipping.

Finally, as his gaze dropped to his hands, I recognized pain, or maybe fear. Fear that he'd get caught? Whichever emotion it was, it revealed Nolan wasn't the shallow, rich playboy he wanted people to believe, but complex, and layered. Possibly, a being granted with the knowledge of someone who lived for centuries, by the story aura—long enough to build those layers. Did that make Mindy one of Dracula's brides?

"Mindy, uh." He sniffed again. "She was worried about Lindsay since she'd sleepwalk during our overnight parties. Real creepy stuff."

Nolan definitely didn't talk like an intelligent vampire, but it could be a mask.

"Wait," I said. I put my pen down and met his gaze. "You keep mentioning Mindy. Are you engaged?"

He cracked a side smile. "This one's a dang good investigator, huh?" Nolan looked at Detective Wilhelm, who only frowned at the compliment directed my way. "I haven't proposed yet, but—" With his back arched, he dug a small jewelry box from his pocket and produced a diamond ring. "I'm planning to do it on New Year's Eve. I bring this with me everywhere, because I'm just excited, you know?" The corny grin on his face corroborated his story. Not only did this confirm he wasn't Dracula, but the knowledge of his impending proposal also placed him as the character Jonathan, in the novel, AKA Mina's fiancé, and the lawyer who worked on Dracula's estate.

"Are you a lawyer?" I asked. Detective Wilhelm shot me a glare. I was sure to get an earful about whatever earned his disapproval after Nolan left.

"Me?" Nolan asked. The flushed look on his face told me I'd guessed wrong on that one. "My dad wishes. I created VacayDays. It's like Airbnb, vacation rentals, and whatnot. My old man thinks I'm lazy but I make good money. Besides, it leaves more time for sailing. I just got my own sailboat." He wiggled his eyebrows, an odd expression of pride but it suited his pretentious vibe. "I even got some of my tenants into sailing with me."

"Do you know if any of Lindsay's exes needed money?" The detective asked, directing the conversation back to the correct focus. "Maybe some of them showed violent tendencies?"

"I know it sounds bad," Nolan said with a rake of his fingers through his hair, "but we really only hang out with other people of… our status. Some of her exes couldn't keep up with our lifestyle. And the violence thing, I don't know, Man. Everybody loved Lindsay, even Garen, and she broke that dude's heart."

"Garen?" I kept my eyes on Nolan and scribbled the new information by feeling. *Garen = Morris?* If he dated Lindsay, he matched the character named as Lucy's suitor from the novel. If nothing else, it was one more tie to track Dracula.

Nolan nodded. Every move he made sent a whiff of overpowering cologne that made my throat tighten.

"Yeah, her ex-boyfriend," he said. "We were bros while he and Lindsay dated. But then Mindy wanted me to stop hanging out with him after their big breakup."

"Can you give us Garen's contact information?" The detective passed Nolan a blank piece of paper.

The rest of Nolan's information confirmed him as Jonathan Harker from Dracula. But if he wasn't a lawyer dealing with the villain's estate, how would I connect the two?

The detective barrelled over the conversation with a barrage of extra questions, which I used to try tracing the characters. I'd already written Nolan off as innocent, but I needed every piece of information leading to the person Dracula's story aura had landed on.

"Mommy?" Wendy piped up, and I twisted in my seat to see she'd stood. Before she said anything, the little dance she performed told me everything. "I need to go potty."

As much as I didn't want to miss the details, mom-duty called. I excused us and hurried with Wendy to the restrooms. I stood guard outside the single restroom while Wendy did her business.

The Brothers Grimm would be glad to know I'd found a living character. Nothing would make me happier than sending those two ghosts back wherever they'd come from. Supposedly, solving this murder would do that.

I let my mind work the case while I observed the routine work of officers in the station.

Nolan truly seemed to care about Mindy, and if he cared about Mindy, he'd want to help catch the person who'd killed his girlfriend's best friend. He'd definitely have given us the murderer's information if he had any leads. It was clear Nolan didn't know who'd attacked Lindsay, which meant it wouldn't be as easy as following him to Dracula.

The detective's door swung open across the station, and Nolan stepped out. They shook hands vigorously, each man trying to out-testosterone one another.

"Wendy?" I knocked on the restroom door. "Are you almost done?"

If we hurried, I'd have time to ask Nolan a few more questions like: *have you seen anyone particularly pale?* And, *do any of your friends have fangs?* But worded better, of course. I was a journalist, after all. When my head didn't pound like the Little Drummer Boy's sticks, I was pretty good with words.

The toilet flushed in response.

A whiff of the familiar cologne caught my attention, and I spun around. Nolan had stopped near the station's front desk to answer his cell phone.

"Nah, Man," he said. "It's the only castle on my list."

Castle? Like, the castle Dracula called home? I shuffled closer, hoping he wouldn't notice me sneaking up behind him to eavesdrop.

"Yeah, it's rented out through the year. The dude paid in cash and everything. But it's definitely big enough for a kegger."

My heart skipped a beat, and it had nothing to do with the small hands that suddenly wrapped around my waist. Wendy attached herself to my side, while my brain worked overtime.

It all made sense. Nolan wasn't a lawyer dealing with Dracula's property, like his character, Jonathan. Instead, he owned the property the murderer lived at, through Vacay-whatever.

Easy peasy lemon squeezy. The answer was right in front of me. All I had to do was check Nolan's company's website, determine which rental looked most like a castle, and pay the murderer a visit.

Case closed + happy Brothers Grimm = Wendy free from their story crap.

I squeaked, trying to contain my excitement. I didn't know what to do first, call Kai or sharpen a stake to kill the vampire with, before he could get into a battle that'd lead to Morris's—or Garen's—death.

Giddy now, I found my foot tapping, pulse picking up speed, and bladder suddenly full. *Talk about mom-duty.* After carrying and birthing a whole human, I couldn't hold my pee as long as I did when I was a spry, young lady.

I spun around, grabbed Wendy, and shoved through the restroom door.

Chapter 14

Play Your Clues Right

Splitting my attention between the investigation and mom-life, proved trickier than I'd expected.

Thick, swirling steam wafted up my nose. Peppermint flavoring gave my huge mug of coffee a Christmas spice, while Wendy enjoyed the same taste in her hot chocolate. Cats that were tangled in strands of Christmas lights decorated the outside of my mug, and once I slurped down the bucket of caffeine, I'd see the words at the bottom that read: *Meowy Christmas*.

Hopefully, by then my headache would subside and I'd get a boost of energy to get me through the night.

With the steaming cocoa drink in one hand and the tiny scissors I used to trim my eyebrows in the other, it proved difficult to balance a bullet in my grasp, too. I tucked my mug between my folded legs, squeezing it with my feet so it wouldn't spill, then focused on scratching the sharp point of the scissors into the side of a bullet. I was terrible at carving, or etching, or whatever craft this would be considered, but at least it resembled a cross. Hopefully, Jacob Grimm and this Agnes character were right. Supposedly, a blessed weapon, any weapon marked by a cross, repelled vampires.

I scooted to the edge of the couch, took a break from crafting, and tapped my phone's screen. Eight was late for Wendy to still be awake. I wished I could crawl into bed beside her and cuddle, dreaming of sugar plum fairies, but Kai's flight landed in a few hours. With him home again, I didn't dare waste another night. Not when I could locate Dracula, save some lives, and appease the ghosts.

Wendy giggled as Kevin McCallister once again thwarted the burglars in *Home Alone*. Instinctively, I put my hand under her mug, ready to catch it if it slipped from her fingers, while she wiggled and squirmed on the cushion beside me.

Other than the mini hot chocolate station, complete with marshmallows, peppermint chunks, and caramel candies, the Coffee Table of Evidence took on the role of a conspiracy board. Red sticky notes contained all the real-world pieces of evidence including the tree of Lindsay Dew's friends and acquaintances. On blue, I recorded details about Nolan and his business that the detective and I had uncovered during the interview. I reserved yellow for anything directly related to Dracula and vampires since it was the most urgent.

I peeled a yellow note off the glass and considered the list of ways to end a vampire.

Decapitation and burning. Wooden stake. Sunlight. Bullets with a cross scratched into them.

The peppermint coffee soured on my tongue. Tonight, maybe hours from now, I'd either have to shove a stake through an undead serial killer's heart or…I swallowed, chop off his head.

Killing Dracula would twist the story, saving Morris's—or Garen's—life and spare Mindy from turning into a vampire.

Just when the paint cans knocked out the movie's burglars, a chill swept the room. I shot to my feet and scooped the mug of hot chocolate from Wendy's little hands.

"Time for bed!" I announced. My daughter already suffered visions of Neverland, she didn't need to experience more ghostly visits. The temperature in the living room dropped so quickly that my throat hurt from the icy air.

As expected, Wendy moaned and groaned with a dramatic collapse against the couch cushions. Her entire body transformed into a wet noodle, each limb supposedly too heavy for her to lift. With her nose in a pillow, she rolled around repeating "please".

"You can finish the movie tomorrow, I promise," I said. Could I promise anything to her? How much time did I have before the mermaids under her bed became real and pulled her into Neverland? If she followed the story as it was written, she'd become friends with the mermaids and find endless joy in tormenting Captain Hook.

My daughter was better than that, more than a character. Wendy was a dynamic, complex, unique person. An eternal existence in the box of a character wasn't right. She deserved a choice, to become anything she wanted, and I'd fight for that choice, even if it took a thousand solved murders to appease the Brothers Grimm.

I crouched and scooped Wendy up, who tried her hardest not to smile as I tickled her.

"We'll watch The Grinch too," I added. "And go to the playground."

"Okay." she sighed. "Will the fairy be at the park tomorrow?"

I froze while bent over to plop Wendy on her bed, but it had nothing to do with the cold wafting in from the ghost-infested living room. My heart skipped a beat. I wanted to brush it off and ignore it— after all, what could Tinker Bell hurt? But Tinker Bell wasn't the problem. It was what she represented. Also, what kind of creep had turned into a fairy and come to my daughter's window? A crick split through my lower back and I dropped Wendy on her comforter.

As if she read my mind, Wendy crawled under the blanket and then pointed to the window. "I like playing with Travis, but he can fly and do magic and I can't, so it makes me feel bad."

"Travis?" I asked.

Wendy nodded, as she wiggled down into the mound of blankets and stuffed animals. "He sits in the back of the classroom and always makes Mrs. Skipper mad when he throws paper airplanes at her."

Tinker Bell was in Wendy's class. *Of course.* The pixie followed Peter everywhere, so it only made sense.

My stomach twisted and groaned, either a reminder that I hadn't eaten more than a few bites all day or it was responding to the stress swirling in my brain. I'd been so focused on Wendy, I didn't think of the other innocent children the story aura might sweep up. Fairy tale plots didn't care if the person was young or old. If they fit the description, it settled quickly and quietly stripped them of their freedom.

"Maybe we'll skip the park," I said, my determination doubling down to win the Grimm brothers' help.

I checked under her bed, bundled her in a blanket like a burrito, and gave her a kiss on the forehead. The bedtime routine went easier than expected without Kai's special voices he'd always use to have her stuffed animals say 'goodnight'. Pigtails poked out from the top of the blanket as she snuggled down into the comforter and the pillow sunk around her head.

"I love you," I said, as I pulled the door closed to a crack.

"Mommy." she peeked out, nose at the edge of the butterfly blanket. "Is Doctor Van Helsing going to fix you?"

The squeeze in my throat caused me to cough. My heart pounded despite the blast of extreme cold in the living room.

I cleared my throat, trying to keep it steady. "What?" It still came out sharp and startled, so I took a slow breath before continuing. "What do you mean, Wednesday?"

"The doctor in the book at the library. Is he going to fix you?"

Did I have a disease she could sniff out like a dog? The dang nurse at the hospital must have worried Wendy. I was *fine*.

"Fine," I blurted out. "I mean, I don't need to be fixed, Honey, I'm okay."

Wendy pursed her lips, considering this. "But you got bit and then the next day we read about a doctor in a book. And you look really, really tired like a sick person."

Ouch. Kids knew how to punch a girl in the gut, but she wasn't wrong.

"I don't want you to sleep in the dirt," she said.

"What?" *You lost me, Kid.*

"In the book, you read that the bad guy slept in a dirt box with coughing and the bad guy hurt the sick lady at the hospital. And then she hurt you."

Dang. Wendy was smart, too smart. And observant. I'd read pieces of Dracula, including a speed-read of the end where the characters hunted the vampire. From what I could remember, they get into a battle with Dracula's servants, then seize his coffin, finally cutting off his head in a teamwork attack.

"Oh, you meant coffin," I said, putting the words together. "I'm not hurt." Even as I said it, my hand left the doorknob and instinctively covered the scabbed-over vampire bite.

My grip tightened on the door frame with my other hand. Not only did Wendy have Neverland to deal with, but she also suffered with a mom who hunted fairy tale monsters rather than a PTA professional like Yoga Mom. On top of that, Wendy worried for her mother's life—something no child should have to face.

"What about the bad guy who hurt the sick lady? Will he hurt you too?" she asked, eyebrows squished together.

I swallowed. If only my daughter's life could stay innocent, sweet, and devoid of villains and stories that steal free will. The option wasn't mine but reserved for women like Yoga Mom. I needed to do the best with what I had, which required an all-nighter to track down Dracula and decapitate him.

"I won't let him," I promised—one I could keep since death wasn't in a Keeper's cards. To encourage Wendy's curiosity, I added, "and I'll have the doctor to help me stop the bad guy."

My daughter's nose wrinkled, and her head cocked to the side. "Van Helsing stops him?"

"Yep, good old vampire slayer." I gave her a thumbs up.

"But it was the other boys."

I furrowed my brow. The chill against my back fell to the recesses of my attention. Despite my slight shivering, I ignored the ghost's presence for Wendy's sake.

"What other boys?"

Wendy shrugged, then tucked the blanket under her chin and burrowed back down into the bed. "I don't remember." Her voice trailed off with a sigh and her eyelids dipped, heavy.

"She's right, you know?" Jacob spoke from behind me in long, exaggerated words that grated on my nerves.

I chewed on the inside of my cheek to keep from snapping back at him.

"Goodnight," I whispered, my daughter's eyes shut. I carefully closed the door before spinning around to see the brothers standing on the other side of my kitchen counter.

"Jonathan and Morris kill Dracula, not Van Helsing," Will said. "If you ever need help on the stories themselves, we can be of service. It is your job to find the people who've become these characters."

Jacob nodded along, before adding another question. "Have you found them?"

I padded across the kitchen tile in my fuzzy socks, heading for the pot of cold coffee. "Investigations take time," I said, after taking a sip directly from the pot. It tasted like the dirt in Dracula's coffin and I coughed. My stomach growled, hungry for the dinner I'd picked at but never eaten. Nothing sounded tasty and even my coffee didn't satisfy.

"That didn't answer the question," Will again. "We want to go home."

"Then leave," I said.

"We can't. Not until we know our world won't be destroyed."

I slammed the pot down against the counter and sighed. "I don't know what that means but I have enough destruction right here. We have a deal. All I have to do is find his house and I'll have your murderer." The clap of my hands slapping together made Jacob jump and the slightest bit of satisfaction trickled through me. Or was that the chill turning my blood to ice? "Boom! Solved."

The brothers exchanged glances that didn't sit right with me.

"Look," I started, a surge of energy coursing through me. It'd been a long time since caffeine worked this well for me. Too bad I couldn't fathom taking another sip of the coffee. Instead, my stomach roiled with an intense craving that I couldn't place. It felt like pregnancy all over again. "I've identified Jonathan as a guy named Nolan. I plan to use him to trace my way to Dracula."

"And?" The bushes that hung over Jacob's eyes peaked.

"And I'll cut off Dracula's head."

Jacob's hand slapped his throat, with his mouth gaped and his eyes bugged. It seemed he was choking, while Will had the opposite reaction. No fear showed in his expression. Instead, anger twisted his face with a grimace and a fiery gaze.

"What?" I shrugged.

"You must not," Will managed, his voice a growl. "You cannot. Remember your daughter. Remember our arrangement and—"

"Will." Jacob tried to grab his brother's shoulder. I blinked, unsure of what I saw. Instead of his hand swiping right through Will's ghostly body, his palm landed solidly on his brother's arm. "Look."

Their wispy, spectral shapes filled in with the faint look of a disfigured skeleton.

My mouth fell open.

"We're becoming part of this world again," Will said, inspecting his arm with his brother's touch had landed. "No…"

Zombies flashed into my mind again at the sight of them. It looked as if their human bodies, long decayed and turned to nothing but bones, had taken over their ghostly existence. I frowned, feeling the tightening of time like a noose around my neck.

"What's happening?" I asked.

"Fix this," Will demanded, without an explanation. "You will fix this, Keeper. Let characters do their job, and help them find the way. We can't help you if you don't…" his voice gave out.

"I'll kill Dracula," I added.

Jacob's arm shot out, pointing a long, skeletal finger toward Wendy's bedroom. He opened his mouth, but no words came out. The vigorous shake of his head told me he didn't agree with my plan.

But ending the villain was my only option. I'd only agreed to solve the case for them, but that didn't include letting the murderer get away with…well, murder.

The Brothers Grimm blinked, distorting like an old TV, and then disappeared.

It left me gasping. Despite what I expected, my muscles didn't ache after the painful chill. On top of that, my headache subsided to a dull pinprick at my temples. In fact, I felt amazing.

I hurried around the counter and dropped onto the couch. After peeling a fresh sticky note, clicking my pen, and pulling up Google on my phone, I doubled down on the investigation. I'd make good use of this surprising energy, even if it killed me. Or whatever one says when they're immortal.

Nolan's website hurt my eyes with bright colors and sunny pictures. I scrolled through dozens of photos of gorgeous houses, apartments, and condos all around San Francisco Bay. Some rentals were right off the shore, which offered a luxurious and expensive vacation. Among the tall, modern houses was a dark-framed building with thick columns on either side of the black front door.

In the description, they labeled *it a 'castle-inspired architecture'. Bingo.*

By the time Kai walked through the door at half-past two in the morning, travel-weary and smelling like airplane pretzels, I'd drawn my plan of attack. The green sticky notes listed every weapon I'd bring, from a wooden stake to a solar-powered flashlight.

With a pink sticky note still attached to my thumb, I stood and wrapped my arms around Kai's neck.

"I missed you," he said when I pulled away. I plucked the Post-It off my finger and scanned the scribbled plan.

Wait for dawn. Sneak into Dracula's house. Chase him into the sunlight wielding a stake.

"What're you doing?" he asked, watching me pull a rain jacket onto my arms. I'd will the hood to do the job for me but with the random hauntings, I didn't want to get caught out freezing again.

"I have to kill Dracula."

After living with me for a decade, nothing shocked Kai anymore. Or so I'd thought. He furrowed his brow and inspected my eyes.

He ran his thumb along my jaw. "You look…different. Are you okay?"

"You know what I'm going to say." I slipped on my sneakers, not caring that I'd be in a hood, a rain jacket, and sweatpants when I confronted the vampire. "It can't wait any longer." Tinker Bell Travis and Peter Wendy haunted my mind's eye. At least with them, I didn't feel the chill of death, just the choking squeeze of losing a child. *Yep, that's worse.*

"And are you sure that you don't need help taking down a super-fast, incredibly strong, undead creature?" his hand trailed my arm then found my hand, our fingers intertwining. "I'm worried you're not getting enough sleep with everything that's going on. How's your head?"

I took a sharp breath. Kai smelled delicious and the sudden urge to kiss him, maybe bite his bottom lip, and his earlobe, and neck, over-came me. I shook the thought away and gave him a smile.

"Actually, I feel better than ever," I said. "Like if I were at a carni-val, I'd whack the hammer game and win."

"Nobody wins carnival games," he said, returning my smile. It was proof I'd convinced him of my strength and surety. "They're rigged."

My husband dropped his armful of luggage and used his free hand to snake his arm around my waist. When he pulled me into him, I expected to melt in his arms. Instead, I found myself kissing his throat, listening to blood pulse through his veins. Visions of sinking my teeth into his flesh flashed through my mind and I pulled away, gasping.

"Are you sure you're okay?" he asked.

I nodded, gnawing on my bottom lip.

Kai squeezed my hand for a boost of encouragement, but all I could focus on was his heartbeat. My teeth bit too hard, drawing blood from my lip and leaving a twinge of metallic taste at the tip of my tongue.

"Rigged or not, watch me win this."

Chapter 15

All Sizzle and No Stake

Gusts of salty air blew up from the coast. Out in the neighborhoods with the high-income families, the houses were built further apart, which allowed for the wind to pass through easily. Though cold, the damp chill didn't compare to the atmosphere the ghosts carried with them.

I didn't so much as shiver each time the breeze blasted hair back from my face and cut through the layers of a rain jacket, hood, and shirt.

I opted to walk the few blocks to Carrion Court, knowing I'd be more discreet as a pedestrian on San Francisco's streets, than when I'd inevitably struggle to parallel park in the neighborhood. In the light of day, I might have contacted Detective Wilhelm and bribed him to use police resources to dig up dirt on the person renting Nolan's Vacay castle. But I wanted to catch him just after he fell asleep when I'd have the upper hand. Literally, holding a stake.

Right over his heart that didn't beat.

Despite the sleepless night and long walk, my strength stayed steady. I'd killed a werewolf to save my life six years ago. Tonight, I'd add a vampire to that count to save others.

I turned the corner, spying the dark house at the bottom of the hill. The court ended with Dracula's castle in the middle, just off the coast of the San Francisco bay. As I stalked closer, the crash of waves hurt my ears. Each time water lapped against the sand, I flinched as if it were fingernails scraping along a chalkboard. The smell of exhaust and salt stung my nose, turning my stomach sour. Even the tickle of my short hair brushing against the middle of my neck intensified.

How could I feel so strong and in so much pain at the same time? I shook it off and pressed on, focusing instead on the house at the bottom of the hill. There, I'd confront Dracula, avenge Lindsay and her mother, and end this classic horror once and for all.

Goosebumps pricked my neck, then crawled down my arms, disappearing beneath my clothes. I'd suffered headaches as an immortal, but didn't expect a fever too. I dug into the diaper bag I'd refashioned into a backpack for recycling.

I pulled my phone from the side pocket and opened my call list. Scarlet's name appeared over a hundred times when I'd tried to contact her and she didn't answer. Our boss's test had her fully invested to make it onto the team as an investigative journalist at Bay Side Media, but that didn't stop me from begging for her help.

How could I be so sick and yet immune to death? I needed whatever insight she could give me. If I confronted Dracula and ended up vomiting on his bat wings, or whatever, it wouldn't put me in the advantage for a fight.

The screen's bright light seared my eyes, so I narrowed them to slits and held the phone out. The ringing echoed in my ears, even at arm's length and without the hands-free mode on.

"Hey," Scarlet answered, her voice so loud I slapped my free hand over my ear.

Relief flooded me at the sound of the former Keeper's voice. She didn't have all the story cycle answers, but she had experience.

"Scar, oh my gosh." I breathed. "I didn't think you'd actually answer. Carlo said you've been swamped."

"Undercover actually," she said. "I don't use my phone a lot. I'm posing as part of this cult and they don't allow technology."

"A cult?" For a moment, my own problems faded. It felt good to focus on something else and maybe help Scarlet again. "Are you staying safe?"

"Actually, I'm great at this. They live as if it's the eighteen hundreds and that was my favorite century. But they don't get any of my references." She laughed. "The murder is already solved by the detectives down here, but I'm about to get an inside scoop on how they get money. I think they're actually dealing major drugs and the cult is just a front. But I haven't proved it yet."

"Wow," I said, floored. "That's amazing! Pam is going to worry you'll take her spot. I'm so incredibly proud of—" The sharp scent of iron overwhelmed me. I gasped and the grumbling in my stomach drew me to the smell, as the odd craving built.

"Mari?"

I licked my lips, and my tongue snagged on the tip of my tooth. Warm blood filled my mouth. I spit it onto the concrete, shocked by the sudden wound and my hand shot to my canine teeth.

The smooth surface had extended to twice its normal length, and my teeth came to a point as sharp as a sword's edge. *Ebenezer Scrooge, I'm a vampire.*

"Mari? Are you there?"

The cross necklace I'd thrown on as extra protection, burned against the skin on my chest. I dug my hand down the front of my shirt and yanked the chain against the back of my neck until it snapped off. My palm sizzled where the cross touched my flesh. Quickly, I shoved it into the rain jacket's pocket.

"It's all Twilight over here, Scar."

Scarlet understood the reference immediately. Her obsession with movies and TV usually distracted her from helping me, but it was part of her charm.

"Oh no, Dracula?" she asked.

I nodded then realized she couldn't see me. "He turned a young woman and then she bit me. But I'm the Keeper, so I'm safe, right?"

Scarlet's silence only further unsettled me. "Mari, I don't know. I only sealed that story once in the last century, and he never came close to biting me."

I stopped and placed my palm against a cool concrete wall. Was that why my coffee tasted like dirt? The taste for blood both sharpened my senses and made me sick at the same time.

"Oh," Scarlet continued. "But I *did* sick from the girl in *Little Women*. I caught the disease she had and was ill until I got medicine. You can't die, but you can suffer."

"But you healed," I said, trying to make sense of it all. "And I've healed rapidly before, too."

Another gust of wind carried the scent of iron with it, and my interest was piqued. My vision sharpened, and I honed in on a black sports car parked in front of the house at the bottom of the hill.

"My body healed fast but only things it knew how to heal normally. I'd never come in contact with that sickness before *Little Women*."

"Wait, you had Scarlet Fever?" I asked, amused by the irony of it.

"Your body won't know how to deal with becoming a vampire. Mari, you need to get checked—"

I scoffed. Scarlet too? I couldn't get away from people telling me to rest when all I needed to do was hunt the villain killing innocents.

"What's a hospital going to do for me?" I asked.

"I was going to say, you need Doctor Van Helsing's help. He's seen vampirism before."

Blood flooded my senses. Everything was tinted with a shade of red, while the metallic smell and taste took hold of me. Scarlet's voice faded and the faint pulse of a human's heartbeat pounded in my ears.

"Hey Scar?" I said. I squeezed my eyes shut and prayed that when I opened them, the red tint would be gone. The crash of the distant waves, so prevalent and painful in my ears said otherwise.

"Yeah?"

"Jacob Grimm said someone named Agnes attacked Dracula with cross-marked weapons last century, is that true? Does it work?" I asked. In a flash of paranoia, I patted the side of my jeans to double-check I'd brought my gun. Hopefully, the blessed bullets worked against vampires as he'd claimed.

"Agnes?" her voice was quiet and laced with an emotion I couldn't put my finger on. After a moment of silence, she cleared her throat and spoke. "Uh, yeah, I think so. That sounds right, but I really don't remember much of my hunting days anymore. The more human I become the less Keeper I feel."

The thump, thumping of a nearby heart drowned Scarlet's words that only sounded like rambling to me now. I hung up the call without a goodbye and focused on nothing but the heartbeat. It flooded my eardrums, pounding with the force of a toddler beating the ground with his fists during a tantrum.

I followed the sound until it led me to a car with two dudes passed out in the front seats. One held what looked like an empty bottle of beer and drooled on his shirt. While he looked drunk, the other guy's chest didn't rise or fall as clearly.

I squinted, spying two small holes in the second dude's throat.

Drunk Dude stirred, tossing and turning in the driver's seat before he blinked and squinted at me.

A laugh startled me and I whipped around to see a girl stumbling out of the castle-like house. She leaned against one column, carrying her high-heeled shoes in one hand, then she shoved off and sauntered down the steps. With her, was a girl who looked slightly less hungover. She had her phone to her ear, as she spoke the address into it.

"Can't we just sleep here?" the barefoot girl moaned.

Her friend shook her head and shivered. "The guy's a freak. I thought we were making out, but he bit me so hard it drew blood, and then he licked it. I want to get out of here." The girl's voice shook and my gaze narrowed in on the red dripping down her throat.

"Scarlet," I whispered. "I have to go."

Before she could protest, I ended the call and tucked the phone into my pocket.

Sudden, intense anger surged within me at the person who'd become Dracula. For the story aura to select him, he'd already preyed on women, likely horrifying them and hurting them without a care for their lives.

The door swung open, crashing into the wall and a muscular, clean-shaven man stood at the threshold. His jawline rivaled Henry Cavill, but he looked older, too aged to be hanging around college girls. Salt and pepper coloring altered his hair's dark shade of brown. The over-priced brand of exercise clothes he wore didn't look like it'd ever seen a wrinkle, much less been to the gym.

"Hey, you ladies don't have to leave," he drawled. The swagger in his stance barely concealed his predatory position, as he towered over the two girls. "Come here."

He grabbed the barefoot girl and pulled her toward him. She squealed in drunken delight and called him professor. *Ew.* Her friend screamed and tried to shove him with little success. Dracula barely moved an inch.

I stayed in the shadows near the wall and drew closer, readying the stake in my fist.

When I reached the bottom of the hill, I emerged from the darkness. Dracula sunk back into the dimness of the entry, pulling his barefooted victim with him. Only a faint flicker illuminated the inside of the house, visible through the open door. The friend followed, yanking Dracula's arm in a failed attempt to free the drunk one.

The girl tried to calm her friend, telling her it was fine. I snorted. *Yeah, about as fine as I am.* Absentmindedly, my tongue flicked to the growing fangs at the top of my mouth.

"Stop," the friend shouted, as she threw her body weight against the vampire, hands out."She's drunk, leave her alone."

While he was distracted, I crept up the front steps and flexed my fingers, ensuring my grip on the stake. I'd come up with a plan that'd give me the advantage, but the victims in front of me didn't have time to wait.

"She likes me," he said. Dracula trailed his nose along the girl's throat.

She giggled and wiggled her eyebrows at her friend. "Come on Jen, he's sexy."

"Ugh." The friend groaned in disgust and swiveled. "I'm leaving."

When she stepped across the threshold, it gave me a clear shot—if only I had my gun. Why didn't I remember to bring a blessed bullet before I was in the thick of a fight? *Curse my foggy brain.* If I had time to sleep, maybe I'd think straight and remember what Jacob had said.

Dracula opened his mouth as the drunk girl curved her neck, ready to be kissed. It was obvious she had no clue he was about to drain her blood then pass out in a coffin for the day. The light of the faded bulb in the entry glimmered against his pointed tooth. It grazed the girl's flesh.

"Hey!" I yelled. "Let her go!"

Dracula's gaze flicked to me. The girl was oblivious, basically limp in his arms while her friend dodged out of the way, gasping and hurrying past me down the steps.

The flat shape of his mouth curved into a cruel smile. "We're just having fun," he said. Without missing a beat, he sunk his fangs into her throat. The action was a clear middle finger to me. Despite the sharpened wood in my hand, he didn't consider me a threat.

Energy coursed through me, either from vampirism or rage or a mother's sheer determination to end this story and get back to my daughter.

I lunged at him, shoving through the doorway. Foggy brain and impulse struck again. I didn't consider the girl's safety as he held her in front of him, a human shield blocking my access to stab him through the heart.

"Who are you that you think you can fight me?" he asked, venom in his eyes. It was the same cold-hearted look I'd seen in other murderers, those without remorse—those who'd kill again and again for the thrill and game of it.

To my horror, bile rose in my throat, and I almost spewed all over him. I swallowed to force it back down and flexed my hold on the weapon.

"I'm a hunter," I said.

His smile wavered, and recognition dawned. Either he somehow knew about the story cycle and that I'd come to destroy him or he acknowledged the determination in my gaze. He allowed me to back him against a closet door in the entryway with the girl as his protection.

Dracula's eyes searched mine, and I recognized the same hunger in him that I felt. "You're just like me."

The suggestion boiled my blood

If I couldn't thrust the stake into him without hurting her, it was a waste to hang onto it. I tossed it to the side and grabbed for the cross necklace. Steam rose from my fist but I acted quickly, smashing it against his face.

With my free hand, I scrambled for the iron switchblade tucked into my belt, but he shoved the girl at me and we both went down.

She was unconscious, eyes rolled back and a limp weight on top of me, as her faint breath blew puffs of white air in the chilly night air. Pushing her off was easy thanks to the vampire's strength I'd gained, but Dracula was faster. He lunged for the stake and pinned me back against the cold, marble floor.

Long fangs bared and took my breath away. Memories of Jameson's deadly jaws messed with my head, but my heightened senses and speed gave me half a chance to fight back.

Dracula raised the stake, ready to destroy me with the same attack I'd planned for him. I walked right into his home and handed him the weapon. *Stupid, stupid, stupid.*

My hands shot out and blocked his arms from coming down. Our strength nearly matched, and he groaned, frustrated that I could hold him at arm's length.

"You can't kill me," I said, hoping that'd stop him from hurting me. Death or not, I didn't want the pain that came with a stake in the heart.

It depends on you. Will's threat, or warning, or whatever, came back to me and that miracle mom-strength combined with a surge of vampirism I enjoyed. In a moment of determination, I arched my back and twisted, throwing Dracula off balance.

The split-second gave me an opening to yank the switchblade from my belt. I sliced it through his arm and the stake fell from his grasp. It rolled across the marble.

In a flash, Dracula stood and stepped back, with not so much as a stumble over the girl's collapsed body.

I rolled to my stomach and reached for the stake before scrambling to my feet. I gripped the stake and spun around. By the time I faced him, he'd transformed. Instead of the vampire in a too-tight gym shirt, he'd shapeshifted into a wolf the size of my couch with black and gray fur.

Not only did his newfound shape make it difficult for me to reach his heart, but the fur also protected his skin from the iron in the crucifix and blade.

The beast stood with one paw on his victim's chest. His jaws opened slowly, baring bloody fangs. Drool dripped from his black lips onto the girl's contoured cheeks.

I understood.

It took everything I had to lower the stake and back away. My chance was gone. Maybe not gone, but I couldn't sacrifice this silly drunk girl's life in an attempt to destroy him now.

Dracula's snout raised, arching to show every one of his sharp wolf's teeth. I almost tripped over the little ridge of the threshold as I stepped back.

"Don't hurt her," I begged. It was my fault. He'd toyed with her as a vampire, but now he threatened to devour her, all to hold power over me.

He dropped his head, growling, then backed into the dark hall until I could only see the glimmer of his predatory eyes.

The shadow swallowed him. In a moment of reprieve, I took a breath, trying to relish the smell of the sea air and ignore the girl's faint pulse.

I tucked the stake into my backpack and dropped to my knees. The girl moaned and rolled her head to the side when I struggled to drag her out of the house.

I collapsed on the porch beside the unconscious girl, my strength suddenly sapped. Yellow light filtered in beneath the porch's overhang. The back of my neck, between where my hair ended and the layers of clothes began, prickled and burned.

I gasped and slapped my hand against the back of my neck without thinking. The pain doubled, and I seethed, quickly yanking the hood over my head.

The natural glow of morning beamed down and mixed with an odd, bluish illumination.

Dawn had arrived, and brought with it, the sudden sensitivity of a sunburn on my skin.

And two skeletal brothers.

Chapter 16

Every Vampire for Himself

Not them again.

Jacob and Will's ghostly shapes with partially formed skulls and skeletal structures would scare anyone. Except for me, of course. I was too busy being afraid of sunshine like a cockroach.

Speaking of which, I scrambled away from the morning sunlight and pressed my back against the wall beside the front door. The ghost's presence froze the dampness on the porch's steps to slick icy slabs. Icicles transformed the drips from the overhang's gutters into sharp, transparent weapons.

"This is all wrong." Jacob's voice cracked like a boy in puberty. "She's doomed us."

Will frowned at me. "You were supposed to follow the plot and let Morris and Jonathan hunt him."

From burning skin to the sudden chill, my body flip-flopped. It left me shaking and huddled against the wall, the way a scared child might.

"I don't care. You owe me," I said. "I solved it and brought you straight to the murderer. That was the deal. Now smite him, or something, he's hurt enough people. I…" I looked at my hands, scratched from the stake. "I failed to stop him."

At the mere suggestion, their expressions twisted from grimaces to gaped mouths and bugged eyes. Both of the brothers looked frozen in shock, but it wasn't at me. I followed their line of sight, my spine popping as I twisted.

At the threshold, stood a man. Instead of Dracula's muscular body and sharp jawline, the light from inside gave shape to the lanky guy with a bushy beard. A black glow radiated over his shoulders.

He rubbed his eyes and leaned one arm against the door frame. "Who're you?" Confusion quickly flipped to concern as he narrowed his eyes and fixed his gaze on the girl laying in front of me. "Is she bleeding? What the hell happened?"

The man took two giant steps and crouched over her. "What did you do?"

"Me?" I squeaked, my voice rough. Of course, Jacob and Will had vanished in my time of need and the witness, the girl's friend, was also long gone.

He cursed and raked his fingernails through his short curls. "I thought I had him," he mumbled.

"Yes," I managed. Exhaustion, the beat of his heart, and the smell of blood on the girl's neck as well as her faint pulse, all combined to throw my focus. It was all too much. Vampires, the threat to Wendy's freedom, and the investigation. Not to mention, the ghosts who haunted my every thought and held my daughter's story aura condition over my head to do their bidding. I'd led them to the murderer. That man was clearly Dracula, yet they only looked more frustrated and horrified.

I cleared my throat and put more effort into my voice. "Your friend attacked—"

A blaring siren cut off my words. Red and blue lights flashed as a trail of police cars barreled down Carrion Court. I struggled to my feet, ready to speak with the officers and enroll them to help me locate the murderer, again.

By the time they parked and hopped out of the car, an ambulance had turned the corner. Our party of three quickly became many and relief flooded me. The barefoot girl would get help and we'd apprehend Dracula.

I struggled to my feet and pointed to the victim. "He attacked her."

The lanky guy's statement drowned my voice out. In any other situation, I'd have control. I'd approach the cops with confidence and aid them in completing the investigation.

But they stood in the morning sun.

"Garen Quincy," the lanky guy said. "I don't know who she is." Garen nodded toward me. "The front door was open, and she was sitting out here with Tiffany."

Garen? If I was correct, this was Morris, the man who would succumb to injuries after battling Dracula. What was he doing in Dracula's house? It didn't make any sense. Was this modern society messing with the classic's plot again?

The officers confirmed Garen's identity after he pulled his driver's license out of his wallet. He offered anything they needed, answering questions I tried overhearing. The addition of the guys who'd passed out in the car, and a yawning girl from inside the house, made it difficult to listen to the conversation.

Paramedics and partiers crowded the porch. Suddenly, a dozen hearts beat too close and my knees wobbled. The weak, energy-sapped feeling reminded me of early pregnancy when nausea refused to let me eat. While my senses sharpened, intense hunger drew my attention to the mention of blood.

"Looks like a laceration to the neck and a blow to the side of the head," a paramedic said. Together they worked to get Barefoot Girl, AKA Tiffany, onto a stretcher.

A blow to the side of the head? My investigators' instincts forced through the vampirism that overwhelmed my body. Tiffany must have hit her head against the hard marble when Dracula dropped her.

No, *I'd* broken her fall. Had I hurt her when I'd rolled her off of me? It had all happened so fast when Dracula pounced on me, and I didn't know my strength with the inhuman abilities transforming my body.

It was an accident. Surely, the doctors would see the bite in her neck when they looked closer, and it'd build my case against the man renting this house.

"Ma'am," the female officer interrupted my thoughts. The handcuffs on her belt clinked and the smell of her blood temporarily blurred my vision. I blinked and gave her my attention.

"There's blood on this…thing," the male officer said as he picked up the stake with a napkin and inspected it.

Both cops and Garen snapped their eyes to me. I opened my mouth to explain Dracula's attack in a way that they'd understand. After years of working with Detective Wilhelm and helping him understand supernatural suspects without suspicion, I'd honed the skill. But today, I struggled to find a word other than vampire.

I followed where their gazes had landed to the red stain streaked across the front of my jacket. *Ebenezer Scrooge.* When Dracula shoved Tiffany at me, it must have smeared blood on my clothes.

"You're going to need to come down to the station to answer a few questions."

"No, I'm on a case," I said. "The man who attacked her is inside. We have to find him. I have reason to believe he's the suspect in another murder."

Garen's interest was piqued. He lifted his chin and narrowed piercing blue eyes at me.

The male officer stood and faced Garen. "We'll need to talk to everyone involved."

Despite what I knew, what I'd experienced, he denied Dracula's existence. He shook his head. "There's no one else but us," he said. "I don't know what she's talking about."

"But I heard you say—"

Garen raised his voice to interrupt me. "She must have broken in." Like Jacob's long, accusatory finger, Garen pointed at me, and dread slammed into the pit of my stomach. As if on cue, dark clouds shifted to cover the sun. A light storm had rolled in from the coast, and a reprieve from the threat of sunlight boosted me.

"No," I said, more confident now. "No, I saw an older man harassing two young women."

"Two?" the female officer asked.

"Yes, one of them ran away when I tried to help."

As the paramedics evacuated the porch, carrying Tiffany with them, Garen stepped closer to us. His eyes searched mine and his lips parted. Recognition seemed to dawn, and he gasped.

"She's lying," he said, suddenly backing away. "She's lying, she definitely attacked us."

"Come with me." The female officer waved for me to step in front of her.

"No—"

Garen hyped up his bros. "We don't know her, right?"

The drunken men from the car folded their arms and frowned at me. The one who'd been bitten only held the position for a moment, quickly unfolding and scratching at the scabs on his neck.

The other guy corroborated Garen's story and added his own flair. "Hey, I think I saw her creeping around the house last night."

I couldn't deny his truth. *Crap.*

Garen nodded. "So, she totally tried to kill Tiffany!"

"No!" I backed away, putting space between the cops and me.

"She's dangerous," Garen shouted.

The male officer raised his hands, trying to calm the big, fat, lying turd. I frowned, hunger and rage combining. I'd come so close to apprehending the villain in Bram Stoker's story, only to piss off the gods who controlled my daughter's free will, and have this frat-boy-looking jerk, the same guy whose life I was trying to save, fabricate that I'd attempted to murder his friend.

"Wait," I said.

"There's blood on her hands!" Garen pointed.

Frustration mounted as I turned my hands over and inspected the dark blood crusted on my palms. Why was he doing this? What in the wonderland inspired him to blame me, when he was the one partying in Dracula's rental? I needed to call Nolan. And Detective Wilhelm. And Kai. And summon some gosh-dang Grimm ghosts.

"Screw this," I mumbled, as I shoved my hand into my rain jacket's pocket and grasped my phone.

"Gun!" The male police officer knocked his coat out of the way and reached for the weapon in his holster.

The yawning girl's mouth opened for a scream this time and the female officer ducked and barreled toward me, the heroine, apparently. She slammed into me like a linebacker and we crashed against the porch. It was the second time someone had pinned me to the floor in the last few hours. *Why me?*

At least with Dracula, I was moments from destroying an undead serial killer.

This time, I was the one whose skin burned from the painful touch of iron. My reactions were quick but my head was too muddled. Before I could speak, she'd yanked my arms behind me and pinned my arms, twisted and aching against my back. Cold, hard handcuffs slapped around my wrists.

Last night, I was strong enough to hold back Dracula, growing into my super strength. But today, hunger roiled in my stomach and the lack of sustenance left me weak, not only in my arms and legs but mind, too. I couldn't focus. I only managed a thought of gratitude for the cloudy sky as the officers peeled me off the porch and shoved me down the steps.

And what about sleep? Vampires weren't immune to exhaustion.

I relented, obeying their instructions to dip into the backseat of the cop's car. Raindrops dotted the black cement and pattered against the vehicle's roof. On the way, I'd request they call Detective Wilhelm. I'd get my time to speak and defend myself, but for now, I only wanted to lean against the headrest and close my eyes. If I calmed my mind, I'd piece together Garen's goal in accusing me. And maybe, if I had time, I'd find and recruit the aid of Doctor Van Helsing to reverse this process of vampirism.

But first, jail or not, I'd find a way to summon the Brothers Grimm and tell them their wish had come true. Morris was in Dracula's house. It was as close to the correct plot as possible, for now.

The officer plopped into the front seat and fired up the engine.

The steady fall of rain showered the car, lulling me to take a death breath and let my muscles relax. Going to jail was not the bee's knees, but at least I'd have a moment of rest.

And while I was arrested, Wendy was freed thanks to my efforts. Because *screw saving Garen.* Maybe Jacob and Will were right, I'd let the story play out as the plot was written, which meant the guy whose lie had me slapped in handcuffs, would die.

The car turned, and I had to twist my neck to see Garen grow smaller and smaller from my view out the back window. At any other time, I'd want to save everyone's lives, even dudes like him, but now, that feeling of worry for others was distant—unreachable.

You just secured your own death, Dude. And despite how weird it felt, I didn't care. I didn't care at all.

Besides, I'd do anything to save my daughter, my own blood. Even if it meant a sacrifice or two.

Raindrops distorted my view of the very guy I'd just wanted to save, and I smirked.

Chapter 17

In a Pickle at the Police Station

Moonlight glinted off of a knife in Garen's hand. Darkness surrounded me but I caught glimpses of Garen and a clean-cut guy I vaguely recognized as Nolan. Where was I? They both held weapons and approached, step-by-step.

If I ran, it'd be into the unknown, the blackness, it could be as equally dangerous. What threats lay there? I needed to stay and fight. My heart pounded, and I brought my hand to my chest, feeling the beat that didn't match my new, undead body.

For a moment, the inside of the men's skulls, bones, and teeth flickered, over their faces like masks and their feet disintegrated into a transparent vision. I blinked and reached for my eyes but couldn't feel my hands except for the rawness around my wrists.

Nolan and Garen weren't coming for me.

Fangs emerged from the darkness, massive and dripping with fresh blood. Instead of the vampire's pale, pretentious expression, fur covered his face, and it looked like bad CGI in an old Wolfman movie.

I sucked in a breath. A stake, switchblade, and water bottle materialized in my hand. I furrowed my brows and squinted at the water bottle. The universe gifted me these for a reason, but I didn't feel thirsty.

I shrugged and uncapped the bottle. Mist escaped, forming in the shape of a crucifix. Holy water?

A deep scream echoed into the blackness. I snapped my head up to see Nolan on the ground crouching and choking. Garen had lost his knife to Dracula, who pinned the blade to its owner's throat.

All I had to do was tilt the bottle out and thrust. It'd splash the blessed water on the vampire, boil his skin, and save both men.

Garen whimpered. The scent of bacon, sizzling and bubbling with grease wafted from behind him. I was so deeply and painfully hungry.

I followed the smell, stepping over Nolan. Garen coughed and begged for me to help but I only cared about what lay ahead of me.

The guttural screams behind me didn't matter anymore.

I launched forward, gasping for air. Vampire and hunters had vanished, replaced by a stark, cold room. The thin mattress didn't cushion against the hard cot. My back twinged, tweaked from whatever weird position I'd fallen asleep in.

Fluorescent lights blinked and buzzed overhead, which made the cell feel more like a hospital room than a jail. The high, barred window to my left offered no light. I'd slept the day away.

"Good morning, Sunshine," Detective Wilhelm greeted me, before taking another huge bite of a fast-food biscuit with cheese and bacon. Grease dripped down the side of his chin, following the frown line to his jaw. Apparently, where the detective dined, it was a breakfast-served-all-day kind of joint.

My stomach growled.

Everything came back to me in a rush of memories that had nothing to do with vampires and ghosts—they weren't from today. Years ago, I'd been locked in this same jail, held in the cell directly across from my current one, and arrested for the murder of an innocent woman. She'd been in the wrong place at the wrong time, crossing with a fractured fairy tale because of modern society's taint on classic stories.

After his last bite, the detective crumpled the greasy paper from his meal and wiped his hands on his pants. "We've been in this pickle before, haven't we?"

I rubbed my forehead. The migraine was long gone, replaced now with a sinking hole in the pit of my stomach.

"I didn't attack that girl," I said, already defensive. Hunger made me cranky, and the need to confirm my deal with the ghosts was like insatiable starvation. "I need to summon them…" I mumbled as I glanced around the empty cell. Should I pray like Hook did? Or pull from other folklore when it came to summoning spirits? The options were vast, but the lack of resources in the cell severely restricted me.

Detective Wilhelm sniffed and shoved his hands, including the one full of trash, into his coat pocket.

"I predicted you'd lose it someday. Women aren't built to see death that often. But attempted murder…" he whistled. "I'll admit, I didn't see that one coming." He laughed and shook his head. "Didn't think you had it in you."

Little did the detective know, I'd gutted the serial killer who'd swallowed me whole. But I didn't have the time for, or interest in, proving myself to Detective Wilhelm.

He rambled on as I dropped to the floor and used the dust to draw a circle. That was how people summoned spirits, right? I'd watched enough paranormal shows to remember it, but the Brothers Grimm weren't like other supernatural creatures. I rubbed out the circle and tried a rectangle that could vaguely be considered a book.

"Hmm."

"I don't know what arts and crafts you've got going on, Rowan, but if you work with me on the murders of the Dew women, I'll get you out of this assault charge you've gotten yourself into."

Was Barefoot Girl okay? The question teetered on the tip of my tongue but I couldn't muster enough concern to bother asking. I had the ghosts of stories past to summon and a few demands to give.

"Rowan?" he barked.

I looked up.

"You're acting weird." He scrunched his face, which only made his receding hairline more obvious.

Was I? *Huh.* For the first time in a long time, I felt good. I'd rested, I'd solved the murder, and found Dracula, basically, I'd freaking crushed it. This felt better than after I'd absolutely killed a workout goal in yoga. I'd set out to banish the story aura that haunted my daughter, and the spirits that haunted me. Now, the only thing left was confirmation.

"Anyway." Detective Wilhelm coughed up phlegm and cleared his throat. "Mr. Rowan called me. He wants to have a talk with you. I can't blame the guy. If you were my wife, I'd give you a good, long lecture."

"Kai?" I stood. *Right.* My husband. He'd still be at home with our daughter—the same daughter I'd set out to free. The whole reason for my goal.

I smirked. *Perfect.* I didn't need to create a summoning circle, I just needed Kai to bring Wendy down here so I could see for myself that the story aura had vanished. And then what? Send the Brothers Grimm back to the graves they'd come from?

"That sounds good," I said, under my breath. "They don't need to boss me around anymore. I'll do whatever I dang-well please, especially with this super strength and—"

"Rowan!" He shouted. "For heaven's sake, you're an embarrassment to yourself. If I let you out of here to make a phone call, do I need a straight jacket?"

I bared my teeth.

What the hell? I. Bared. My. Teeth.

"Yikes," I whispered. Detective Wilhelm was a sexist pig, sure, but he wasn't dumb. Maybe I needed to listen to him. I took a deep breath and shook my head. "No. Sorry, I'm just really, um…" What? Hungry? Obsessed. Yes, that was it. I was obsessed with helping my daughter. And that was a good thing—totally a good thing. "I'm really frustrated." It was the truth. I wanted the answer that I'd succeeded in my goal, or in other words, fulfilled my side of the deal and thwarted the Brothers Grimm's insistence that I do as they say.

The detective entered a passcode into a screen that unlocked my cell. I stepped out and followed him to the phones on the wall where the arrested were allowed contact. From this perspective, the station looked dull and cold, rather than busy and full of life.

I pictured Wendy hopping out of the restrooms just as she had a few days before. Except now, she wouldn't have the green glow of the story aura, pinning her to Peter Pan's plotted existence.

Detective Wilhelm nodded to the phones. "You've got five minutes. Then I want to chat about any information you've nailed regarding the Dew murders."

I dialed the number for Kai's cell phone and leaned against the wall. The click on the other line told me he'd answered.

"It's me," I said. "Are Wendy's vision's gone?"

"Whoa, Mari?" Kai said.

"Of course it's Mari." I scoffed and gripped the phone tighter. The steady beat of dozens of hearts faded from my attention as I dove into the question I'd been dying to get an answer to. "Did the Brothers Grimm do what they promised? I found Dracula, so they owe me. Honestly, at this point, they're getting what they want because I'm ready to tap out of this story and—"

"Mari!" he interrupted. "What is going on?"

"Oh, I got arrested."

A sigh came from the other line followed by a moment of silence.

"Did you hear me? I need to be bailed out and to see if the story aura is off of Wendy." The words spilled out of my mouth and I didn't care if anyone overheard.

The heavy scent of iron wilted. The flow of fresh blood didn't intrigue me as much as the victory I'd achieved in solving this murder and closing the deal.

"Because if it's not," I said, "I'm going to find a way to make Jacob and Will suffer. I'll fly to Germany, dig up their corpses, and kill them again if I have to."

"Oh." He laughed without joy. "Right. You've just been arrested for the attempted murder of a college girl, yet somehow you already have plans to go ghost-hunting in Europe."

I turned and faced the wall, speaking with my voice lower now. "How did you know that?" I'd skipped sharing my supposed crime, but he already had the information. After twisting back around, my gaze landed on the back of Detective Wilhelm's head as he poured himself a cup of coffee. From my vantage point, I could see through the open door of the cop's lounge area. He turned around and spotted me glaring at him.

So much for looking like I'd gotten my marbles back. But I didn't care. Screw the detective and the ghosts and everything that wasn't a success. After I confirmed Wendy's freedom, I'd give a giant middle finger to the living fairy tales and throw myself back into my job to focus on winning a Pulitzer Prize. I'd never forgotten that lifelong dream, but being the Keeper of Stories didn't lend a lot of extra time either.

It'd be one success after another.

I smirked.

"Mari? Did you cut out?" Kai asked.

"I'm here."

He sighed again. "You're not yourself and it's worrying me."

"Are you going to get your butt down here and bail me out, or what?" I tapped my foot, impatient with this game of concern for my health or sanity or whatever it was.

Another moment of silence. "Scarlet told me how it works," he said, quieter now. "I didn't believe her but I can hear it in your voice. This isn't you."

"What the hell is that supposed to mean? Do you think I hurt that college chick?" *Ugh.* Since when did I call young women by the same nickname Detective Wilhelm used?

Speaking of the devil, the detective invaded my personal space with the bitter stench of stale coffee on his breath.

"Time's up." He flicked his finger toward the phone.

"I thought it was my mind playing tricks on me before you left last night," Kai said.

I took a deep breath. Maybe Kai had picked up on my little obsession. But focus wasn't a bad thing, and if I could ride this high of solving the Dew's murder, saving Wendy, and fulfilling my agreement with the ghost gods, I could accomplish so much more. Forget the Pulitzer, I might even have the energy to decorate homemade Christmas cookies and deliver them to my daughter's teachers like Yoga Mom. And look good doing it.

"I have to go," I said. "Dig into our emergency fund if you have to. I'll see you in twenty."

"Okay," Kai agreed. "I love—"

I hung up the phone and spun around, nearly colliding with a dazed detective. Detective Wilhelm was distracted admiring a woman who'd just walked in with a low-cut shirt. She screamed at the officer at the front desk about a noise complaint. The sound pierced my ears and sensory overload returned like a freight train barreling through my station.

I slapped my hands to my ears and let Detective Wilhelm guide me back to the cell. On the way, we swapped theories about the Dew murders.

"Trust me," I said. "He's your guy."

"And you expect me to listen to you when you're not even in your right mind?" He laughed and shook his head.

I stopped, turned around, and let him bump into me while he was too busy wiping crumbs off of his shirt. "I'm giving you the murderer's address and you won't even check it out?"

Detective Wilhelm sniffed and straightened. "Walk me through what makes you think it's this particular person. You don't even have a name."

He had me there. I never caught Dracula's name, but I knew he was a professor based on Barefoot Girl's words.

"No," I said. "But Nolan will, the murderer is one of his tenants. I went back through the list of people who knew Lindsay Dew and traced it to him."

The detective arched an eyebrow bushy enough to rival the brows of Jacob Grimm. "That doesn't explain why you'd have reason to suspect a random tenant."

Ebenezer Scrooge. He was right, and it left me scrambling for an excuse. The further I dove into hunting fairy tale monsters, the less I wanted to fabricate explanations for people like the detective. But his help came in handy and I needed him to solve this murder, effectively clearing my name.

The smell of coffee faded and the station's ringing phones muted as we stepped into the back where they hid the criminals. I behaved by stepping into the cell as expected.

"The ex-boyfriend. I scrambled. "I, uh…" my gaze darted around the dismal cell, bouncing from the bed to the window. "I had a hunch that he could be involved even though Nolan claimed Garen had no hard feelings after the breakup. Something seemed off when Nolan told us Mindy didn't want him around Lindsay's ex." It wasn't a lie. Why Nolan even mentioned that, had piqued my interest. "So, I followed Nolan and found Garen at this other guy's house. If you cross-reference the marks on the neck of the victim I supposedly assaulted, you'll find it consistent with Lindsay's injuries."

"Hmm." Despite my detailed description, Detective Wilhelm only shrugged. "Sounds all wrapped up with a nice bow like a Christmas present. But, I'll give it a look."

He slid the cell's door shut so hard it slammed and echoed through the hall. With that, he disappeared, and I was left alone with my thoughts.

Even though I'd see Wendy soon and get out of this hellhole, I scraped the recesses of my brain for summoning ideas. It wasn't like I had anything better to do trapped in an empty jail cell.

Plus, even if they held up their end of the deal, it wouldn't be a total waste to pay them a visit. Or have them pay me one, considering I'd bring them into the cell with me. I'd tell them what they'd been taunting me with.

"It depends on you," I repeated. "They can deal with the stories they recorded. It's not my responsibility." I'd hang up the hood. Hell, they could give it to Johnson for all I cared. I'd tried to save Garen's life, and he didn't want it. No more Mister Nice Mari. No more twisting stories to save lives. I was hungry for the success I felt when I found Dracula again—to get back to murder investigations and give it my all.

I scooted off the edge of the cot and dropped to my knees again. The concrete was cold even through the fabric of my pants and the hood that encircled me. With the dust, I made small checkmarks each time I filed a new idea about summoning away.

What would it take to summon a god?

Lightning? Some Greek gods came down to mingle with human women if the ladies were hot enough. I snorted. I couldn't imagine Jacob or Will being interested in anything other than fairy tales.

"Maybe it isn't about summoning them as gods," I thought aloud. Maybe it was about them as librarians.

Books. And…more books?

Footsteps interrupted my thoughts. One after another, the approaching fall of several feet echoed in the empty hall. I stood, shook off the dust, and readied to see Wendy devoid of the green story aura glow.

Kai stepped into my line of sight. With his hands shoved into the pocket of his sweatshirt and brow furrowed, I immediately recognized the look of guilt. Instead of our daughter, Kai brought with him another woman.

The older, heavyset woman looked vaguely familiar with her white curls cropped and coifed close to her head. Suspects, victims, and other faces flipped through my mind's eye until I realized where I'd seen her before. Of course, now a certain pitch-black glow emanated from her.

"Mari," Kai said, reading my thoughts. "This is Nurse Betty."

When my mouth fell open, the sharp tip of one of my fangs grazed my bottom lip.

"Nurse Betty," I repeated in a whisper. AKA Doctor Van Helsing.

Chapter 18

You Can't Teach a New Vampire Old Tricks

On the other side of the cell's cold, iron bars stood the character known for hunting vampires. Except, of course, in the real story of Dracula, Van Helsing doesn't kill the villain. That victory goes to the other two men, one of whom framed me for attempted murder.

I raised my arm, weakly pointing at the nurse and trying to form words. "How?"

My husband pulled his hands from the center pocket on the front of his sweatshirt and produced a mess of sticky notes. He answered my question in one phrase. "Post-Its." Kai reached out with a handful of the colorful pieces of paper I'd scribbled theories and evidence on. "It was a shot in the dark, but your theories are always solid. So I gave the detective a call, and he helped me track her down." He tilted his head toward Nurse Betty. "Just heads up, you owe Wilhelm a reason this will help him solve the murders."

"Kai!"

He shrugged. "Worth it. Scarlet told me about her fever and how she couldn't heal from it without help."

I snatched the mess of papers from him and peeled each one off of the other. A crease ran down the center of the note that read: *in-home nurse = Van Helsing?*

My handwriting was sloppy, but I wasn't the doctor in the room. I looked up and met Kai's gaze then flicked my attention to Nurse Betty.

The kind old woman looked exactly like the type of nurse you'd want at your bedside during a dangerous fever or uncomfortable sickness. But I wasn't the one in danger.

I shifted my attention back to my husband. "Where's Wendy? I need to know if the aura is gone."

Kai raised his hands, either in surrender because he knew I'd kill him, or to calm me—which also made me want to kill him. A good bite to the neck would do the trick...I shook my head and tuned into his words just in time.

"With Tala," he said. "She and Mr. Geppetto are back early from their San Diego Christmas. And I know what you're thinking. The answer is that she has mentioned no mermaids or fairies."

"Okay." I exhaled through circled lips. "What about bail?"

My husband wagged his finger at me. "I know that look. You're pissed which means I'm only safe on this side of the bars."

I folded my arms, complete with an eye-roll for his dramatics. Totally ticked off or not, I considered myself a civilized... Keeper? Criminal? *Vampire? Nah, that ain't me.* Pulitzer Prize winner and absolute Grimm god crusher? *I'm good with that.*

"Kidding. Look, I just want you to hear her out," he said, with a wave of both hands at Van Helsing. The nurse offered a tight smile with concern lacing the corners of her wrinkled eyes. If I wasn't behind bars, I almost expected her to reach out and embrace me in a warm, grandmotherly hug. But this was no Mrs. Potts from the animated Beauty and the Beast, or Mary Poppins. Apparently, she dealt with vampirism.

"Do you know I'm..." I paused and glanced at Kai. With a slight shake of his head, I understood.

"Suffering?" Nurse Betty finished for me. Though I wouldn't agree that super strength, extra speed, and heightened senses counted as suffering. She stepped closer to the bars, reaching through with a gnarled, but warm and comforting hand on my wrist. Her skin felt twice as hot as mine and I wondered if she noticed the distant, nearly nonexistent rhythm of my pulse. "Miss Dew had the same condition. Doctors couldn't help her but the blood transfusions kept symptoms at bay."

"What symptoms?" I asked.

"The earliest onset of symptoms included allergies to the sun and her own jewelry, loss of appetite, weakness, as well as anger and irritability."

Kai coughed to conceal a smirk, and I almost lunged at him with my hands going straight for his throat…a delicious, soft, warm throat. A shudder rippled through me. The thought of biting flesh made me sick. See? I wasn't a vampire.

"Can we just hurry this up?" I pulled away from her, shoved the sticky notes into my pants pocket, and stepped up to where the cell door would slide open. "I have a lot on my to-do list and a mountain of goals to crush before the New Year."

Solve murders.

Win awards.

Be better than Yoga Mom.

Become a billionaire.

End world peace—I mean, world hunger.

Speaking of hunger…

"Mari!" Kai snapped me back to reality. "Listen to her, please." Desperation creased his brow where his overgrown hair hung into his eyes. Normally, the look of love and concern would have my heart skipping beats, but I felt nothing.

Van Helsing took a deep breath and continued. "Later Miss Dew suffered delusions and even got aggressive. Visual symptoms manifested like overgrown teeth. I heard she even attacked a visitor at the hospital."

My hand shot to my neck where the bites had scarred over.

"But before you reach that stage, I believe the condition is reversible by resuming normal activities."

Unimpressed, I folded my arms. But I stayed silent and let her finish because my normal activities already included solving murders.

"Mental health has a great impact on our physical condition," she said as Kai nodded along, fully engrossed in her theory. "When Miss Dew spent time with her loved ones, the condition showed signs of reversal. The more she behaved as she once did, the more her sense of humanity returned. Though I can tell you, it will get worse before it gets better."

I narrowed my eyes and glanced between them. "So you're prescribing I act normal?" It took all I had to stifle the scoff. Never had I considered myself an average Joan. Add the immortality times two, responsibilities as the Keeper of Stories, and a daughter whose classmate was a pixie, and my oddities only multiplied. Normal wasn't a part of my vocabulary then, or now.

Van Helsing, Nurse Betty, whoever she was, nodded. "I'm recommending that you hang on to your sense of self. The more you're with the ones you love, the better you'll connect with your humanity. You're in control of this condition." She tapped her head for emphasis on the aspect of mindset influence.

It sounded like a load of crock. But hey, fairy tale princesses and the monsters of their stories were real, so what did I know? Only a few years ago, I would have considered anyone claiming ownership of a magical hood a liar. Now, I lived that reality.

I reached for my throat and absentmindedly twirled the strings that kept the hood tied, the only part of the garment that showed unless I willed the rest to materialize. The red ties knotted around my fingers, pulling tighter the more I twisted.

"That all sounds really vague," Kai said, directing his disappointment to Nurse Betty. "Is there anything more concrete we can do to help?"

"Absolutely," she said. "A heavy dose of vitamin D."

I snorted, and she cocked her head. A quick glance at Kai told me he, too, found immature amusement in her choice of words. If nothing else was normal, at least I could rely on my husband to be a complete and total dork with me.

"Getting a tan from natural sunlight is best," the nurse continued. "Also, you'll want to file down overgrown teeth. And, now, this one is controversial but effective." She paused.

And for what? Was I supposed to sit down? I had places to go and people to see, not time to waste.

"He should employ regular use of an AED machine when you feel your heart rate dropping."

I arched my eyebrow. "You, uh." I laughed. "You want my husband to use a defibrillator on me?"

Nurse Betty didn't so much as flinch and I saw the Van Helsing in her, kindness mingled with determination that was inspired by an intense and admirable intelligence. I swallowed the lump in my throat as if it were the truth itself. After a moment of silence between the crowd of three, I nodded.

"Promise?" Kai thrust his arm through the bars and offered me his pinky like a child making a deal on a playground. The simple gesture was a delight. To my surprise, his warm finger wrapped around mine actually made me excited to spend an evening with him. One evening, then tonight I planned to return to write a killer article—*the* article that would shoot me toward fame.

"Will you let me out now?" I asked.

My husband pursed his lips. "You're not going to… get aggressive, right?"

I shook my head and smiled to drive the point home. Unfortunately, the points of my canine teeth poked out between my lips and dug into my soft, pink flesh. *Crap.*

"I won't bite," I said. Unless biting meant writing. And solving murders. Also, winning awards. Plus, trumping Yoga Mom's display of parenting perfection. The rest of the list replayed in my mind like a broken record or an obnoxiously catchy song that sticks to your brain.

Kai called for Detective Wilhelm who sauntered to the cells. Without thinking, I hummed the theme of Baby Shark. Really, it should have been the song from Jaws with the rage I felt watching the detective take his sweet time.

He hiked his pants up to his heavy belly then punched the code into a screen and verified it with his fingerprint.

"Good on you for taming that wife of yours," the detective said with a testosterone-filled slap against my husband's back. I frowned but didn't let it get under my skin. If I let every rude comment bother me, the city's defibrillators would be out of commission from overuse.

Instead of gripping my hands around the detective's throat, I took a deep breath and considered the words of the only woman who knew how to cure vampirism—or my *condition*, as she called it.

I stepped out of the cell and followed Kai to the front of the station. While I waited to retrieve my belongings, we bid goodbye to Nurse Betty. She took one last long look at me, inspecting my eyes with her intense gaze before accepting my hand for a shake.

When she took it, she leaned in and whispered. "You're welcome."

Apparently, my face displayed the complete shock I felt inside because she lingered. After digging out a pair of oval glasses from her purse, she straightened and stared me down.

"I know you didn't hurt that girl," she said. "I've been watching Professor Vaughn for two years now. He got sick back when I was the campus nurse at the college where he teaches. Later, I noticed he spread it to Lindsay, so I took a job as her in-home care to try to help her."

She gave me all the answers. Excitement bubbled, and I couldn't stop the smile that revealed my fangs. Nurse Betty only eyed them with wary interest. The striking blue in her eyes seemed to pierce my withering soul. Did she know the truth about vampirism?

"Did you tell the detective?" I asked. "He's working the Dew murder case."

When she nodded, not a single white curl moved from its designated place. This woman was more put-together than Yoga Mom—if that were possible.

"It's why you were released without bail. But just like all the other cops I've spoken with, he doesn't believe Professor Vaughn is as dangerous as he truly is." With each word, her voice dropped quieter and quieter. She quickly glanced at Kai who gathered my phone, purse, switchblade, cross necklace, and rain jacket. The counter was full until he scooped everything into his arms.

"I don't want your condition to get any worse," she whispered now.

"But the professor needs to be apprehended, and I believe you might have the strength to take him down before anyone else gets hurt."

From what I'd read in Bram Stoker's novel, Van Helsing headed the hunt to destroy Dracula. The doctor was the brains of the operations, a natural leader because of his amicable personality and significant intelligence. Nurse Betty's attempt to guide me to *apprehend* the vampire made sense. But Dracula wasn't my problem anymore, and I had enough on my to-do list already.

"Look," I started. "Detective Wilhelm is smart enough to bring backup. With enough of them, the cops will get him."

"Please." She gripped my forearm. "Before he hurts any more girls at the college."

"Okay. Sure." I lied.

The slight squeeze she gave me before releasing my arm told me she knew I hadn't agreed to anything. Frown lines tugged at her stern, flat mouth. Before she could protest, or beg, or whatever embarrassing desperation she had planned, Kai edged his way into the conversation.

The pile in his arms was pushed between us. Nurse Betty lifted her chin, took a step back, and offered a goodbye with the slight dip of her head.

Clearly, I'd royally pissed off Van Helsing. *Whatever.* I'd found the murderer. Wasn't that enough? Someone else could clean up the mess. Let the cops do their jobs and leave my schedule open to cross off more of those goals before the year ended.

I'd saved my daughter, successfully fulfilling my deal with *gods* no less, and now I was ready to sink my teeth into the next achievement.

As soon as we stepped out of the police station and into the busy streets of San Francisco, I picked up the pace. Kai hurried to jog behind me.

"Are we training for a marathon now?" he huffed.

Marathon? I mentally added that to my list of goals I wanted to crush.

"Earth to Mari." he waved his hands, huffing, and puffing as we climbed the hill away from the station. "Our house is that way." The point of his finger in my face reminded me of the obnoxious way Jacob

Grimm had tried to push me around. It only irritated me and encouraged me to walk faster toward my goal.

"I want to stop by the office and see if Pam is working late," I said, without so much as an extra breath. Surely, my boss would have leads for me to follow a new story. With my newfound strength, speed, and heightened senses, I'd squeeze a few investigations in before rejecting my vampiric self—or whatever Van Helsing had prescribed. If I could use the condition to my advantage, maybe I'd solve a few murders at lightning speed or write a mind-blowing article. It'd only catapult me closer to that Pulitzer, and then fame and fortune were just around the corner.

"What about checking on Wendy?" he asked.

I slowed my roll. He was right. Though I'd found Dracula, I didn't have confirmation if the Brothers Grimm upheld their end of the deal. Kai couldn't see the story aura and it could have been a coincidence that Wendy didn't mention new visions of Neverland.

"Fine." I swiveled on my heel and linked my arm through his. "Let's go."

We walked fast enough to draw more than a few looks. Kai's gasps for breath annoyed me but I dragged him along, impatient to attack my to-do list. To be better. To achieve perfection. It was so close, I could taste it. Or my fang caught on my lip again and drew blood.

San Francisco pedestrians dodged out of our way but nobody protested. Maybe it was my ghostly pale skin or the shine of my teeth jutting out from my top lip. Either way, I didn't care what they thought, I'd wipe the floor with anyone who dared cross me.

I glared at a couple whose gaze lingered too long as we climbed the staircase outside our condominium's building. They hurried past us and Kai begged me to slow down.

"Why?" I finally stopped once we reached Tala's front door. The scent of her famous cinnamon rolls wafted from the other side. My stomach rumbled, but I ignored the call to hunger. Successful people didn't have time for holiday treats.

Kai blinked rapidly and then rubbed his eyes. "Your eyes are red.

We need to reverse this transformation ASAP. You look like Edward Cullen."

I tilted my chin back, letting the dim light in the outdoor hallway flood my face. "Nah, I'm hotter than him." Since my lighthearted joke didn't land, I knew my husband was more serious than he'd ever been.

"You promised you'd try to…" his voice trailed, and he looked at his palms as if they held all the answers. "I don't know, heal from this?"

"Yeah, sure." I nodded. Though I barely gave it a second thought, Kai seemed to relax. He believed me.

"Good." He grabbed my hand, lifted it to his lips, and planted a kiss. "I almost thought I'd lost you to The Vampire Diaries."

I pulled my hand away and curled my fingers into a fist. Three knocks on the door were never enough for Tala to hear so I banged seven times. "I see you've been browsing my streaming queue."

Kai laughed and shrugged. "So, while you file your fangs, I'll order ramen, and we'll still have time to catch the Christmas Parade on Main tonight."

The list didn't match my plans for the night but I'd let him believe it for a few more minutes. My schedule looked more like *confirm success on the Grimm deal, then head to the office to work overtime,* effectively launching me to the top of my field.

When Tala finally answered, swinging the door open, the scent of sugar and cinnamon assaulted us. The beaming smile across her face rubbed me the wrong way. Except her joy had no reason to irritate me. I shrugged off the weird feeling and tried to remember how I used to feel about this woman I considered Wendy's secondary grandmother.

Tala patted Kai's back as he stepped inside and announced that our daughter was in the kitchen decorating cookies.

I lifted my foot but all the strength in the world couldn't help me bring it down to the other side of the threshold. The door frame seemed to hold an invisible barrier, blocking me from entering.

"What's wrong?" Kai turned around.

"I can't…" my gaze dropped to the door frame at my feet. I

strained, grunting like an egotistical bodybuilder at the gym. An impossible force pushed against my foot.

"Come to the kitchen and tell me what you think of this new icing recipe," Tala shouted as she bustled her way toward the bright, tiled room at the back of the condo.

All at once, the pressure released, and I stumbled forward. The pink, shaggy rug was coming up fast but my reflexes were faster. My hand shot out and grabbed Kai's shirt. I used the fabric and my epic, new arm strength to break my fall. Kai helped by pulling me up.

I straightened and shook the hair from my face.

"Mommy!" A tiny body slammed into my legs, almost knocking me back the other way.

A blinding shade of green glimmered around her head and shoulders. A sickening thud dropped to the pit of my stomach like an anchor.

No. It can't be. I'd failed.

Although I'd found the murderer, I didn't complete the deal. Or the Brothers Grimm were cruel, lying gods and had tricked me.

My lip twitched. Instead of fear or sadness, I only felt frustration now, the anchor in my gut twisting and grinding. Pure, intense anger built inside me.

"Mari?" My husband furrowed his brow. With his hand in mine, he squeezed to direct my attention to him. I offered him a glance, and he mouthed *you promised.*

Yeah, so did the Brothers Grimm. I shook my head and peeled Wendy off of me. "I have to go."

A typical summoning would take too long. Surely, the Grimm gods couldn't deny my success if I finished the events of *Dracula*'s narrative.

Despite my ability to move faster than a normal human, Kai snagged my arm before I backed out the door. His hold didn't dig into my arm and he didn't insist because my husband wasn't the demanding sort of spouse. Instead, the flat line of his mouth and slight uptick at the center of his eyebrows framed the combination of love and sadness in his eyes.

I wanted to pull away and resume my plan of action but the look stopped me dead in my tracks. Maybe Doctor Van Helsing's prescription had power behind it. I'd spent half of this day with Kai now and I felt a stirring somewhere deep inside me that encouraged me to linger with him a little longer.

"Please," he said. The sound of his voice decided for me. He'd dropped his volume to a whisper, keeping the words just between us. "You can't help her when you're not you anymore."

I sucked in a breath and the fact that I didn't run out the door was all the promise he needed. Kai let go, crouching and taking Wendy's shoulders into his hands now.

"Are you ready to go to the light parade?" he asked, and it inspired a squeal of glee from her. Our daughter glanced between us with her delighted expression quickly falling at the look on my face.

I tried to smile. *Parade first, then the goal.* Besides, I couldn't give in entirely to vampirism if I wanted to be a great mom, journalist, and investigator. The fact that I'd be restricted from going out into the daylight would squash those opportunities.

Tala yelped from the kitchen. A knife clattered to the tiled floor as blood spilled over her finger. My vision blurred, then sharpened. All senses heightened and even the sound of my breath hurt my ears.

It took everything I had not to dive into the kitchen and go for the blood. Tala wrapped a towel around her finger and ensured Kai that she was fine. I didn't even want to drink blood, but my body still reacted the way a vampire's body should. If my experience, not even fully vampiric, was this strong, how did Dracula not attack every creature with a pulse? Especially if he hadn't fed in a while?

Giving him Garen might prove easier than I'd thought.

Parade first. Parade first. I repeated the plan to remind myself that it was necessary to keep me from becoming a monster.

But the second item on my to-do list rivaled for my attention: push the story along, sacrificing Garen's life to Dracula, and seal the classic horror's plot, once and for all.

Chapter 19

Just What Doctor Van Helsing Ordered

An array of baked goods covered every surface of Tala's kitchen from reindeer-shaped cookies, to oversized cinnamon rolls, and homemade chocolate truffles. Kai had dragged me back into the house after I'd tried to leave. Rich, smooth icing stuck to the tip of my tongue when I went to lick the cinnamon roll Tala had shoved into my face. Between the flavors of nothing and nothing, a hint of sugar melted in my mouth. Or was I imagining the taste I once knew?

I tried again, accepting the cinnamon roll. This time, the taste of nothing only made me want to throw the pastry across the kitchen. I pictured it sticking to the window that overlooked San Francisco's streets below. The roll would slide down, leaving sticky, nauseating residue along the window pane while I turned and attacked my husband.

All I had to do was sink my sharp teeth into his exposed neck to taste something again. Though if I stopped and thought about drinking blood for longer than a second, it made me gag.

Forget food and blood, I didn't need to eat. I needed to use my immortality for a worthwhile pursuit like becoming the best mother, parent, journalist, investigator—screw it, *person*, in the world. The human and vampire parts of me clashed while residual thoughts of being the Keeper of Stories clung to the back of my mind.

"Parade first," I muttered the reminder.

With a lot of long thank you's, too-tight hugs, and annoying armfuls of Tupperware, we finally made it out of Tala's condo. The blast of cold, winter air down the open hallway refreshed me. Night had arrived in all its glory with darkness in the sky, tainted by the city's stupidly bright lights.

We bundled Wendy in a coat so thick she looked like a marshmallow and could barely bend her arms. Every glimpse of Christmas distracted her, and the short walk to the street in the parade's route took longer than necessary. I tried to stay calm by repeating Kai's words.

You can't help if you're not you.

How about, I can't be the best human if I'm a vampire?

I smirked and accepted that motivation for now. Bodies crowded the streets, milling about, laughing, and waiting for the parade to begin. Some brought folding chairs from their homes while others sat on the curb, wrapped in coats and blankets. Normally, I'd crave to have one of the many paper cups with steam drifting out of the top. Tonight, cocoa and coffee didn't interest me.

Wendy pointed to the red ribbons on every streetlamp. At least the pieces of holiday cheer temporarily brightened the city. Christmas lights blinded us from seeing the crime, litter, and puffs of car exhaust. It was a nice, if not naïve, reprieve.

We wiggled our way to the edge of the sidewalk where Wendy could catch sight of Santa's sleigh. Hundreds of heartbeats pounded in my ears, drowned only by the blasting jingle bells and Mariah Carey's voice echoing from the speakers on parade floats. While the singer belted out verses of a popular Christmas song, viewers cheered and children scattered into the gutters to grab candy. I squinted to make out the banner on the front of the red and green float that showered the streets with candy. *Pediatric Dentistry.* I snorted and shifted my gaze to the next source of entertainment.

It took every ounce of self-control I could muster not to disappear into the crowd where Kai couldn't haunt me with his loving eyes.

Somewhere, in the city of San Francisco, Garen lived and breathed when he should be dead. Dracula's story needed to end for me to triumph in the deal with the Brothers Grimm.

I shifted my weight between my feet, frustrated at the never-ending floats that rolled by with their stupid banners. Women dressed as sugar plum fairies shined with ridiculous smiles and I returned every cheerful expression with a frown.

Kai nudged me in the ribcage, and I shot him a glare.

"Look, it's you."

My gaze followed where he pointed. A float pumped fake snow into the air, partially obscuring my view of the giant sleigh full of toy bags. Instead of a jolly old man with a bowl full of jelly, someone in a green, fuzzy costume sat in the sleigh's bench.

"Ha. Ha." I said, with a shake of my head. While I didn't care for Christmas, or people as much as the next person, I wasn't a Grinch. Besides, my flat, pissy, vampiric attitude was only temporary until I crossed off a few goals.

"I can't see," Wendy whined.

I rolled my eyes at her and stepped back before she could touch me. The action earned me a sharp look from my husband. I only shrugged and tried my best to ignore our daughter's shrill voice.

Kai crouched and scooped Wendy onto his shoulders where she giggled and pointed to a group of people in the parade who walked dogs. The front of their line displayed a handheld banner that announced they were from the local animal rescue. The big dogs marched along, happily soaking the attention of friendly parade-goers who patted the puppy's heads. The smaller dogs yapped and skittered away from loud noises and bright lights.

"I want to ask Santa for a dog!" Wendy announced to the world, her arms in the air.

"Okay, Wednesday," Kai said.

I arched my eyebrow and turned to him. "You're kidding, right?"

His slight shrug nearly earned him my fist in his face. *Whoa.* That was violent. I didn't—I wasn't like that. I only attacked bad guys, murderers, and creeps in the name of justice. I shook my head and shoved the urge to hurt the person I loved away.

Irritability and anger. Aggression. Pieces of Nurse Betty's list of symptoms came trickling back to me, prickling the hairs at the back of my neck. I swallowed and narrowed my gaze on the dog walkers, trying with all of my might to return the smile of the woman carrying a Chihuahua who wore a sweater that asked for donations in bright, bold print on the fabric.

"I want a wiener dog!" Wendy shouted and pointed to the hot-dog-shaped Dachshund who trotted along the street with stubby legs.

"Hell no," I said. "They bark and yap and dogs stink. Plus, they're ugly, dumb creatures that—"

"Mari!" Kai's nudge to my ribcage wasn't as playful this time. He poked me with his elbow to interrupt my tirade.

"What?" I snapped. "We're never getting a dog."

Undaunted, Wendy shrugged and shifted gears. "What about a kitty?" she gasped. "Or a hamster!"

"No. None of them," I said, glaring at her until Kai's peaked eyebrows drew my attention. My husband narrowed his eyes and held my gaze.

This was my husband and my daughter, why did I want to yell at them? I loved them more than anything, but I couldn't feel it except in glimpses when I forced myself to stop and shut everything else out.

Finally, it was possible to let my shoulders relax and step closer to them. I reached up and held Wendy's hand then offered a genuine smile at Kai.

"Maybe a hamster," I said. Warmth flooded my chest. Was that my humanity fighting against the infection of a vampire's disease? At first, it felt good, like taking a drink of hot chocolate on a cold, winter day, but when it reached my extremities, it clashed with the chill within me. Pin prickling sensation stabbed my arms and legs, which only made me itch to get away from there.

As soon as I tried watching the parade again, too many sounds and smells assaulted me. I hated the Christmas lights that blinded me and every rhythmic beat of the living souls that surrounded us.

At the tail-end of the local rescue's section, puppies trained to carry small buckets approached people in the crowd. Some dogs sniffed at the leftover candy while their walkers tugged them away.

"May as well let them eat it," I said. At least then the parade would end and I'd get the hell out of here. *Screw getting better.* I was perfectly fine.

"What?" Kai leaned closer.

"I said," I raised my voice. "They may as well let the dogs eat the chocolate so that they die!"

The parade drowned my shouting from reaching most people's ears, but those nearest us turned and gave us shocked stares.

Still too close to my face, Kai spoke again. "I don't like how you're acting. It's worrying me."

I frowned. "Well, don't." I refused to meet his gaze. The more I looked at my little family, the more I realized they were a distraction. Instead of watching a parade, I should be hunting Dracula, and then starting a new investigation. How would I win a Pulitzer if I was wasting my life away with a worry-wart of a husband?

"Why won't you look at me?" he asked.

I only shook my head and crossed my arms. His voice sparked more of the heat in my chest that only hurt when it met with the chill of my slow vampiric blood flow. Human and undead creature tendencies raged within me. My faint pulse still thumped with an irregular beat.

Kai let go of Wendy's leg to reach for my hand. I flinched and stepped back. The people behind us didn't appreciate me bumping into them.

"Mari?"

I wanted to look at him. *No, I don't. I want to win. I want to be the best.*

"Leave me alone," I said, keeping my eyes distant and fixed on a streetlamp past the parade. If I looked at him, I'd feel the needles all over me again. But my husband always helped which meant I had to be the one to put my foot down.

Kai crouched, letting Wendy hop off of his shoulders.

"Let's just go grab some hot apple cider at Starbucks and—"

"Nope." I shook my head. "No."

The battle within me left my mind ping-ponging between the possibilities. If I became a vampire I'd be stronger, but then I wouldn't be the perfect human mother and journalist that I pictured in my future. This wasn't the moment to decide, not while the glow still radiated around Wendy, reminding me I'd failed. I just needed some space, then we'd try a family dinner, maybe Christmas crafting together to help fight off the vampiric side of me.

Back-and-forth, the argument consumed me and I just needed it to stop. I needed quiet.

I glimpsed Kai stepping toward me out of the corner of my eye.

Finally, I looked up at him. "Get the hell away from me!" Before he could reach me, I turned and shoved through the crowd.

"Mari!"

Bodies pressed against me with the prickly human warmth. Hearts beat everywhere except within me. Mine had slowed to a crawl so weak that I couldn't feel if I was alive or undead.

Jingle Bell Rock blared from the float where a man dressed as Santa Claus waved. A little boy screamed and stepped on my foot as I pushed past a large family.

"I just need quiet," I said.

The crowd thinned as I stumbled away from the street roped off for the parade. *Feliz Navidad's* chorus faded as I rounded the corner and spied the tall building that housed our condo. Every stride I took grew in size as I stomped toward home. Overhangs sheltered the residents' designated parking spaces, casting yawning shadows into the middle of the lot. I followed the maze of cars through the parking lot toward the staircase on the building.

The small play structure that our Homeowners Association demanded exorbitant fees for caught my eye. I broke from the course and hiked into the little playground. The gate slammed shut behind me and I plopped on the bench.

Cool air graced my face. I leaned back against the bench and took a slow breath. Vampire. Mother. Keeper of Stories. Journalist. I had a lot of pieces to my puzzle but I wasn't sure which ones I wanted to keep.

The twinkling stars that dotted the sky were barely visible thanks to the city's light pollution. I let my eyelids fall, enclosing me in darkness.

Unfortunately, a spirit's illumination pierced through surfaces like eyelids and my hands. I slapped my palms over my eyes and groaned. The bluish light that interrupted my peace and quiet could only belong to one entity—a god.

"What's up?" I mumbled.

Jacob spoke first. "Are you afraid of us?"

I sighed and let my lips bubble in a raspberry as I blew out a breath.

"Of course she's not, if our Keeper of Stories fears a couple of skeletons then we have a bigger problem on our hands," Will said.

Right. As if a fear of ghostly bodies wasn't normal. Hey, maybe I had hope yet. As far as I knew, vampires weren't afraid of anything except werewolf boyfriends in a vampire, human, wolf love triangle.

I opened my eyes just to glare at the *Pirates of the Caribbean-*looking creeps. "What do you want?"

"As you can see," Will started, waving to the pieces of rotting flesh hanging off his bones. Was their godhood stripping away? The process of reverse decomposition and dying seemed to have taken hold. "Time is running out. Do you have a plan?"

"I found your murderer." I spoke between my teeth. "Why didn't I get what I wanted?"

"Do you mean to ask why your daughter is still cursed?" Jacob asked. Long, scraggly hairs reached down from his eyebrows and nearly poked him in the iris.

Cursed? I'd never considered that term for it, but it struck a chord. I opened my mouth but Will interrupted before I could answer.

"We saw the man you say is Morris at Dracula's house. Why isn't he dead yet? Why is the vampire still alive?"

My gaze wandered past the ghosts and glazed over as I stared at a random car in the parking lot. With what little energy I had left, I shrugged one shoulder. Hopefully, it communicated how little I cared for the Brothers Grimm. I wanted to succeed and fulfill my end of the deal, sure, but making them happy wasn't on my radar.

I licked my lips, snagging my tongue on my fang. "I haven't figured out why Garen was there, okay?"

"What are you waiting for?" The older of the two brothers stepped out of the bark that surrounded the play structure. The bones in his foot crunched against the sidewalk's concrete.

"I needed some rest," I said.

"This is a test, Keeper." The holes in Will's skull pointed toward me but he didn't have eyes, not even ghostly ones, anymore. "Will you pass?"

The mere suggestion of my failure royally pissed me off. I straightened, sliding my feet off the bench and slamming them against the sidewalk. "Of course, I will!"

"Good." he nodded.

Jacob dropped his hand on his brother's shoulder. This time, it landed. They were more solid, even, than they appeared.

"Morris dies," he said, the partial flesh on his face spread into a weird smile. "Did you hear that? Morris will die. Dracula will die. They'll die."

"I heard, I heard." Will shoved Jacob's hand off of him and then wiped his shoulder as if cleaning off his brother's germs. He focused on me again and dipped his head as if giving me a slight bow. "Whatever it takes to seal the story."

"Even death." The ghost of Jacob Grimm grinned.

With that, they vanished.

I stood and shoved through the gate into the enclosed play area. The night was in full swing now, and as a vampire, hunting a vampire, it was the perfect time to kill.

I stalked out of the parking lot and into the quiet streets of San Francisco, following the memory of the route and the salty, sea air.

Chapter 20

Another Nail in Dracula's Coffin

Blood stained the beams on the house's porch. I only noticed because of the smell. The sharp scent of alcohol hinted that someone had scrubbed it after our altercation. Except it wasn't rubbing alcohol that burned my nose. I approached the front door, careless about alerting Dracula because of the pounding music.

Never had I expected modern-day Dracula to be a rich, older, playboy who partied too much. But, I guess it made sense. Nobody else could afford to rent a waterfront castle in San Francisco. Though his status as a college professor didn't match his wealthy lifestyle.

Hip-hop music boomed from inside the house. I tried the doorknob, ready to enter as if I were another person invited to the party. The door creaked when I pushed it open.

I expected the invisible barrier to stop me, but nothing prevented me from stepping inside. I chalked it up to the fact that this wasn't a human's home, it was where Dracula lived. Reports of injured women stopped in the past day, making me look guiltier and the vampire hungrier, I assumed. As far as I knew, Dracula needed fresh blood to survive. And what better way than to throw a house party where drunk people passed out, ready to be drained dry?

Carefully, I stepped further into the entry which opened up to a spacious living room.

Instead of a room full of college kids, a lone figure sat on the couch. I stepped into the entry, tip-toeing to peer inside. Curls covered the back of the man's head, and when he turned, I caught sight of a bushy beard.

A video game flashed on the screen. The game's character ran with a gun out in front of him. He ducked to dodge sight from an opponent, then crouched behind a piece of a broken spaceship.

Heightened senses and investigator's skills had me scanning the entry, living room, and the winding staircase that led to the second story. A chandelier sparkled above us but instead of traditional light-bulbs, dripping, wax candles flickered with gentle flames. How anyone reached it to light the wicks, I didn't know.

Unlike other party houses I'd seen, beer cans didn't litter the floor. But a full bar lined the open space beneath the staircase. I pinpointed it as the area from where the alcohol smell wafted.

Faint light glowed from the hallway upstairs and I guessed Dracula had awakened, or would, soon. If I wanted to leave the vampire a tasty treat and close this story, I needed to get it done. Maybe I'd even get back in time to put Wendy to bed. I tried to care about my family but the investigation was far too interesting.

"Hello?" I said, pretending to have just arrived.

Garen twisted on the couch to find the source of the voice. The video game controller slipped from his fingers and clattered to the floor. The sight of a young man playing games on a console didn't match the castle's marble flooring and vaulted ceilings.

"You." He stood.

I licked my lips and nodded. An elaborate lie formulated in my mind that'd help me pull Garen toward Dracula. With the vampire busy fighting him, I'd swoop in and decapitate him.

"What?" The question came out in a stutter as he stared at me. I had no idea what he really thought of me, just that he'd framed me for attempted murder.

I raised my hands in mock surrender and walked toward him. "No hard feelings," I lied. "Look, I came here to warn you. You're staying in someone else's house."

"Yeah." he folded his arms. "I know, I'm his roommate."

Whose roommate? The vampire, or Nolan's?

"Um." I wracked my brain for more lies to help me. "I, well your roommate is dangerous. He…" what could I say? *The truth.* "He attacked several students of his. I'm out because the cops know I didn't hurt that girl." Curiosity and experience drove me to mention his twisted version of the incident. "But you thought I did. Why?"

"Why are you here?" he asked, ignoring my question.

"I told you," I said, as I stepped closer. "I don't want anyone else to get hurt and your…" my gaze searched the candles, the blaring speaker attached to a phone, and the overpriced couch. "Your roommate is unpredictable."

His Adam's Apple bobbed from a hard swallow. Garen raked his fingers through his beard on his way to folding his arms. "So, what? You came here to save me?"

I nodded. "Exactly. Can I turn this down?" I pointed to the small speaker that thumped with music.

The question garnered no response. Garen only stared at me, so I pressed down on the volume button until it didn't pound in my ears.

"Where is your roommate?"

He pursed his lips then nodded toward the staircase behind me. "Sleeping. Who are you?"

"I'm Mari Rowan," I said. It felt good to tell the truth. "I'm an investigative journalist. I track killers and report on them to help keep the public informed and safe."

The reminder of the woman I once was, triggered a quicker heartbeat, almost enough for me to call it normal. But it quickly dropped again when I thought of the reason I'd come here. The deal with the Brothers Grimm wasn't done until Garen—and Dracula—were dead. "Vaughn killed one of his students and her mother, on his way to get to the daughter."

Garen's lip twitched. He rubbed his face, to his beard then looked away, breaking our shared gaze. Each gesture and flinch revealed a secret beneath the surface.

"But you knew that, didn't you?" I prodded.

Garen only sniffed.

"Is that why you framed me for the attack?" I stepped closer, the tips of my fingers tracing the back of the couch. Again, he said nothing, no defense, no argument, so I pressed further. I sensed that he wasn't throwing me out because of… fear?

I continued my theory. "Professor Vaughn is your friend."

Nothing. Garen only released his folded arms to scratch at the back of his head.

"Do you harass and hurt women too?" I asked.

Finally, that sparked a response. "Hey. Whoa."

"Fine." I nodded. "If you just take me to him, I'll tell the cops you cooperated and you won't be questioned." It sounded legitimate, though Detective Wilhelm would never actually listen to me and I had no power to make such a claim.

Now that Garen looked at me, his expression transformed. From guilt to a defensive stance, his face twisted and eyes bugged. The sweat lining his brow and upper lip, as well as the racing heartbeat, revealed a sudden shift to…fear.

I glanced behind me, expecting to see Dracula emerging from his coffin somewhere upstairs and taking the steps one by one with spooky confidence. But like most of Garen's responses, there was nothing.

"Garen—" I turned back to see he'd dodged around the couch and made it to the front door.

"Stop!"

The insane speed with which I crossed the room and snatched his hand surprised even me. Though he was large, I had no trouble pinning him in place with the grip of only one of my hands. I could get used to these vampiric powers.

Garen's chest rose and fell rapidly and his gaze searched my face, darting from my eyes to the fangs peeking out beneath my top lip.

It was all very dramatic, and I didn't have time for it. I could easily drag him upstairs and feed him to Dracula, but a twinge deep down in the pit of my stomach caused me to pause.

"You're a vampire," he breathed.

Well, that was unexpected. The constant twists and surprises in this fractured classic would have driven me nutty if I wasn't convinced I'd end it within minutes.

"You're just like him." The quiver in his voice filled me with a sickening power. I shoved the weird, egotistical feeling away.

"No—"

Before I could insist that I wasn't a murderer, he cowered away from me.

"You're going to kill me, aren't you?" he predicted.

I swallowed. Though his pounding pulse drew my eyes to his throat, I wasn't thirsty for Garen's blood—not unless it was Dracula who spilled it right before I cut off Dracula's head.

"How do you know about vampires?" I asked.

He shook his head while his mouth hung open, wordless and breathless.

"Is it because of Professor Vaughn? Are you his pet? What is this?" Anger built inside of me and I liked how it muted the more human parts of me, namely the guilt that hovered because of what I was about to do. "Then you won't mind if I take you to him."

I yanked him along with me, my fist full of his shirt's fabric. Thanks to my strength, he had no choice but to follow. The flash of my gun tucked into my jeans probably didn't hurt either.

We reached the bottom of the staircase before he sputtered.

"Wait! Wait." he begged.

But I didn't stop. The plot of Bram Stoker's novel needed to end. I'd seal this story now and curiosity for Garen's side of the story couldn't even stop me now.

His shins banged into the steps as I dragged him up the staircase. Garen tried to go deadweight on me after struggling was unsuccessful.

"Please, please stop."

"You can't be afraid of him, you live with him," I said, as I shoved him in front of me, keeping my grip on his upper arm. "He probably won't even hurt you, right? You're his partner in crime. Do you invite the girls to a party here where he could drain them? Huh?"

"No!" his voice squeaked, and I almost felt bad for digging my fingernails into his bicep's flesh. "I would never. I was trying to stop him. Professor Vaughn is terrifying and the cops never helped because he would always talk his way out of everything. But I knew he was guilty. I knew he hurt Lindsay."

I stopped halfway up the staircase and turned to him. "How does moving in with him help?"

He took a shaky breath and glanced around. "I don't really live here. I was just crashing on his couch. My buddy, Nolan, he owns the house, and I was trying to build a case against Professor Vaughn so I pretended it was all about using the biggest house in the city for parties. Then I noticed the professor was weird. Like, at first, I thought he just slept during the day so he could stay awake and party at night but then I caught him. I—I thought I'd lost my mind but..."

"What? Get to the point, Garen." I lightened my grip, knowing I'd outrun him if he tried to escape, anyway.

"Professor Vaughn changed into a bat. Just like that." he snapped his fingers. "Lindsay was my ex, and I noticed the professor had taken an interest in her. I asked him if I could throw a few keggers at his house and he agreed because I said I'd invite Lindsay."

My eyebrows shot to my hairline. "So, you did bait the women."

He rubbed the palm of his free hand over his face and sighed. "No, no—"

"Oh, come on Garen." I didn't care about his feelings anymore. Experience with serial killers taught me to be tough, so this was a piece of cake, especially with my own feelings muted. Would my vampire side help me get into the mind of murderers? The thought of losing my humanity sent an involuntary shudder through me for the first time.

"I never brought Lindsay here. In fact, I told her to stay away, but he invited her."

"And you're just the vigilante who wants to avenge your ex-girlfriend's death? Hadn't you been broken up for quite some time? I heard you took the end of your relationship well."

His eyelids rolled, and he pinched the bridge of his nose. "It wasn't about Lindsay. I think the professor had his eye on Mindy next."

"Nolan's girlfriend?"

Garen nodded. "I told her to leave town."

"And she listened?" I asked, skeptical about the twist of everything.

"That's right. I swear I tried to get the cops involved but Professor Vaughn always smoothed everything over. So, I took matters into my own hands but I wasn't ready to tell Nolan that his tenant was a freaking supernatural creature. I didn't want him to laugh in my face and then tell Mindy…" his voice trailed as his eyes searched the plain, empty wall behind me.

The house, like most vacation homes, was devoid of anything personal, but even for a rental, this was exceptionally cold. Dracula didn't have a family, but I did and I was on a mission to save my daughter.

"Nolan didn't know any of this?" I asked.

He shook his head. "I couldn't risk him telling…" again, his voice trailed. He didn't want to admit something to me and that was fine. We'd wasted enough time. I didn't really need all the details other than to satisfy my curiosity.

One more question nagged me. "I still don't get why you framed me when you had proof and cops willing to believe you that Professor Vaughn attacked that young woman."

He eyed me warily, landing his gaze on my fangs. "When I realized you were a vampire, too, I just wanted you gone as fast as possible."

Vampire. *I'm a vampire.* Maybe it was already too late for me, but it wasn't for Wendy. If I couldn't be the best human, I'd be the best supernatural creature.

I grabbed a fistful of Garen's shirt sleeve and turned him around.

This time, when Garen begged, I tuned it out. The only thing I heard when I dragged him up the staircase, was something about how Dracula had laid low the last couple of days. According to the bait himself, the monster upstairs was hungry. How easy would it be to open the enormous bedroom's double doors and throw Garen inside? Dracula wouldn't be able to resist a fresh breakfast after a day of not feeding, especially with the presence of the drink consuming his desire.

All I had to do was help Garen bleed, a little.

Chapter 21

Vampire in a Vacation House

Victory was so close I could taste it. Sure enough, when I shoved Garen through the double doors, we found a coffin. Professor Vaughn had really dedicated to his Dracula persona and I couldn't blame him. The vampire side of me overwhelmed me, hovering in every thought and feeling—or lack thereof.

Even the coffin, in all its splintery, wooden glory, looked comfortable. Did I just admit I wanted to sleep in the dirt? The scent of damp soil filled the entire room, so I didn't have to open the coffin's lid to see the natural mattress Dracula used.

"Please, he'll be waking up any minute," Garen said. The look of wrinkled desperation on his face aged him several years. No longer did he look like a tough college kid, but a man at the end of his life.

I averted my eyes, not allowing his pleading to change my mind. The eyes always got me with their windows to the soul and whatnot. I shoved Garen forward, who stumbled and nearly fell on top of the coffin.

He didn't run, knowing now that I'd move faster and block him with the unnatural strength coursing through my body. With my gaze fixed on the coffin, I dug out the switchblade from my boot and flicked it open.

With whip-speed, I snatched his wrist and turned it up, exposing the blue veins that bulged beneath his flesh. The pulse of blood rushing through them made my mouth twitch. I licked my lips and quickly planned an escape. I'd give him a minor cut, then duck out of the room before the blood consumed me. From the hallway, I'd ready in a shooting stance and aim my gun loaded with blessed bullets at Dracula's head.

"Please." The begging grew more desperate, embarrassing even, as Garen dropped to his knees in front of me.

I closed my eyes. *Don't look at him. Just do it. Cut him. End this novel, now!*

With a shaking hand, I pressed the blade against his wrist. I looked away, keeping my head turned and eyes on the door where I'd escape in moments. Out of the corner of my eye, I saw his head droop, and it seemed he'd accepted his fate.

Whatever it takes to seal the story.

"Even death," I whispered. Where had I heard those same words?

Ebenezer Scrooge. Did I just quote the Brothers Grimm? The soulless, gods removed from humanity who cared nothing but for their goals to keep the stories correct and separate from the real world? Even at the cost of an innocent person's life.

I swallowed the lump in my throat. Soft whimpering pricked my ears, and I finally forced myself to look at the man I was about to get killed.

It's for Wendy. I'll be saving lives when Dracula comes out and I kill him. The weight of my gun felt heavier in its holster, pulling against my pants. I'd tell myself whatever I needed to get through this.

"Whatever it takes…" I breathed. My stomach twisted until it turned upside down and bile rose in my throat. "Even…" I couldn't bring myself to say the next word. No amount of super strength or tendency to vampire violence would bring me this low. A thousand memories swirled through my mind as if I was the one facing death.

This isn't you.

Despite my avoidance of Garen's gaze, the image of another pair of desperate eyes haunted me. Even when I closed my eyes, I saw my husband, my daughter, Tala, and Scarlet. Everyone I loved filtered through my thoughts. What if they were the ones destined to die because of a story's plot? Would I feel the same and finish the events of the book?

Kai was right. This wasn't me, because I was nothing like Jacob and Will Grimm. The thought that I'd listened to them ignited a million feelings from rage to pure, gut-wrenching sadness. Never had I been so disappointed in myself than when I emulated the soulless spirits that haunted me.

Tears flooded my eyes in a sudden, intense rush of emotions—all the emotions I didn't feel since becoming a vampire. Before I vomited on Garen, I let go and stumbled back, doubling over at the waist.

Garen gasped and struggled to his feet. He stood, frozen in place as he watched me. I slapped my hand to my chest to feel the thump, thumping of the humanity within me.

My heartbeat had returned.

The victim ran past me, disappearing out of the bedroom door. I had no doubt that Dracula would beat me in a fight, even as a Keeper, so I couldn't blame Garen for running. Even though I couldn't die, the pain of being torn from limb to limb or drained of my blood was too much for my exhausted mind and aching body to comprehend.

As the strength faded from my muscles, the familiar pressure of a migraine returned. I struggled to drag one foot in front of the other. I followed where Garen had run, taking myself down the hall before Dracula woke.

Walking proved harder with my heavy legs and dizzy head. The slow creak of a door opening came from behind me and I pushed myself to move quicker. I paused at the top of the stairs. Could I shoot Dracula faster than he'd charge me? I knew he wouldn't hesitate to take me down after our first altercation.

My hands shook when I pulled my gun out and turned around. With my legs in a firm stance, hip-width apart, I raised my gun. Burning exhaustion rippled through my triceps as I gripped the weapon and aimed through the open door.

Dracula emerged from the coffin, tall and ominous. I squinted but couldn't focus on him when everything in my vision melted together like an old TV screen right as it turned off. I blinked and tried to clear the migraine's poison from my eyes.

I flicked off the gun's safety and exhaled. The smooth, cold feel of the trigger pressed against the soft spot of my finger as I struggled to put weight behind it. My shaking hand refused to cooperate and before I pulled the trigger, a crash echoed from downstairs.

Slowly, Dracula approached me, unbothered by the gun in my hands. *Work hands. Work!*

"That won't stop me," he said.

"They're blessed—" I managed before two men wielding massive butcher's knives shoved into me.

Nolan knocked me to the side, and my knees buckled, finally giving out.

"Wait!" My voice came out weaker than my body felt. They didn't hear me but I tried, anyway. "Garen's going to die."

It was just as Bram Stoker wrote it. Both men, Nolan and Garen as the characters of Jonathan and Morris, barreled toward the vampire with stainless steel weapons. Together they'd bring him down but Garen would die if I did nothing.

Nolan threw himself at the vampire, thrusting the knife out in front of him. He pointed it at Dracula's throat but fell short when Dracula leaned back in a movement far faster than a mere man could follow.

Dracula slammed Nolan to the side and then turned to face his friend. I pulled myself to my feet and attempted to aim, again.

"Garen, get out!" I screamed. "He'll kill you!"

Nolan scrambled for the knife he'd dropped, distracting Dracula just long enough for Garen to rush him like a linebacker. Together, vampire and victim crashed to the ground, but the struggle only lasted a split-second before Dracula wrapped his hands around Garen's throat.

I needed Nolan out of the way so I could bring down Dracula before Garen got killed.

"You're blocking my shot!" I screamed. Either he didn't hear me or he didn't care. All I needed was a moment with a clear shot at the monster, but the chaos didn't allow for a split-second of reprieve. Nolan dropped to his knees, wielding the butcher's knife and waiting to swing at Dracula once Garen pinned him.

But he didn't know the supernatural strength behind the vampire's power, and Garen was rapidly losing the battle. I had seconds to interfere before Dracula either strangled him or…

"Ebenezer Scrooge," I cursed. The vampire disarmed his attacker and gripped the knife.

I shifted my weapon's aim to the coffin and fired into the box of dirt. The warning shot cut through the grunting and shuffling of the fight, though victim and vampire didn't stop their struggle. The shot achieved what I'd hoped. Nolan reacted by ducking and snapping his attention to me.

Quickly, I flicked the gun to the left to tell him to move and the threat of the weapon forced him to obey.

I squinted and double-checked the safety before aiming, once again. With the bodies in a pile on the floor, I couldn't get a good line of sight and didn't dare risk hurting the person I was trying to save.

The vampire's speed made it impossible for me to aim, so I rushed him, ready to jab the barrel end of the weapon into Dracula's ribcage. If only I'd come prepared with a stake but my impulsive obsession with sealing the story had muddled my common sense. And now the headache, the lack of rest, everything culminated to make taking on a vampire an impossible feat.

But I still had to try.

My heart pounded as blood rushed to my head, deafening everything around me. Nolan shouted something that I couldn't understand through the waves of my pulse, crashing and beating against my skull.

I rushed Dracula, finally ready to take the shot just inches from the center of his chest where a heart didn't beat. But the vampire was too fast as he dodged out of the way in less time than it took me to blink.

A groan full of agony and fading strength echoed above the sounds of the scuffle. Garen rolled to the side with his own blade jutting from where his body housed his spleen.

With intense force behind his unnatural strength, Dracula smashed the outside of his arm and open palm into my collarbone. The hard bone in the heel of his hand crushed my windpipe, and I slammed into Nolan and we both fell to the floor.

I gasped for breath and rolled to my back, relishing the adrenaline that finally kicked in and dulled my aches long enough to move.

Dracula backed to the open window where the moonlight shined through and illuminated his open, empty coffin. I wouldn't get to my feet fast enough, so I reached for the gun again, hoping beyond hope I could take a shot before he jumped. My stomach flexed as I extended my arms and aimed from where I lay on my back on the floor.

I pointed at the soft spot between the muscles at the back of his neck and pulled the trigger. The shot quieted everything, stripping my ability to hear Garen's last, gasping breaths, and Nolan shuffling behind me.

At the same time, Dracula's form shifted. The cross-etched bullet zipped through the air where his head had been. For a moment, I thought he'd vanished. I squinted at the small, fluttering body that flew out the window.

I rolled to all fours and stood, rushing to lean against the window frame before my knees buckled again.

A small, brown, ratlike creature with leathery wings took flight in the night sky.

Dracula had escaped and left me with the guttural, sickening sounds of death behind me.

Chapter 22

Boys Will Be Vampire-Hunting Boys

"Garen!" A shrieking voice pierced the silent night.

Nolan tried to stop her, but a skinny, young woman with shining dark hair shoved him away. A black glow that matched Dracula, Nolan, and Garen, surrounded her body, too. She dropped to her knees and cupped Garen's face in her hands.

Instead, of dragging her away, Nolan did the smart thing and dug his phone out of his pocket. I should have done the same but I couldn't move. With his forehead in his hand, Nolan crouched where he stood and described the situation to the emergency line.

The muscles in my legs screamed at me and I sank to the floor with my back against the wall. The window's frame dug into the back of my head as I caught my breath and watched the woman hold her dying friend.

Dying…because of me. I'd come here impulsively and forced a fight before I was ready. The weight in my gut twisted and my stomach tightened. Salt stung my eyes as tears tried to form but dehydration prevented more than a slight wetness at my bottom lid. Lack of food and water from when I was a vampire, left me recoiling into myself, weak and light-headed.

"Mindy," Garen breathed.

Mindy? Was this the same Mindy that Nolan wanted to propose to? Of course, she had the undeniable proof of characterhood in the form of a dark glow. My brain tried to wrap around the situation but I was a breath away from fainting and likely confused at the sight.

Mindy dropped her forehead to meet with Garen's. Right there, in front of her boyfriend, she used her hands to tilt Garen's chin up and lay a kiss on his lips. Her tears dripped on his cheeks and slipped down the side of his face, wetting the curl of hair just above his ear. If this were a Disney movie, rather than a real-life tragedy, her cries of adoration would spare his life.

"I love you," she sobbed.

I glanced at Nolan who'd hung up the phone and stood. He swayed in place, staring at his girlfriend and dying friend as they kissed again. By the hurt that wrinkled his face, their interaction shook him as much as it did me.

Had I confused the characters? Maybe this wasn't the end of Bram Stoker's novel where Morris died. Maybe the paramedics would arrive in time to save him. Maybe we had another chance to come after Dracula, together. I clung to this possibility, and the glimmer of hope kept me from giving in to unconsciousness.

Dark hair spilled over Garen's torso as she leaned over him and gasped. The sight of the knife in his side drained her face of blood. Her lips parted and shaking fingers tentatively grazed her mouth.

Blood bubbled from between his lips and he coughed, rolling his head to the side. "What are you doing here?" He tried to reach for her face but she grabbed his hand and held it instead. "Nolan." he breathed, as he struggled to look around.

"I don't care," she said. "I don't care. I came back because I wanted to tell Nolan the truth about us."

Blood mixed with her tears and leaked down Garen's chin. If only I could move, I'd tried to help, but the slight shift of my head sent my head spinning.

The story aura's glow around Garen's body faded before I noticed the rise and fall of his chest had stopped. Open, unseeing eyes stared at the woman who apparently loved him, his friend's near-fiancee. Sadness struck me like a knife to the heart and I knew my humanity had returned, though I could still smell blood too sharply and feel the pulse of the other two living persons in the room.

Mindy buried her face in Garen's chest and sobbed.

"I don't..." Nolan spoke up, taking a step toward the unexpected couple. "I don't understand."

You and me both, Buddy. I coughed as bile burned my throat and left a bitter taste on the back of my tongue.

When paramedics flooded the room, Mindy fled to her boyfriend's arms, but he didn't return the hug. I struggled to my feet and tried to skirt around the outside of the crowd to slip out. Surely, the detectives on the case would believe Nolan's tenant was dangerous after tonight. But I doubted they'd find Dracula.

As I shuffled toward the door, I caught pieces of Mindy's story between sobs. Her shoulders shook as she leaned into Nolan's chest and strands of dark hair stuck to the tears on her cheeks.

"I'm sorry," she said, begging for his forgiveness. "We loved each other, and I didn't know how to tell you."

Nolan didn't respond. All of his swag and ego that I'd witnessed during our interview had vanished. He was a changed man after fighting for his life, watching his friend succumb to his injuries right before his eyes, and discovering his girlfriend's infidelity.

"I was going to make it right," Mindy insisted.

"I can't talk about this," he said.

She wiped away the tear that beaded on her top lip and then frowned. "As if you didn't sleep with Lindsay. Garen and I actually loved each other, we were going to elope."

Ebenezer Scrooge. That solidified it, I'd messed up and misidentified the two characters who took down Dracula at the end of the novel. Modern society struck again, fracturing the fairy tale, or classic literature, into unrecognizable pieces.

Or maybe it was simply the complexities of real life that couldn't handle the basic, restricted world of fiction. In the novel, Mina loved Jonathan and Morris was simply Lucy's ex-suitor. Today, with real people, Mindy carried on a relationship with both Garen and Nolan, and both men were considered Lindsay's exes in one form or another.

Bram Stoker's horror turned into a soap opera really fast. Paramedics attempted to revive Garen with chest compressions until one of them announced they'd reached the stage to call the time of death.

Before they could declare it, effectively sapping the last bit of consciousness I clung to, I slipped out of the bedroom and down the stairs. Thanks to the hood, I willed it to cover my body in clothes that resembled the emergency responders and the cops who ran into the front door didn't give me a second–glance.

I hurried out into the night. Once past the porch overhang, I faced the moon's glow and stared up into the night sky where the light of a distant airplane blinked.

In moments, the Brothers Grimm would likely arrive to tell me I'd failed. Not only had I gotten the wrong man killed, but my stupidity also resulted in Dracula's escape. Now a supernatural serial killer roamed the streets of San Francisco, and I couldn't even claim that the ghosts owed me Wendy's freedom.

I'd failed them, myself, Garen, and worst of all, my daughter.

I ran my thumb along my top lip until the soft flesh snagged on the sharp point of a fang. With my forefinger and thumb pinched around the tip, I squeezed and snapped it to the side. The point cracked off, sparing the rest of my natural tooth. I followed suit on the other side, breaking off the last piece of the monster that I'd become.

If nothing else, at least I'd gotten my humanity back.

Chapter 23

Lies, Tigers, and Monsters, Oh My

The front door's hinges creaked when I pushed it open. I cringed at the sound that disturbed the quiet of the late evening. The screen on my watch told me it was nine at night, almost two hours past Wendy's bedtime. Apparently, I hadn't looked at my phone all night, because my watch displayed a notification of a dozen text messages from Kai.

I stepped inside and carefully shut the door, leaving the chill of the winter night to blow through the open hallway.

The lump on the couch was way too large to be my daughter's snoozing body. A fake fireplace crackled on the TV and a withering candle burned on the tall kitchen counter across the room. The glow of the Christmas tree lights kept the room colorful but not bright enough to disturb sleep. The white noise of the repetitive fireplace on the screen likely drowned out the soft snores I assumed to hear from Kai.

I crept inside, not wanting to bother him after having already disturbed his peace during our fight. After abandoning him to take care of Wendy, with no explanation of where I went, I expected him to be both hurt and angry.

"You're alive." A voice came from the red and green striped blanket. Kai pulled himself up to sit, using the back of the couch as a grip. "I called you, a lot."

"I'm so sorry," I said. I dipped into the cushioned chair that sat kitty-corner to the couch and grabbed the pillow stitched with a smiling snowman on the front to hug. "You didn't deserve any of that. I was way out of line." The pressure of my hand against my forehead temporarily relieved the pain that'd come back in full force since the adrenaline dwindled. I rubbed my eyes and shook my head. "I just…"

My husband scooted to the end of the couch closest to my chair and took my hand. "I know, you weren't yourself." He brushed his thumb over my lips and a faint smile spread on his face. "But you are now? Should I grab a defibrillator?"

With his eyes fixed on the spots where my fangs had jutted from my mouth, I knew what he meant. A small smile curled onto my face. Even during the most intense, serious moments of our lives, Kai kept his sense of humor. He never went dark.

"Yeah, Nurse Betty was right," I said. "About everything. Spending time with you helped, but it definitely got worse before it got better."

Kai nodded. "Plus, it's pretty rad that I can say I met Doctor Van Helsing."

I laughed and rolled my eyes, a common combination of reactions whenever I conversed with my husband for a few minutes. The act of normalcy felt good, like a small burst of energy that kept me upright long enough to check on Wendy then sink into the couch beside Kai and swallow my pride.

The soft, worn cushions tried to lull me to sleep, but I needed to admit something before dreams took me. I sat crisscrossed and faced my husband.

"She's still asleep?" he nodded toward Wendy's bedroom door.

I nodded. "Except she rolled over when I cracked the door, so I hope I didn't wake her." After picking at my fingernails and taking a cleansing breath, I looked at Kai. The TV's glow lit up one side of his face, showing the lines that creased the skin beneath his bloodshot eyes. He reflected my exhaustion. Kai didn't sign up to marry a woman who killed monsters—investigate murderers and write about them, sure, but not hunt them. The guy deserved a break, yet here I was about to ask him to track and destroy a literary vampire with me.

Before diving into the request, I chewed on my lip. "I need your help. I…" I looked at my hands as they twisted the fabric of the blanket Kai had been using. "One of the guys involved in the story died, and it was my fault. Then Dracula escaped. I have to find him."

"How can I help?"

"I just need backup. I have to kill him, Kai."

He nodded, taking in the fact that we were going to go on a couple's hunt for a supernatural serial murderer. "Okay."

"Okay." I leaned into him for an exhausted attempt at a hug to show my gratitude. I opened my mouth to tell him we needed to wake Tala and tell her we needed an emergency babysitter. Destroying Dracula couldn't wait. "We…" my voice came out in a whisper as the warmth of my husband's arms and the fireplace's crackling convinced me to close my eyes, just for a moment. The soothing darkness and soft couch would give me a second wind to get up and find the villain.

Just one minute…

"Look at that lazy woman, just snuggling her husband when evil walks the city streets," I said, pointing at myself.

From this view, outside of my body, I could see everything. The complete picture was painted in front of me, a mom curled up with her husband, passed out on the couch in a small living room. I tsked and shook my head at the disappointment that was Mari Fable Rowan.

Who dared rest when she had a story to seal and a child to save? Sickening. I squinted and leaned over my body which was curled like a snail in her shell under the red and green striped blanket. I frowned at the messy hair that covered her face. Once the emergencies were resolved, I desperately needed to cut those split ends so she—I mean, I —didn't look like such a slob.

Me? Wait…she?

It dawned on me that I could think and move and…this wasn't a dream.

"Good morning, Sunshine."

I jumped and slapped my palms to my chest. Horrifying zombie creatures stood between me and the front door. I backed away until the kitchen counter dug into my spine.

It was Will who'd spoken first, and I decided Detective Wilhelm was *definitely* named after him.

"What in the wonderland is going on here?" I asked as I pointed to the second me who cuddled Kai on the couch.

"This is the last bit of connection we have to our power on the other side," Will said. "We are using it to show you the future."

"You really can't let a girl rest, can you?" I scoffed. Not that I wanted to sleep when guilt ravaged my insides and I knew I needed to avenge Garen's death.

"It was a Dickens to pull this off." Will frowned.

"Come," Jacob said. The pieces of flesh that dangled from his bones made my lip curl in disgust. Their bodies had partially reformed, reversing their deaths and stripping their status as gods. The process of decomposition happened backward, effectively pinning them to their once-human existence in the natural world. This world.

"Do you trust us?" the other brother spoke again, extending his half-rotted arm out to me.

"Definitely not."

"Too bad," Will said with a twitch of his eyebrow.

A deep rumble rippled beneath my feet. It rattled the pictures on the wall and built, shaking and trembling everything around us. I gasped and reached for the counter to steady me but the earth quaked again and threw me to the side.

The TV crashed to the ground, smashing the screen into dozens of pieces. I shrieked and crawled across the floor toward Wendy's room when the shaking ceased. A massive, deafening roar echoed from somewhere in the city.

"What in the…" I breathed.

Jacob looked at Will with slight concern creasing his brow. "What is the beast called?"

Without taking his eyes off me, Will answered. "Godzilla, I believe."

My mouth dropped open. Once I gained control of my jaw again, I shook my head and refused to accept what he'd said. "No, no, no way." I twisted and scrambled to my feet. "Wendy!"

"She's not there," Will said.

The door slammed open to reveal an empty room. I held onto the walls to keep me upright as I struggled to push open my bedroom door, still calling for Wendy.

A lump lay in the center of our bed but I quickly saw that it wasn't Kai. One of my coworkers, Elsie, was fast asleep under the covers. Color was drained from her face and her hands were crossed at the front of her chest like a body posed for burial.

A haunting laugh chilled my bones, and I spun around. Twisted, black horns vanished from an open window on the other side of the room. I ran to the window in time to see a horned woman, take flight. When she slammed into the ground, her body transformed, shape-shifting like Dracula did from vampire to wolf. But this creature grew an elongated neck and breathed fire from her black snout.

"Maleficent?" I whispered.

Pedestrians on the streets below screamed and ran for their lives. Maleficent responded to Godzilla's roar with a burst of flames and a shriek of her own. I looked up to see the tip of the dinosaur-like monster's head past skyscrapers. He must have taken another step because I had to grip the window's frame to keep from falling when the earth shook.

A building I didn't recognize caught my eye. It didn't match the rest of San Francisco's architecture, instead, much taller and all black except for the fiery oval at the top between two spires.

The oval shifted and moved until the black slit in the middle was pointed at me. I backed away from the window, suddenly realizing it was the Eye of Sauron.

"This isn't happening," I said, curling my fingers into fists.

"Not yet," Will said.

"Will you follow us now?" Jacob asked as he buttoned his coat and beckoned for me to exit the bedroom and follow them out the front door.

I did, in a daze, wanting to shut my eyes and make it all go away. If they could show me how to make sense of this awful nightmare, I'd follow until I figured out how to wake up and end the visions of evil sugar plum fairies. Of course, there was nothing sweet about Maleficent.

Time moved too fast and yet slower than I could comprehend. We walked a path I knew well, taking the sidewalk that led straight into Pioneer Park. Though the city had transformed, and not just into a villain's playground. Some buildings were different, rebuilt in a style I'd never seen before with more geometric shapes and little windows. Was I seeing the future just as the Brothers Grimm had claimed?

Screams and cries of help sounded all around us. It was carnage and chaos and I could only imagine Jaws swam somewhere near the coast of San Francisco's Bay along with Ursula and dozens of other monsters that ravaged innocent people.

The trees at the entrance of the park grew over the walkway, reaching with long, crooked branches out to block our way. I dodged around them and hoped the splintered ends didn't turn into fingers that could grab me.

The flick of a long, orange tail caught my eye, and I squinted at a creature perched on a branch above. I saw his eyes first with their yellow glow. After a slow blink, his tail followed suit, lazily lifting and then falling. I recognized the smooth, shining orange and black fur and the cat's eyes as a tiger, likely from *The Jungle Book*, but I couldn't remember the character's name. The name Rudyard Kipling had given his literary tiger was on the tip of my tongue but the scene drew my attention away.

We stepped into the park that had followed the modernization of the buildings. The playground looked safer, maybe so safe that a child would consider it boring. My eyes quickly bounced from the short slides to the jagged, glowing crack that split the center of the park in two and opened to another world.

Steam wafted from the portal as colors ebbed and flowed on the other side, shifting and rippling through the shades I recognized as the story aura's glow. This wasn't like the doorway portals Scarlet had created, or the one I'd trapped Johnson in just a couple of years ago.

Instead, the opening looked alive, pulsing and breathing and teaming with the disturbed life of another dimension. The crack was ten times the size as the doors Scarlet had used to step through, shifting her from one area of story aura to the next.

I shuffled toward it, struck with awe and silence and breathless fear. It towered over me like a dark magic version of a skyscraper. Its haunting glow had consumed the park and turned into a ghost town except for Shere Khan at the entrance. Other villains likely hid in the darkness of the walking paths that branched in several directions.

"Do you see what you did?" Jacob asked.

Wow. He may as well have said, *welcome to the rotten fruits of your failure.* This was nothing but a nightmare, which meant I didn't cause this. It had to be a dream. Right? *Yes...maybe.* A shudder rippled through my body, or ghostly figure, or dreamlike existence—whatever I was.

"Don't get your bloomers twisted, Jake," Will said.

Jacob folded his arms. "Impossible," he said, "because I'm not wearing any."

TMI, Dude, too much information.

"Is this Neverland?" I finally pieced the memory of Hook's drawing together and mentally laid it over the vision of this portal.

"Essentially," Will answered with a nod. "This is the rip between the story world and Earth. What you're looking at now is how it will be after you've twisted more and more stories and sealed them with the wrong endings."

I shook my head, but the denial didn't stop the Brothers Grimm.

"We didn't know when you would be ready to see it," he admitted.

Jacob stepped in and continued the explanation for his brother. I only glanced at him then my eyes darted back to the rift between worlds.

"It has been a long time since we were humans on this Earth," Jacob said. "Our best understanding of life here is through the stories humans write."

"What he's trying to say is that we modeled our approach to

connect and communicate with you using the plot from one of the best stories of all time," Will explained.

I reached out and dared to touch the edge of where the worlds had ripped. To my surprise, the jagged lines inside the rift felt smooth and velvety beneath my fingertips. The rift reminded me of horrors and fantasies and science fiction portals I'd seen in movies. Instead of a wardrobe, as in *The Chronicles of Narnia*, it resembled ripped fabric, like when Wendy scraped her knee on the concrete and tore her jeans at the knee.

The rift shifted into the shape of a giant piece of furniture, with my hand on the knob of the open double doors. My breath caught in my throat and I backed away from it. The moment I wondered where the rift's original manifestations went, it returned to normal with the jagged lines and rippling colors but a tiny piece of thread had pulled out, and snagged on my fingernail.

I gasped and looked at my hand then back at the rift.

The Brothers stared at me with confused curiosity. Had they seen it change, too? Their focus on me said otherwise.

"Stop twisting the fairy tales, Keeper," Jacob said, stern demand lacing his usually upbeat and awkward voice.

"Let Morris die and destroy Dracula or the rift will tear open and more than our spirits will come through. Terrible monsters and villains will roam your city and take everything from you." Will had stepped in front of me. The only eyeball that had formed so far, burned with fury in his skull. He glared at me with all the seriousness of a monster himself.

"Did you never wonder how you could become a vampire?" Jacob asked with his head tilted like a confused dog. "You're not part of *Dracula*, but with the veil so thin, anything ever suggested in fiction can become real."

"How do you expect me to kill a vampire who can shift into a bat and fly away?" I asked, trying to gain the advantage in this argument. They'd invaded my house before and my mind now. Running was impossible, considering this was my nightmare in my brain, but I could keep my dignity and confidence.

"Ah, yes." Jacob grinned. The rotting flesh of his lip only added to the frightening look of his smile. "You're talking to gods who are all-knowing when it comes to stories. Even the pieces the author never included." He giggled like a little girl at a slumber party and I frowned at his giddiness over the horror story that'd consumed my Christmas season. What did that have to do with anything? "Dracula has to have fed, a lot, on fresh, virgin blood in order to change forms."

"Can we focus? Will growled and shot his brother an annoyed glare. "We demand that you follow the stories and build the barrier between worlds again."

They bounced off of one another. Jacob nodded along with his brother's suggestion then repeated the same sick words from before. "Anything that seals the story, Keeper. Death included."

"I won't let innocent people die," I said, though my voice didn't sound like my own.

"What about Morris? Start there," Jacob said. "It will only get easier. All you have to do is read the stories and fix their plots. Like an editor, if you will."

"I don't expect weirdos so far removed from humanity to understand." I glanced at the rift, curious if it would shapeshift into a wardrobe again.

"What about Wendy?" he asked.

"I'll find another way." My eyes trailed the jagged edges of the tear between worlds.

Though it couldn't get smoother, Jacob ran his palm over the front of his coat. He did it even more often than before, likely because he knew how disturbing his appearance had become. Though I didn't miss the long, curling eyebrows that nearly poked him in the eyes.

"I'm baffled by your interest in the man who became Morris. Do you love him? Why protect him?" he asked.

"Do I need to say it again? I won't let innocent people die."

Will sighed and threw his hands in the air. He rubbed his face over his beard then placed his hands on his hips, with his head shaking. "There is a veil blocking the story world from this one, but you've thinned it. Right here, when you should have died to the wolf, it started fraying and our spirits were pulled through. If you don't keep the stories to their plots….this future, this destruction—" he waved his arm out, panning the park as if I could see Maleficent, Shere Khan, Godzilla, and the Eye of Sauron right here, right now. "This is the destiny of you and everyone you've ever known."

Fire raged within me, ready to rival the fury in the god's eye. Who was he to threaten me with this vision? How could I trust these lying creeps when they'd made me a promise?

My lip twitched then turned into a grimace that I hoped looked worse than the Grinch. "You said that you'd help me save Wendy from being bound to *Peter Pan*, and she still has the story aura," I said. Saliva caught in my throat as I spat out the words. "I solved the murders, like you asked, and she's still trapped!"

"Keeper…" Jacob tried to calm me with his palms raised in surrender but I stepped back.

"No," I said. "How do you expect me to trust you?"

"This is the reason she can see Neverland, Mari." Will used my real name, likely another one of his attempts at connection with a human he didn't understand. He pointed to the rift behind him. " Let Dracula kill Morris and it could save Wendy."

"I–I can't…"

This is your fault. Mari!" his arm shook and the flesh on his fingers quivered. "Mari! Mari…"

"Mommy."

I shot forward, my feet landing on a shaggy carpet and forehead colliding with Wendy's nose.

"Ow," she complained. Her hand covered her nose where I'd bumped into her.

"Wendy." I breathed and reached for her shoulders. After glancing around and ensuring that no ghostly skeletons haunted the living room, I faced her. "What is it? Did you have a nightmare?" The word taunted me and felt weird to speak aloud after what I'd just experienced. Was it real? The bit of frayed thread on my fingernail proved it. I curled my hand and looked at Wendy again.

"No," she said. "I heard you talking to Daddy last night, and I had an idea."

I furrowed my brow but stayed silent to give her space to talk.

"You're looking for the bad guy in the library book, aren't you?"

Dracula. Maybe I shouldn't have read her excerpts from the classic horror. I answered with a nod.

"I know how to find him." She smiled, proud of herself.

"What?"

My daughter beamed. "I listened really good. The characters in the book followed the bad guy all the way to where he tried to run away. It was by the water, like when we get ice cream on the pier."

I wracked my brain, trying to recall the end as Bram Stoker had written it.

"So maybe he's there." Wendy shrugged.

She was right. The story aura would draw Nolan to track down Dracula and as his tenant, he might have a shot at finding him with all the professor's identifying information. If I found Nolan, I'd find Dracula.

And I'd destroy the vampire for what he'd done to those young women, imaginary nightmare rift or not. As for Wendy's tie to *Peter Pan*…there had to be another way.

Chapter 24

A Christmas Eve Kill

The day flew by with a dozen preparations that included chipping away at the leg of an old kitchen chair we'd found in the condo's shared dumpster. Wooden shavings speckled the floor, and I scolded Kai for sharpening the stick over our shaggy rug where splinters would hide between the threads and stab our bare feet. He shrugged and dragged the knife along the leg to carve one last time.

The sharp point came to a tip that resembled the fangs I'd snapped off. Tonight, we'd find Dracula, but I had no intention of showing up unprepared. This time, I'd carry every weapon ever said to hurt a vampire.

A ring trilled in my ear as I pinched my cell phone between my face and my shoulder. I took the stake Kai had just created and analyzed the shape and weight. I gripped it to see if I could wield it easily enough without splinters terrorizing my palm.

The other line rang and rang and rang until it went to voicemail. Nolan's bold voice spoke a few lines about VacayDays and invited the caller to leave a message. I groaned and swiped to end the call then tapped on Detective Wilhelm's contact info. When he answered, I tossed the stake back to Kai. I threw my husband a thumbs up for the hard work, before pinching my other ear to hear the detective more clearly.

After giving me some grief, Detective Wilhelm agreed to use police resources to track Nolan's cell phone. The fact that I knew a few details about the second incident at the rental castle helped him believe I had a lead.

"Call me when you find him," I said.

"Fine." He breathed into the phone. "But this better not be a waste of time. I still don't see how locating that college kid will lead us to the murderer. I cleared him in my interview, he isn't our guy."

"No, but he knows him. Drac—" I stopped myself and cleared my throat. "Professor Vaughn was his tenant and I'm willing to bet Nolan will be out for revenge after his buddy got killed."

"If your wild theories hadn't worked the past, I wouldn't be doing this," he said with a grunt. Before I could respond, the line went dead.

I peeled the phone from my ear and made faces at the screen, mimicking the detective's words. "Your wild theories." One day maybe, Detective Wilhelm would afford me the respect other investigative journalists received when they helped solve a crime. But today was not that day.

A knock sounded at the door and I answered to pay the person delivering our mobile food order. I hugged the bag of warm burritos wrapped in foil. The smell of seasoned chicken and salsa delighted me. After several days without a normal appetite, I was ready to eat a horse, or just a massive burrito stuffed with rice, cheese, and beans paired with a Pepsi for a hit of caffeine.

I'd eat healthy after the holidays. For now, I needed sustenance and energy and at least it wasn't blood that I'd need to suck from another person's neck.

We sat at the Coffee Table of Evidence and built a tree of sticky notes to visualize our plan. On the red notes, I wrote the worst possible scenarios and how we would respond to them. With the yellow papers, the scenarios we envisioned were slightly less critical. Finally, green offered trouble but of significantly less intensity. These included situations like *if the blessed bullets don't kill Dracula and he turns into a bat, Kai will be ready to catch him with the butterfly net from Wendy's science kit.*

Wendy munched on a tortilla chip and tried to sound out a word on one of the Post-It notes.

"K, k, iii, ll," she said, reading the scribbles on one of the red pieces of paper. Kai and I exchanged glances but kept quiet. Though Wendy wasn't afraid of much more than mermaids, we didn't want to risk sending her over to Tala's house after explaining killing and death.

My phone vibrated from the corner of the coffee table where it nearly buzzed right over the edge. I plopped my burrito down, having it stand up on the plate like a Guinea pig on its haunches so that the insides of rice and beans didn't spill all over the place.

I scooped the phone into my hand and swiped to answer. The detective was curt but thorough.

"Nolan's on the move," I said. After wrapping the foil over the rest of the burrito, I stood and told Wendy to grab her pajamas. Hopefully, we'd be back soon and she wouldn't have to spend the entire night at Tala's house where Wendy claimed it stunk like old socks. Maybe the kid needed a checkup on her sense of smell because sugar cookies and banana bread smelled nothing like clothing.

Kai shoved the stake into a backpack right next to a water bottle he had the youth pastor that lived in the condo downstairs bless. That guy definitely thought we were crazy now.

"Crucifix?" I asked as I carried my shoes to the living room chair.

Kai nodded. "Check."

"Holy water?" I leaned over to tie the laces of the sneakers that I'd bought for jogging years ago. Now, I'd only use them to run headfirst at fairy tale monsters.

"Check," he said with a wiggle of the plastic bottle to show the water splashing around inside.

Wendy bounded out of the bedroom in mismatched pajamas. The Jack O' Lantern shirt clashed with her red, candy cane-striped pants. The teddy bear in her arms had seen better days, too. Stuffing poked out from where the seams had frayed around one of its ears.

"Stake and garlic?" I asked.

"Check and check."

"Mister Bo?" Wendy said, holding the beloved stuffed animal up as if she were Rafiki and the teddy was Simba. I'd watched Lion King way too many times not to see that scene when she lifted her toys in the air.

"Check," Kai said. A smile tugged at his lips as he offered to hold Mister Bo while Wendy pulled fuzzy boots on her feet to walk across the hall.

I hopped up and trailed through the door behind them. I pulled the gun from my holster, looked inside, then tucked it away again. "Blessed bullets?" I muttered. "Check."

Tala and Wendy stood at the threshold of her front door and waved as we walked down the hallway. Three hugs weren't enough when we'd said goodbye. I turned and ran back for another quick squeeze and left Wendy with a kiss on the top of her head.

"I love you," I said.

The warmth from our last hug faded too quickly when we went down the stairs and climbed into the car. No wind or rain slowed our short drive to the pier, but the holiday traffic did.

The weather had calmed for the holiday which brought crowds of last-minute shoppers to the streets. We parked as close to the beach as possible, then walked along the pier for the rest of the way. More people than usual darted from here to there, waiting at the crosswalks with us and disappearing into shops. We fit right in as we hurried to follow the directions to the location Detective Wilhelm had pinged.

Though no wind or rain threatened us, the chill of the crisp air soaked deep, even cutting through the hood's protection. The phone's GPS directed us to a shortcut down Soup Cracker Street that allowed us to pass the pier and reach the area where the ocean met land.

"Wendy predicted this," I said. We followed a wooden staircase that led to the beach. The bottom of the posts that held the steps in place disappeared beneath layers of sand.

"What?"

"Wendy." I raised my voice to be heard over the rush of the waves crashing on the shore. "She didn't just listen to the story, she picked out details like clues. Not only did she tip me onto tracking Nolan, but she mentioned Dracula would be by the water. This was how it happens in the novel. Dracula tries to escape while Van Helsing, Morris, and Jonathan hunt him down."

Shouldn't you be proud? This is how the story was written. I flicked my gaze to the heavens, though I knew the Brothers Grimm weren't there. Wherever they were, at least it wasn't here. They wouldn't appreciate my plan to destroy the vampire before he hurt the person who'd become Morris.

Despite the dim light of the shore at night, I could see the outline of Kai's jaw and cheeks shift. I knew him well enough to fill the rest in with my mind's eye. His crooked smile had me flushed with heat in my neck and crawling up to my ears as if we were college kids again, walking on the beach on our second date.

"What?" I asked.

"She's just like you," he said. "I wouldn't be surprised if Wendy grows up to be an investigator or monster—"

"Don't say it." I stopped him. Though *monster hunter* wasn't the worst title. I brought down the creatures that attacked and killed innocent people and it aligned with my goals as a journalist, to keep the city safe.

The little blue dot on my phone's screen quickly slid closer to Nolan's location. We were closing in on him.

"He's here," I said, lifting my phone. "Let's hurry."

We lay low, talking quieter than the crashing waves.

"So, what will stop Dracula from shifting into a bat and flying away?" Kai asked.

"He needs to feed to be able to do that," I said. "And Detective Wilhelm confirmed that there were no reports of any recent victims. It's pretty specific too, has to be virgin blood—never tainted by another vampire."

My husband frowned. "Spooky."

Walking in the sand slowed us but we picked up the pace to balance it out and save time. The empty shore seemed to go on, endless and exhausting. If we weren't on a time crunch to catch Dracula before he left the city, I'd enjoy the calming sounds of the ocean. The rhythm of the waves would lull me into a false sense of security if I wasn't careful.

After hiking in the sand for what felt like an hour, a dark shape formed in the open ocean. I squinted and let my eyes adjust to the distance. The closer we came, the easier it was to identify the tall, billowing triangle as an open sail on a beached boat.

"This is his," I said. "This is what Dracula was going to use to escape, no traces left behind. He'd start fresh in a new city." Frustration at his two other escapes built, and I nearly kicked myself. I'd been impulsive not once, but twice. Twice, the monster slipped through my fingers as easily as sand.

We followed the shoreline several more steps until the blue dot indicating our location nearly covered where it tracked Nolan.

"It says we made it." I tapped my phone to reload the page. Nothing changed, still showing that we'd found our target.

"I don't get it," Kai said, as he turned and scanned the beach. "There's nobody here. Not as far as the eye can see."

I followed more of the same behavior, panning my gaze around the area. Like Wendy, I wanted to pay close attention and catch any details. I'd kept the flashlight on my phone turned off, not willing to risk announcing our arrival to Dracula or spooking Nolan as we stalked him to this isolated area of the city's shore.

"Where are they? And where are the cops? Detective Wilhelm said he'd meet me here."

The empty beach left me with chills. Clouds rolled in and blocked the moonlight's glow from brightening our path through the sand. The damp smell of coming rain mixed with the scent of the sea.

We traced the area where the tracking link pinged Nolan's phone, searching for anything that would give us a clue. Was the app wrong? Did the detective lead me on a wild goose chase?

Speaking of the devil, my phone blinked with a notification. Detective Wilhelm's name popped up at the top of the screen with a partial message. *Tracked the phone, found...* I tapped the message to open it. *...nothing. Don't waste my time again, Rowan.*

"Ebenezer Scrooge," I said under my breath. "They're not coming."

Kai suddenly stopped and crouched. "Mari…"

Sand rustled as Kai wiped it around. If I didn't know better, I'd think he was building a sandcastle. He pulled something small and rectangular from the sand and stood. It brightened with a light that showed a screen where a picture of Nolan held Mindy. They wore fuzzy beanies and stood on a snowy mountaintop. He looked so happy.

"It's his phone," I said, staring at the face of the man I'd almost sacrificed. *I'll find another way.* I repeated. In truth, I'd avoided thinking too carefully about the moment I'd see Nolan again. Would I be able to spare his life? Or would I succumb to desperation?

I shoved the thought away and tried to shift my mindset. If I looked at this as any other investigation, I'd stay focused and clear-headed. Last night's sleep, though interrupted and jarred with living nightmares, did wonders for me. The migraine was less than debilitating, for now.

Kai stepped forward, bent at the waist with his nose pointed to the ground. "I think these are footprints."

He followed the trail to a rocky outcropping. Waves lapped against the beach behind us.

"There's blood," he said. The wind had picked up now and nearly swept my husband's words away into the salty air.

Blood? Was I too late to save Nolan? Would he die a heartbroken man after Mindy had declared her love for Garen? I didn't know the guy, but I knew he was just a college kid doing his best with his innovative business.

"He needs to feed," I said. Nobody deserved to die alone on the beach as vampire food. "He has Nolan." I patted my side where I'd tucked my gun then took off running toward the outcropping. With Kai at my heels, and our arsenal of vampire-specific weapons, I knew we had a chance. We had the sliver of a chance to stop the serial killer that the detective had given up finding tonight.

The pure blackness beneath the outcropping of sharp rocks concealed everything around us unless we'd turn to face the ocean.

And even there, without the moon, it was hard to make out more than crude shapes in the dark. But the last remnants of my vampiric senses hadn't totally faded, or maybe my time as an undead monster just gave me the experience to smell it.

Blood cut through the scent of both rain and salt. Dracula was here.

Only a sailboat's length away from the outcropping now, I glimpsed movement.

I clucked my tongue to draw Kai's attention, then waved to the backpack. Carefully, he pulled the stake from a side pocket, and slipped the crucifix on a chain around his neck, leaving one hand free.

A raindrop plopped on the skin exposed by the part of my hair. The rain slowly picked up, spotting us with the cold, fresh water.

I nodded toward where something shifted. A shape, one shade darker than the surrounding area moved again. Finally, adjusting I could discern a head and shoulders, but the legs looked extended far too long to be attached to the same body. Hadn't he seen us coming? Or was he too hungry, too weak to notice two figures in the dark?

I nodded at it and whispered. "Light." I raised my hand before he turned on his phone's flashlight. "On my count."

The rhythm of the waves helped me plan the right time to make noise. The fabric of my rain jacket rustled when I reached for my gun. I flicked off the safety and raised it at the shape of a head.

"Three, two…"

Light flooded the beach.

It took a second for my eyes to adjust. I blinked and realized the vampire was too busy, feeding on Nolan's throat.

Based on the college kid's alert eyes, full of fear and regret, Dracula had just sunk his teeth. The distraction provided the perfect shot. Slumped shoulders, and his delayed reaction were clues that revealed his weakness.

He flinched at the light and started to pull his fangs from Nolan's flesh. The slow movements gave me the split-second I needed.

All I had to do was pull the trigger to bury the bullet into the top of the vampire's head. It'd destroy Dracula and save the innocent, stupid for coming here alone, but innocent, young man.

My pulse pounded in my ears. The pace of the rain had doubled, spattering us and the sand with billions of wet drops. It was the only thing that moved at regular speed while everything else seemed to slow.

I exhaled and tried to put pressure on the trigger.

Let Dracula kill Morris. Save Wendy.

My arms quivered from the weight of the decision.

The tips of Dracula's teeth pulled out of Nolan's neck. Blood dripped from his fangs, like the raindrops that trickled down the side of my face.

"Mari." Kai's voice registered between the rain that fell in angled sheets now.

I can save Wendy. My arms dipped an inch.

"Take the shot!" My husband shouted.

Dracula grinned, baring his fangs as he gripped Nolan's throat. His palm was slick with blood but it didn't stop him from squeezing. Why kill Nolan like this now? The vampire had gotten to feed. He was merely playing with his food.

Because he's a monster. But I wasn't. I blinked and shoved the Grimm's haunting words away.

I flexed my arms, pointed the gun between Dracula's eyes, and pulled the trigger. The shot echoed across the beach while the bullet etched with the symbol of a cross embedded in the monster's skull.

Dracula pitched forward and Nolan rolled out of the way, coughing weakly. While he gasped for breath, Kai hurried to help. My arms fell to my side with my gun nearly slipping from my fingers. I sucked in a breath and scrubbed the heel of my palm over my forehead. I marched through the sand, closing the space between me and Dracula.

Rain soaked me, leaving my hair clinging to my neck and face.

Once Kai helped roll Nolan out of the way, he tossed me the stake. I snatched it, gripped the stake with both hands, and buried it into the subdued vampire's back without a second thought. Just as the novel said, his body crumbled to dust. It vanished into the sand as rain pounded it into the ground, effectively burying the monster where he'd tried to escape.

I reached up to lean one hand against the rock. Breath didn't come easily as adrenaline withered. I let my head fall, chin to collarbone. For a moment, I only focused on the rise and fall of my chest and the rhythm of the beat in my ribcage that reminded me of my humanity.

"Mari." Concern laced Kai's voice, and I didn't have to turn to know it was bad news. Nolan had died.

Still, I lifted my head and rolled it to the side. Nolan's eyes were wide open, blinking slowly, but with plenty of life left in them. But pain darkened my husband's gaze.

The hand that held his phone, fell to his lap.

"That was Tala," he said.

My heart skipped a beat, and the natural rhythm was disturbed. The mention of our daughter's babysitter struck me as the worst possible news. Muscles contracted and squeezed my throat as pure fear wrapped its hand around my neck and threatened to choke me.

Kai's face twisted into the visual representation of the panic I'd succumbed to. "Wendy's gone."

Chapter 25

A Hail Mari

No.
No.
No!

I refused to accept the truth until Kai explained what Tala had said. A boy had knocked on their door, and Wendy had insisted he was her classmate. Tala had left them at the doorway, only for a moment, to pull the cookies out of the oven before they burned.

Over cookies.

My daughter was missing over cookies, but I didn't blame the babysitter. This was as the Brothers Grimm had said, *your fault, Mari.*

"I know where she is," I breathed.

Whether the rift ripped when I'd stopped Dracula from draining Nolan's life away, or it was already frayed from Jonathan—aka Garen's—wrongful death. Either way, for once, I appreciated the visions the Brothers Grimm had shown me. Because of them, I knew where the veil between Storyland and Earth was the weakest.

Nolan ensured us he'd be okay, though Kai still encouraged him to call for an ambulance. With my heart in my throat, I ran for the car and Kai followed in my wake.

My feet slammed the wooden planks of the staircase that led back to the streets. Though I ran, smashing my heels against the ground with every step, I felt nothing. Not the sidewalk's concrete beneath my feet. Not the rain that drenched my face and hair and clothes. Not the chill of having been soaked. Not even my racing heart rate.

We piled into the car and Kai peeled out of the parking lot, his lead foot slamming the gas without care for traffic laws. The downpour lightened as the flash of rainfall moved through the city.

By the time we reached the park, the rain had stopped. I nearly fell from the car while it was still moving. Kai brought the car over the curb because it'd take too long to parallel park. Instead, he smashed the button for the emergency lights and left it half-parked.

Though I wasn't asleep, this nightmare was far worse than Shere Khan's threatening gaze from the trees with crooked arms. I didn't want to be a monster like Dracula, but if I could mute the pain and fear of life as a human…

Trees shadowed the park's entrance, like a black hole, ominous and endless in its possibilities to consume everything I loved. The cracked pavement threatened to trip me but I'd take a rolled ankle over wasting another second.

Around the corner, I spied the playground and then the park opened up, in a circle with benches and streetlamps. A child whooped and hollered from his perch at the top of a plastic slide. He waved his arms like little wings then dove down the slide on his belly.

Swirling dark shades radiated with a sickening yet enchanting glow just as in my dream. Storyland teemed with life that followed the narratives of thousands of novels and fairy tales. Somewhere inside, Neverland, the island of lost children, drew my daughter.

The colors highlighted Wendy's green glow as she stood before the rift, small but mighty. The opening was far smaller than in my dream but that offered little comfort. It was plenty large for her little body to hop through, stretched open enough to be considered a door. The rip matched my nightmare in every other way with the jagged edges, and its living, pulsing existence.

A hand shot out from the center of the rift, and my heart jumped to my throat. I nearly spewed it at my feet, still beating. A familiar, brown leather coat hung from the hairy arm.

Johnson.

He stretched and reached for Wendy and she didn't so much as take a step back. Instead, she nodded and seemed to listen to the voice behind the hand.

When I opened my mouth to scream for her to run, nothing came out. Wendy reached out and put her hand in his. I lunged forward and scooped both arms around Wendy's chest to rip her from Johnson's hold.

We both tumbled backward and my tailbone broke the fall. Lightning pain snaked up my spine, but I curled like a cocoon around Wendy to protect her from an elbow scrape.

The arm jutted out, exposing itself all the way to his collarbone. Johnson still wore the jacket that had suffered cigarette burns and frayed at the seams. The small tears in the sleeve mirrored the rift with uneven edges and threads poking out. Though the rift's threads were more like veins, with magical blood coursing through them.

Johnson reached all the way through to the ground and gripped Wendy's shirt in his fist. To my relief, Kai had caught up with us. He scooped our daughter into his arms and backed away as I clutched Johnson's wrist.

I yanked, using all of that adrenaline-filled mom-strength, which was significantly cooler than a vampire's powers, by the way. It achieved the desired effect: Johnson falling through the rift. He tripped over the bottom where the rip between worlds didn't reach the ground.

I grabbed the white, stained shirt he wore beneath the leather coat with the same fistful force he'd used when he laid hands on my daughter. With my free hand, I ripped my gun from the holster at my side all while shoving Johnson upright and against the side of the rift as if the pulsing jagged edges were a doorway's frame. Multitasking was my specialty.

I pinned Johnson between worlds, just as I had when I'd left him trapped in the portal. Though I knew he was immortal, like me, he'd feel the pain of the bullet. With the barrel of my gun pointed straight at the end of his nose, where hairs poked out from his nostrils, I had him under my control. The resemblance to Jacob Grimm only fueled my fire to pull the trigger and end the creep's life.

"What the hell is wrong with you?" I asked, in a voice that might be considered a growl.

"You have that backward, Keeper." Saliva spattered my face as he emphasized my title. "I'm not the one making the wrong choices." His eyes flicked to the pulsing edge of the rift.

It was as the Brothers Grimm had said, my twist of the stories exposed our world to one of fiction. One where Wendy thought she belonged, because of the story aura's poison.

"Mommy!" Wendy shrieked. I glanced at her, an involuntary instinct at the sound of my child's call. "Don't hurt him."

I furrowed my brow but didn't loosen my grip on Johnson's shirt. "He's a bad guy, Wendy. Like the vampire in the library book."

She scrambled from Kai's hold and looked up at me, enormous eyes begging me not to commit this act of violence. Of course, I wouldn't. Not in front of her. But Johnson deserved to fear for his life, or at least pain, until I could get him thrown behind bars and forever keep him from the comforts of his storied home. Let him suffer.

"Wendy," Kai said with a step forward.

But she tugged away and shook her head. "The man told me I could save the world."

My mouth twitched as I flicked my gaze back to Johnson.

"He said lots and lots of monsters will come out of there and hurt nice people if I don't go to Neverland." The quiver in her voice told me she was trying to conceal her fear. Wendy was the bravest kid I'd ever heard of, but I hated that she felt she needed to do this. Her lopsided pigtails had escaped strands of hair that pointed in every direction. It looked as though she'd slid down the plastic slide, after which the static electricity had given her hair the spark it needed to defy gravity.

Kai crouched beside her, holding her arms in his hands to keep her warm. Though I suspected the goosebumps that lined her bare arms, and her shivering, had little to do with the cold.

"Let's go home," he said, in an attempt to calm her and dissuade her from the rift. My husband had little context for the rip between worlds in the middle of Pioneer Park, but he remained calm for Wendy's sake.

"Please, listen to me," she begged. The short pigtails flicked against the side of her head when she snapped her gaze across the park. "Travis wants to go, too. He thinks he can fly when he gets there." She stepped closer to us and pointed into the rift. "I'll be okay." Her shaking voice revealed otherwise.

I followed her gaze past Johnson and into the other world.

"It's a pretty island," she said.

Whatever she saw, didn't match my view. Storyland was nothing but a jumble of aura, glowing so brightly it triggered a full return of the agony in my temples. The migraine was the only thing that could cut through the numbness sponsored by fear and adrenaline. Colors pulsed and obscured vague shapes of a landscape that meant nothing to me. I identified nothing recognizable in the world where real people didn't belong.

A gasp caught in my throat as the colors shifted and formed silhouettes of two standing bodies in the purgatory of story aura.

The Brothers Grimm appeared in their full glory, standing side-by-side without the ghostly mist. Instead of rotting flesh and partially finished bodies, they were whole and solid.

Will lifted his chin at Wendy. "You know what to do, Mari. Let the story be as it was written without twists or changes."

"I can help, Mommy. I want to help just like you do. He said it'd be a big mistake if I didn't go to Neverland and I know you always say that you don't like it when you make mistakes. You save people and do lots of things and never stop and now I can be just like you!"

Emotion welled in my throat. I'd made a huge mistake, and it had nothing to do with twisting stories or letting the rift rip. That was a problem I'd figure out how to deal with, I always did. But the example I'd given to my daughter that it was okay to run yourself into the ground, to chase an impossible perfection at the expense of your life and your loved one's quality of life, was the biggest regret I could fathom. I'd shown her that goals and checkmarks on to-do lists were more important than one's own happiness.

Kai stepped in front of Wendy and bent to pick her up but her tiny hand shot out and gripped the edge of the rift. She held on tightly, refusing to let him take her away.

"No!" Wendy kicked and screamed. "I can be brave! I want to be like mommy!"

I let my head hang for a moment then dropped the gun from Johnson's face. I released him and tucked the weapon away.

"Wendy," I said as I turned and crouched in front of her. My eyes searched the empathy and innocence and pure desire to help in her green gaze. Behind the bravery was a hint of fear, shown in the tiny crease between her eyebrows. "I was wrong."

She shook her head. "No, I've seen it. I've seen you super tired and kind of sick and you still go out and find bad guys." Her bony shoulders rose and fell in a slight shrug.

In my peripherals, I registered Johnson's shadow moving closer to us. Will's voice echoed from the other world and Johnson stopped, frozen in place.

"The Keeper will do the right thing," Will said. I didn't give it much thought as I narrowed my focus on Wendy, someone far more important than the Grimm gods or the other man who continued to haunt me.

"Have you lost your mind?" Jacob argued.

I tuned out their words and cupped Wendy's cheeks in my palms. "You're right." I spoke in the gentlest voice I could muster while the gazes of the gods of story bore through my back and the man I considered a nemesis stood over us. "I have done that and it was a mistake. Mommy makes lots of mistakes, Wednesday, and that's all right. It was silly of me to pretend that I was okay when I wasn't okay, too. I'm not always strong. In fact, I'm scared, a lot."

The little wrinkle of her brow dug deeper. "Really?"

I nodded and took her hands in mine. "Really."

"I don't have to be strong?" she asked. Tears welled in her eyes and my heart skipped a beat.

"Sometimes being strong means taking care of yourself."

The tears overflowed now, slipping down my daughter's rosy, freckled cheeks and dotting the pavement. I wrapped my arms around her little body and pulled her in for a tight hug that we both so desperately needed. She threw her thin arms around my neck and melted into my embrace. Tears stung my eyes.

"I was so scared," she cried. "I didn't want to go because the kids are mean and I don't want to fly. It's too high!"

I squeezed tighter, never wanting to let go.

"I told you so," Jacob's voice echoed from behind me. "She failed. Guardian, grab her!"

Before the meaning of the words registered, shadows closed in. Both Kai and Johnson lunged toward us at the same moment.

The meaty thwack of Kai's fist smacking into Johnson's face alerted me. I straightened and lifted Wendy with me. But with the weight of her in my arms, I moved too slowly while Johnson, immortal and likely more powerful than me, shook off the punch to his nose and returned it to knock Kai out of the way. Kai was thrown to the side from the force of the blow, landing against the pavement with his hands out to stop the fall from hurting his head.

Johnson turned and lunged for us. My heart dropped, knowing I couldn't outrun him or beat him in a battle of strength. He grabbed a handful of my hair and yanked me to the side. With my hands full, I couldn't fight back fast enough.

Johnson ripped Wendy from my arms and shoved me to the ground where my shoulder slammed against concrete, knocking it out of its socket. A bolt of agony rippled through my arm.

"Wendy!" I screamed loud enough to send an echo through both worlds.

"Peter belongs in Neverland," Johnson grunted, as he stepped one foot through the rift.

Another body appeared, blocking the rift's entrance and my view of the gods.

"Like hell she does." A perky, blonde ponytail swung to both sides. Wendy's first-grade substitute teacher stood her ground, firmly blocking Johnson from squeezing through. The schoolteacher sliced the sharp edge of a rapier across the arm where Johnson held Wendy. Immediately, he dropped her, and she broke her fall like a cat, landing on both feet and then quickly straightening.

Wendy kicked the toe of her little sneakers into the back of his knees. It gave Kai enough time to get to his feet and barrel into Johnson.

They both collapsed to the concrete. Everything moved too fast for my throbbing head to comprehend. I struggled to my feet, weaker than I'd ever been. What I'd told Wendy was truer now than ever before. If only I'd taken the time to rest, I'd be stronger now. I'd be the fighter she needed to ward off the demand of the story, and the librarian gods that organized it.

"Go to the playground," I told Wendy, as I stepped up to the rift.

With Johnson temporarily out of commission, Will stepped in. He snatched the rapier from Hook's grasp, while his brother pulled the Captain's hands behind her back.

"Don't let her come here," Hook begged, keeping her eyes on me as they detained her. "It's my home. This is where the magic is for me like you have with your hood."

The mention of the hood that was draped around my shoulders triggered a thought. The memory of my nightmare brought back the moment when the rift had reacted to my touch. It'd formed into the wardrobe from the *Chronicles of Narnia*. It'd behaved like the hood when I willed the fabric to shift and change. I could never be rid of its responsibilities, but I could use its magic.

I unzipped my rain jacket and shrugged it off. With my good arm, I yanked the ties around my neck, letting the hood slip from my shoulders like a red waterfall.

Despite my aching dislocated shoulder, I held the hood in both hands. I hadn't removed it from my body in years, staying the loyal Keeper, and using it to help me find and seal dozens of stories.

Recognition dawned in Jacob Grimm's fully formed eyes. "Keeper, this is a mistake!"

I grimaced "Good thing I'm willing to make a mistake or two."

"No, you'll still be the Keeper of Stories," he insisted. "The fairy tales will still slip through, but you will—"

I threw the hood at the rift, covering his face and shutting up the brothers that haunted me, once and for all. Red fabric billowed into the air, and just like Wendy's hair, it ignored gravity, as the pull of magic sucked it over the rift.

From the corner of my eye, I saw Johnson heaving as he stood.

"Look out!" Kai shouted, but I couldn't look. I couldn't tear my eyes away from the connected threads between Red Riding's hood, and the rift between worlds.

The pulsing magic in the rift's veins thrust out and looped through the fabric of the hood. Like a needle at a seam, the veins sewed the hood into the opening, blocking Hook, Jacob, and Will, from my sight.

The air in my lungs was knocked out from the force of Johnson's impact. He was too late. The rift was sealed, sewn with only patches of colorful light beaming through the threads.

Once again, my nemesis brought me to the ground and a jolt of pain shot through my shoulder. At least it saved me a trip to Urgent Care since he'd probably knocked my shoulder back into place.

I struggled to kick him off of me and glimpse the rift for confirmation that it'd closed. The hood melted into the rip between worlds and, all at once, the magic of Storyland vanished. Pioneer Park returned to nothing but a dimly lit city park and the twinge in my stomach signaled a change inside of me, too.

It was finally over, and I was mortal.

Chapter 26

A White Christmas

Thick blood dripped down my bare arm. Like a drop of red rain, it fell from above and dotted me with the stain of suffering. I recoiled from the bodily fluid, frowning at Johnson as he stood over me.

The deep slice across his arm gushed fresh blood. He slapped his hand over it and then looked at the stain on his hands with disbelief. It wasn't healing—a power I'd yet to fully master. The chaos of the last few minutes rushed me.

Jacob had called Johnson a Guardian.

Of what? Stories?

With the incessant throbbing in my shoulder and temples, I struggled to gather myself and time seemed to move too slowly.

Johnson stepped back, tripping over my foot, and stumbling into Kai. He spun around to face my husband and I twisted to dig my gun out from beneath me.

Before I could pin him with a threat, Johnson shoved off of Kai. He made a break for one of the dark pathways that led through the park. I released my hold on the gun, leaving it in the holster and let my head fall back.

"I'll find you," I vowed. "And you'll be locked away forever."

But not on Christmas Eve.

Footsteps pounded toward me, and I rolled my head to see little pigtails bounding closer and closer. Wendy threw herself over me and tightened her arms around my neck. I grunted at the shock of the weight on my injured shoulder.

The warmth of my daughter's hug draped over me like a blanket of love. I cupped the back of her head in my palm and relished the moment. Kai's shadow cast over us and I squinted to make out his expression.

"We're okay," I breathed.

He nodded, relief relaxing the tight line of his mouth. Without a word, he pointed to the little fairy who still watched us from the playground. Though he looked more like a 'lost boy' than a creature with wings and magic. Of course, all of us had lost our magic. If the story aura still glowed around Wendy—and I suspected it did—I couldn't see it. The hood was gone, and with it, my ability to live forever plus the story aura cheat sheet to find the fairy tales.

"I'll help him get home," Kai said.

I nodded. "Go."

Wendy twisted and waved at her friend. "Bye Travis!"

"No flying?" he shouted. Travis represented Tinker Bell too well with the focus on himself so deep, he barely acknowledged the fighting and chaos that had just occurred in front of him.

She shook her head, sending the pigtails flying from side to side. "Nope. But the funny ghosts said some magic can still get through!"

Ebenezer Scrooge. She was right. This meant I'd still be hunting for monsters and villains but without the hood's aid. Keeping the city safe and informed was why I'd become an investigative journalist, after all. I refused to stop now, especially with everything I knew about the other world of fiction and fairy tales.

Wendy impressed me more every day, especially with her listening skills. A perfect investigator she would make—if she so chose.

"Okay." Travis shrugged and hopped off the play structure's bottom step.

"My daddy's going to take you home," she said.

"Okay."

"Tell him you live in the apartments across the street," she instructed.

"Okay."

"We'll make our own pixie dust with the glitter from the craft cubby in class."

"Okay."

Kai smirked. "This sounds like you telling me what to do."

I rolled my eyes because he knew as well as I did we were a team. Even though I was tasked with saving people from the dark destinies of their story's plots, Kai was just as important with his empathy and knowledge of history. And it seemed our daughter had become part of the team. When Scarlet returned, that made four of us in the fight against fairy tale villains.

Travis skipped in front of Kai as he led him around the corner and out of the park.

Dull aches tormented my every joint and muscle. With the last bit of energy I could muster, I finally pulled myself up and cupped my daughter's hand.

She copied her friend's energetic bounce from one foot to the other as we followed them out of the park.

"Good luck."

A familiar voice echoed but I couldn't decide if I'd imagined it or heard it. Just before we rounded the corner where the trees would block sight of the center of the park, I glanced back.

Where the rift had split open, a small beam of light suspended in the air. It sparkled as it shifted colors in one last reminder that the veil was still thin. The hood's seal was only a temporary hold.

But tonight was Christmas Eve, and I'd promised my daughter that we'd have chicken chow mein and read Charles Dickens's classic holiday story. Much to my dismay. Still, a promise was a promise— which was something another god like Zeus or Odin needed to teach the Brothers Grimm.

When I blinked, the sight of the sparkling light vanished.

We left Pioneer Park in our wake and started down the street that had since quieted. Shoppers had returned home to wrap purchased gifts and families gathered inside, away from the sprinkling rain that returned.

This time, the rain dotted the pavement with slow, heavy drops rather than a storm of sheets. Christmas lights decorated storefronts and the occasional pedestrian hurried to their destination with an umbrella or hooded jacket over their head. The wreaths along the streetlamps gave San Francisco a charming look that I hadn't appreciated when I was a vampire.

"Is Auntie Scar going to open presents with us?" Wendy asked.

I squeezed her hand while I pulled out my phone with the other. I tapped Scarlet's contact info and it only rang once before she answered with an enthusiastic greeting.

"Merry Christmas and a happy new year!" Scar sang into the phone.

"Hey," I said. "Any chance you'll be home in time for Christmas dinner with us tomorrow? I'll make your favorite, Top Ramen."

"If you cook it, I will come." She laughed and quoted *Field of Dreams*. "Seriously though, I'm at your house right now and there is no food in these cabinets." After a pause, she laughed again. "Carlo says he'll hit up his friends at DoorDash before we starve."

After several years of living within modern society and Scarlet had finally assimilated. Maybe too much, considering I didn't always understand the slang she used. But I wasn't so old that I didn't realize to 'hit up' someone meant to contact them.

"He's there?" I asked.

"I can't help it that I'm so popular."

The *Mean Girls* phrase was Scar's odd way of answering with a yes.

"No funny business," I said as if she were also my daughter.

A scoff sounded from the other side. "We're just friends."

"Sure," I muttered. "So, I take it that your little Bay Side Media test is done?"

She squealed exactly like Anna from Frozen—a movie I'd watched too many times with Wendy. "I can't wait to tell you all about it. Pam said I definitely passed."

We paused at an intersection and waited for a car to drive through. A crosswalk chirped it was safe for pedestrians to pass.

"Congratulations!" I said. "That's great news because I'm going to need a lot of your help to find characters."

"What do you mean?" she asked.

"I have a lot I can't wait to tell you, too," I said. "But basically, I'm mortal now and can't see the story aura anymore."

Scarlet gasped so loud I had to pull the phone away from my ear. Before she could dive into a heated lecture about how I should have taken better care of the hood, I spoke into the bottom of the phone.

"See you in two."

With that, I hung up the phone, and we climbed the staircase to our condo. Wendy's little legs must have been tired but it didn't show. She hurried up the steps twice as fast as me and darted down the hall.

When she opened the front door to our house, she threw herself into Auntie Scar's arms. With Kai arriving only moments behind us, it was hugs all around. Carlo smelled like a pine tree and I realized they'd dragged a real Christmas tree into the house and decorated it with scattered, stale, microwave popcorn from the back of our cabinets.

Scarlet and Carlo matched each other perfectly, both awkward in the real world and distant from social norms.

Tala joined the party with a thousand apologies about letting Wendy slip away but I waved it away. The grandmotherly neighbor had no control over the poison of stories on a chosen character. Besides, I didn't want to focus on the negatives tonight.

We were all safe, happy, and home and after plenty of exchanged greetings, everyone agreed to return tomorrow for Christmas brunch.

But not until after the annual reading of *A Christmas Carol*. I let Kai take the driver's seat this time with all of his character voices and dramatic facial expressions.

Tala had insisted the day was too exciting and that she needed to rest at home, leaving us with a group of five. Wendy snuggled in my lap while Scarlet cozied a little too close to Carlo to be considered 'just friends.'

I am as light as a feather; I am as happy as an angel; I am as merry as a school-boy. I am as giddy as a drunken man. A merry Christmas to everybody! A happy New Year to all the world!

As Kai belted the last words of Charles Dickens's famous story, an epiphany came over me.

"Those creeps!" I said.

Everybody turned to look at me and I welcomed the heat in my cheeks that was undeniable proof all vampiric and undead tendencies had disappeared.

Just as the ghosts of Christmas past, present, and future visited Scrooge to change his mind, the Brothers Grimm had taken me through the same steps. While the ghosts in the story taught the main character a lesson, I'd stuck to my guns, literally, and had shot Dracula.

This former Little Red Riding Hood had just lived through Ebenezer Scrooge's story.

"Crazy," I muttered, as I soaked in the love and chatter surrounding me.

THE CRUMBS LEFT on the reindeer plate and the empty cup of milk weren't proof Santa Claus was real. Kai easily could have slipped out to the living room last night and snagged a bite of cookies and milk lent from Tala. The new icing recipe had him raving, anyway, so I assumed it had to be him. Definitely.

Despite the chaos of the day before, a day that felt like it lasted for a week, I'd woken in the wee hours of the morning. Like a child wanting to peek at their stocking, I'd tiptoed to the living room to admire the Christmas trees. Tension clung to my shoulders until I checked every nook and cranny, even spying behind the Christmas tree to confirm no ghosts had slipped into the house.

Maleficent didn't fly and land on our porch and Godzilla didn't shake the ground. Those were future problems I'd find a way to solve, just as I had with Wendy's pull to Neverland and the rift. As long as I got enough sleep and ate a vegetable now and then, I could accomplish anything.

"What are you doing up?" Kai asked. He shuffled into the kitchen, rubbing his eyes with his fists.

"Did you eat this?" I asked. I pointed to the empty plate and the crumbs on the coffee table around it.

"I've been sleeping like a baby," he said. "Nice try pinning it on me though. Just admit you like Tala's new recipe."

"What about these presents?" I walked behind the couch and picked up a box with wrapping paper covered in Santa hats. "I've never seen this wrapping paper before."

"Maybe Tala," he said.

"The door is locked."

Ebenezer Scrooge. I shook my head. Another story had landed, claiming a Christmas character this time. At least Santa wasn't a legend that involved much death and destruction. But how many other characters and stories would arrive that I wouldn't know about? What already existed out there that I couldn't see?

Kai nearly tripped over the coffee table while still rubbing his eyes.

"Are you okay?" I asked.

Irritated, my husband kicked at the table's leg and then glared at me. "Fine. What's wrong with you?"

I shook my head. "Nothing." I let his weird behavior go, chalking it up to exhaustion and too much chow mein from the night before.

The couch looked like an inviting place to snooze, until Wendy woke up and insisted we open presents. I stepped out of the maze of Santa hat presents, and flopped into my favorite spot on the end of the couch where I could lean on the armrest.

"So, when are you going to visit your family again?"

"What's with the third degree?" he snapped. Each time he spoke his voice dipped with more anger.

"Hey, whoa, I think you need some coffee." I raised my hands to signal I surrendered in the nonexistent battle.

"Why does marriage have to be like this?" he asked, as he stomped into the kitchen. He used his open palms to scrub at the corners of his eyes then curled his fists again and rubbed some more. Red lines snaked through the whites of his eyes, shot through with blood. Before I could ask what he meant, he barreled over my chance. "I warned Carlo not to date Scarlet and you better believe I told him why. Once you get too close to someone you see all the ugly inside of them."

A little gasp escaped me. I felt the need to pull the fuzzy red and green blanket off the back of the couch and wrap it around me as a protection against Kai's words. Who was this man? He certainly didn't behave like the husband I knew and loved.

"What?" I squeaked.

Kai blinked rapidly then palmed his eyes again. Where had I heard of this happening before? A boy who suffered with glass in his eyes sounded vaguely familiar but not a story I knew well. The memory came together then quickly stopped at that.

"Maybe it's just cabin fever," he said with the venom in his voice slightly curbed now. "We've been around each other too much."

How? We'd both been swamped, him with his family obligations, holiday chaos, work, and, of course, the haunting of the Brothers Grimm that pulled me away from my husband and daughter. The opposite of what he said was true and none of it made sense. I clutched the fuzzy blanket in my fist as if I could squeeze comfort out of it.

Kai headed for the door. Without even putting his shoes on, he announced he was going for a walk and that he didn't know when he'd be back. The weird, unexpected fight left my stomach twisted and muscles tense, but I didn't know what to say to stop him. I didn't know how to talk to this weird version of the man who was supposed to be my husband.

He swung the door open, letting it smack into the wall behind it.

Tiny swirling snowflakes drifted in through the open door. The delicate pieces of snow landed in the entryway and immediately melted on the floor.

My jaw dropped and even Kai, in his rage, stopped to admire the beauty of it. San Francisco weather didn't include snow. Mister History

Degree had told me many times that the last time it snowed in our city was way back in the 1950s.

Could it be the hold of a story? Had the hood's seal on the rift changed the way the Storyland interacted with our world?

When Kai slammed the door behind him, the force of the air thrust a snowflake across the room.

It landed on my knee where the blanket covered my legs to keep them warm. I stared at it with awe and concern for what I'd done.

"Impossible," I whispered.

Or rather, impossible without the magic of the story world melting into ours. *Or should I call it poison?* I wanted to blame my husband's strange behavior on something supernatural, but I knew my mistakes could have caused the strain in our marriage. Maybe he'd kept it bottled up for so long that after dealing with a vampiric version of me, he just exploded.

Speaking of melting, the snowflake turned liquid and soaked into the Christmas-colored blanket. I curled my legs to my chest, then busied my brain with theories to avoid the hurt in my heart.

I had no proof this snowfall was because of a fairy tale, but I knew better than to rule it out.

Epilogue

Dear Journal,

The city is safe again, for now. I feel like Batman writing that, and also because Kai is the Catwoman to my fight for justice. Lately, he's gone dark, behaving like he's superior to everyone. Especially me.

Now, I'm on edge because we're always fighting. Not to mention the never-ending nightmares that ruin my sleep. When I close my eyes, I see the rift. The aura from the story world shines through the patches that the hood couldn't cover. In every dream I have, the seams unravel. Sometimes it's the fabric of my marriage fraying, and other nights I see Maleficent and Godzilla stepping through the portal to our world.

I haven't had dreams this vivid since I was pregnant with Wendy.

UP NEXT IS ANOTHER WILD, SUPERNATURAL MYSTERY FULL OF QUEENS AND FAIRY TALES. IN THE NEXT BOOK, MARI AND SCARLET WILL TEAM UP AGAIN TO BATTLE THE NEW CHANGES THE STORY WORLD HAS LEAKED INTO SAN FRANCISCO!

PLEASE CONSIDER LEAVING A REVIEW AT YOUR FAVORITE PLACE TO PURCHASE BOOKS IF YOU ENJOYED THIS STORY! ALSO, A SHARE WITH YOUR FRIENDS WHO LOVE CLEAN, SWEET, SMALL-TOWN ROMANCES WOULD BE GREATLY APPRECIATED. MY QUEST AS AN AUTHOR IS TO MAKE OTHERS FEEL SEEN THROUGH THE ADVENTURE OF FICTION. PLEASE REACH OUT TO ME AND LET ME KNOW IF MY STORIES HAVE TOUCHED YOU. YOU, DEAR READER, ARE WHO THIS BOOK WAS WRITTEN FOR.

About the Author

Congenital Heart Defect survivor, Emily Fluke, finds joy and peace through the expression of writing. She is a strong believer that all stories need a little magic and a lot of excitement. Emily and her husband spend their free time wrangling two children and playing video games in their busy California lifestyle. Otherwise, you'll find Emily solving an escape room, running, or writing Magic the Gathering-based poetry.

To stay up to date on new releases and connect with me, visit my website at Emilyfluke.com or follow me on social media under Author Emily Fluke, or @emilyflukefairytales

www.ingramcontent.com/pod-product-compliance
Lightning Source LLC
Chambersburg PA
CBHW061249310726
48971CB00007B/2289